Pr

"My library is full of _____. I am generally not interested in fiction, but this book intrigued me from the first paragraph onward. I *will* be making space on my shelf for this one. What grabbed me? It's simple yet complex; humorous yet tragic; awkwardly romantic; not just another 'good versus evil' novel. *A Severe Mercy* weaves the threads of human events into the fabric of divine purpose and carries the reader along a plot-driven road with bold and unusual characters as traveling partners."

Joel A. Freeman, Ph.D., Author, Veteran Chaplain of the NBA Washington Bullets/Wizards ('79-'98)

"At chapter thirty-one I needed a snack only to continue the book to the end…it was such good reading. It is a true mystery with believable plot and continuous suspense…elegant language with meaningful dialogue…rare… entertaining."

Maria Szathmary, Retired Associate Professor of Economics, Pace University

"Tremendous… keeps you in suspense…especially loved the redemptive thread woven throughout which makes this mystery/love story so powerful!"

Dr. Mark Morin, Author, Missionary, Church Planter, Board of Representatives International Association of Grace Ministries

"*A Severe Mercy* is a captivating page turner, drawing you into the unresolved questions of the past and then catapulting you into present day intrigue. Add in the underlying bloom of rediscovered affections and the universal element of good vs. evil, Lawrence C. Slater has gifted us with a winner! Thoroughly enjoyable from first page to last!"

Joyce Schneider, Author of *Life Is More Than $100 Bills!*

A SEVERE
Mercy

To Tony,
Many blesings !
Lawrence C. Slater

LAWRENCE C. SLATER

TATE PUBLISHING & *Enterprises*

TATE PUBLISHING
& *Enterprises*

Book design copyright © 2006 by Tate Publishing, LLC. All rights reserved.
Cover design by Janae Glass
Interior design by Lauren Weatherholt

Published in the United States of America

ISBN: 1-5988653-7-4
06.16.06

To Marsha, Carrin, Erika, and Tim—all gifts from God.

ACKNOWLEDGMENTS

I would like to thank the following, without whose input and encouragement this book would have been impossible: my wife and best friend, Marsha, for believing in me and the merit of the book; my sister, Sue Gelder, for echoing the sentiments of my wife; Jen Etheridge and her early-on editing amidst a busy home and work schedule; Erika Stell, for producing the first legible copy; Diana Elwell and her assistance in formatting; Donna Razin and her dogged faith and prayers behind the scenes. For all others, friends and family alike, who either read the manuscript or prayed for it, or both—my heartfelt thanks. Lastly, I would like to thank all the folks at Tate Publishing for giving me an opportunity to realize a dream which has been coursing through my brain for many years.

INTRODUCTION

It was known simply as "the accident." To some, the words conjured memories like spirits from a dark pit. To others, like Amber Greene, they embodied heartache and pain, buried under years of frenetic activity and ambition. Touching the pain made her vulnerable again, but offered the possibility of healing. Stern Blankley was vulnerable too, in a way he hadn't reckoned.

Within the bowels of Hollister, New York, dead secrets were coming to life. The light of justice was gaining strength and shadows were fading like morning fog. A collision of the seen and unseen was inevitable. Players entered the stage with unrehearsed scripts, not knowing the roles they played were part of a grand, redemptive scheme. They were players indeed, not puppets; they made choices... choices with staggering consequences.

CHAPTER 1

*L*ocal *football phenom killed in crash.* Stern threw aside the other mildewed memorabilia and drew the yellowed paper from the storage trunk. The article covered the entire front page of the May 18 edition of the *Valley Voice*. He leaned back against the trunk and began to peruse the twenty-eight year old story. The mildew made him sneeze and his face felt crawly. He wiped his cheeks with his sleeve and continued reading...*fatal accident...high speed...tragic death.* The feelings came back: shock, unbelief, guilt. Why guilt? He had nothing to do with the accident, he reminded himself. However, he wasn't totally sorry it happened either.

He folded the paper neatly and tucked it under his arm. A thought tugged his brain. And then another. He hurried down the attic ladder to his second-story office and jotted a title and a name on a piece of scrap paper.

Stern gazed out over the mountains of northern Pennsylvania, notched his window seat back, and fell into a wistful, half-sleep thinking about Amber Greene.

"I look about the same as in high school," she had teased him over the phone.

No doubt, she's remained conceit's handmaiden too.

Her face haunted him as a mother's face haunts a young child. For a moment, Stern imagined her voice, alluring...commanding... secure. He shook his head and blinked his eyes open, focusing on the scenery below, flowing like a ragged, blue-gray river 30,000 feet below the Delta jet. Amber Greene—the passion of his youth for a few crazy months. When Heath Proctor noticed her, Stern was bounced like a besotted troublemaker from an old west saloon.

Heath and Amber. Adonis and Aphrodite. The heavens clapped their hands, and the local high school bowed in veneration of its newly crowned god and goddess. Here was a conjunction of great fortune and good genes, and everyone smiled with terrible pride.

Heath was scouted by Division I colleges his senior year—a sure bet for the pros, the scouts agreed. Hollister High had again finished the football season undefeated, and Heath was voted All-State quarterback and MVP of the championship game. He was headed for Syracuse University in the fall with a full athletic scholarship.

Compared to Heath, Stern was a drone, an inept non-athlete, the consummate klutz, a social dwarf. But he maintained the intellectual edge—the one thing he had in common with Amber.

The people of Hollister, New York, lived in a dream world, mesmerized by media attention and sports hype. Old women cared more about football than knitting and canning peaches. Old men relived their glory days in endless banter about their lost opportunity for the "big time."

Then the bizarre, inexplicable tragedy. A late night, a back road, a speeding car, a lifeless form. The vehicle rolled several times before hurtling off a twenty-foot embankment and landing in the raging, deadly waters. The police found Heath's body floating face down in Sullivan Creek, snagged by a tree root a hundred feet from his Plymouth.

Their god was dead—the victim of a savage fate that wounded the town's psyche and left a numbing pall hanging like an unclean cloud for days. Hollister's craving for glory faded like a blip on a radar screen, and the proud smiles turned to looks of horror.

Was there another car involved, as some speculated? Was it an accident? Was there a cover-up?

Stern opened his briefcase, removed a yellow legal pad, and began jotting down other questions. The book idea was only two weeks old, but his brain was in high gear.

Amber was thrilled with his call, but hesitant when he mentioned doing research for his latest novel. She wasn't sure she wanted to drag her emotions through the sludge of memories just to satisfy his need to write a book. Three decades hadn't erased the hurt surrounding Heath's death.

Stern sighed and thought again of high school. Amber Fern Greene: tall, slender, classic features. The color of her hair and eyes matched her name as if preordained.

Will she recognize me?

He was no longer the gawky, skinny kid, but a solid, well-proportioned, middle-aged man. He'd taken good care of himself, jogging and weight training, and his graying hair gave him a look of distinction (a word he hated, but one frequently used to describe him).

Yeah, she'll know me.

And he hoped she'd notice he hadn't nurtured a midsection bulge. A comparison with Heath crowded his thoughts.

A lot of athletes grow fat after their careers end, and Heath would have been no exception—had he lived.

"Sir, please return your seat to an upright position, we'll be landing shortly," the flight attendant said, interrupting his reverie.

"Sure," Stern said, and snapped the seat up straight.

The flight from BWI in Baltimore to Rochester took just about an hour. The pilot announced they'd be landing on schedule, and the weather was a muggy eighty-eight degrees.

So what? He'd just come from the Chesapeake Bay area.

The plane began to decelerate, but Stern's heart did the opposite. He twined his fingers together, bent them backwards, and cracked his knuckles, hoping no one noticed. He always flew coach, keeping himself attached to his middle class roots. Coach was his comfort zone. Amber would have robbed her mother to avoid the humiliation. *She* was conceited, and *he* flew coach.

She had mentioned over the phone about her marriage five years after Heath's death, and divorce ten wretched years later. She and Jeff Stovall had two children, both girls, now in college. Stern had never married, and his few attempts at relationships were failures. Even his connection with Amber in high school revolved around silly philosophical discussions. They argued metaphysics and epistemology, as if they knew something profound. She was the agnostic, he a militant atheist, although he never quite understood the militant part. The cosmos. Eternal matter. No creation. No God. To believe otherwise was intellectually weak. Recently, he had reconsidered his theory on the cosmos, given the questions of the Big Bang, and even the sacred cow of evolution was limping, wounded by some well-educated thinkers with intellects greater than his—or Darwin's for that matter.

The plane made its final approach and Stern rotated his jaw to ease the pressure in his ears. The tires hit the runway with a smoking thud, the plane shuddering to break the momentum. As they taxied toward the terminal, he practiced a few deep breathing exercises.

Clear your lungs with an eight-count; inhale for four seconds; hold it for seven; exhale again, repeating the eight-count; repeat four times.

The muscles in his neck and shoulders slackened. He checked his shirt collar to make sure it was lying flat, brushed the front of his L.L. Bean slacks, and examined his shoes for scuffmarks. With his handkerchief, he wiped his forehead and nose. He was ready—ready to meet Amber Greene.

And she was ready to meet him, standing with a direct view of the boarding ramp, searching intently as the passengers shuffled through.

Stern took his pulse, waited until several people exited before he arose from his seat, and stepped into the aisle. With his briefcase in hand, he made his way up the sloping ramp and into the Delta

Airways terminal, his eyes scanning for her. Friends, family, and business associates all pressed, hugged, and shook hands, chattering like squirrels. He shuffled anxiously through the crowd.

Then he saw her. It took him a few seconds to catch her eyes. She did a double take, then smiled and waved. The smile struck him. Strange, the impact she still had. The subtle and compelling elegance in her face hadn't lost its appeal. Time and expectation intensified it.

Amber took a step toward him, extending her hand.

"Stern?" Her eyes widened to match the smile.

"Hi, Amber," he said, taking her hand with both of his. "What a pleasure it is to see you again."

"Has it really been twenty-eight years, Stern?

"I guess it was this June." He pulled his hands back abruptly.

"Well," she said, "how was your flight?"

"I'm not a real fan of flying, but it was okay." Standing that close to her sent a rush to his face, which reddened noticeably. She wasn't lying over the phone and could easily pass for thirty. He shifted uncomfortably, and something stirred in him that he'd repressed for years.

"Are you okay? You're not looking well." Amber drew closer and put her hand on his shoulder.

"Huh? Oh, I'm fine," he said, faking a smile. "It was the, uh, flight. Sometimes it does strange things to my head. Takes me a while to land."

Amber nodded as if she knew his thoughts.

CHAPTER 2

It was Amber's idea to meet Stern at the terminal. She had other business to attend to in Rochester, and used this as a reason to rendezvous with him.

"I have reservations for two at Aladdin's at Schoen Place in Pittsford," she said. "It's a short drive from here, right on the canal. A quaint little Greek place with a good atmosphere. I thought you wouldn't mind a leisurely dinner."

"That sounds good to me," he said, trying not to gawk at her, but stealing glances when she wasn't aware.

The escalator clicked and thumped to the lower level of the terminal where Stern retrieved his luggage as the serpentine conveyor spit out its array of vinyl and leather. He rented a car for the drive to a hotel in Hollister and followed Amber's dark blue Lexus into the parking lot at Aladdin's. He pulled alongside her, waiting for her to exit first.

The dinner would give a chance to break the ice with her, to reminisce, to get to know her again, and pick her brain about the accident.

Stern glanced at his watch. Six-thirty. Reservations were for seven. He suggested a casual stroll along the canal footpath.

"I'd love that," Amber said. "I was just thinking the same thing."

"Do you come here often?" he asked, keeping a comfortable distance between them.

"Whenever I'm in Rochester, if I get a chance. I love the canal, love to walk, and it gives me a change of pace and a chance to think. Plus, I'm fascinated with its history."

"I'd like to have been here in its heyday," Stern said. He remembered studying the canal in junior high, New York State history. When he was a child, his grandmother used to play an album with a ballad sung by Burl Ives, and Stern envisioned the ox-drawn barges making their way across the state toward Buffalo.

The early evening sun began to cast slender shadows across the waterway like gray phantoms reaching for the other shore, while the cooling canal breeze gently swept Stern's face. The moment had a sweet magic.

Amber walked at his side, but neither of them spoke much. The encounter had a language all its own. Words would come later. The hushed dignity of the setting struck a chord somewhere deep in Stern's soul.

She broke the silence. "Should we go back? It's almost seven."

"You're right." Stern glanced at his watch again and turned back toward the restaurant. "It's funny how the commonplace can have such an effect on the senses."

"What do you mean?" She strode quickly to keep up with him.

"Just nature. You know, the sun, the wind, the water."

"Waxing philosophical? Just like old times, huh?"

"Well, it has a speech all its own, don't you think?"

"I agree, but I wouldn't call it commonplace."

"Poor choice of words, I meant—"

"I know what you meant," she said, "but I do think we speak so much we can't hear what God is saying through creation, don't you think?"

Stern arched an eyebrow and turned toward her. "*You* believe in creation?"

"Of course."

"You've changed then, haven't you?"

"Don't we all—over time, Stern?"

He paused for a long moment before answering. "Yeah, in some ways, but some things never change."

The air refreshed him and stirred his appetite. He looked forward to whatever Aladdin's had to offer and set his mind on a Greek salad with double olives. He'd never met one he didn't like, and was especially fond of kalamatas.

After a short wait, a hostess escorted them to the dining area overlooking the canal. Stern pulled a chair away from the table for Amber to be seated.

"Thank you," she said. "I feel honored."

"Courtesy should be taught, don't you think?" He moved awkwardly to the opposite side of the table and took a seat. "It's kind of a lost art."

"It would be novel, but I think most women like it."

The waiter—a skinny, swarthy young man with an aquiline nose—appeared out of nowhere with menus, introduced himself, and with the flourish of a skilled conductor, graced the table with two large glasses of water and a basket of bread.

"Be right back for your order," he said, and disappeared into the crowded dining room.

Stern followed his moving form. *Probably a college kid working his way through school.* The waiter reminded him of his own days as a bellhop at a Jewish resort in the Berkshire Mountains of Massachusetts. He'd carried bags for Sam Levenson and Beverly Sills's mother, and could make a hundred dollars in tips on a Sunday, if he hustled his rear-end off. Part of his assigned duties was to prepare coffee, tea, and buttermilk for the aging socialites after they returned from the Boston Symphony Orchestra's performance at Tanglewood. *Good fringes, too,* he remembered. Fourteen dollars a week, room and board, and anything you wanted to eat of the leftovers. The smell of the kitchen lingered in his mind like, well, like the smell of a kitchen.

Quick Boy returned as promised. Stern ordered a deluxe Greek salad with house dressing on the side. "And extra olives, please."

Amber had the souvlaki plate, one of Aladdin's specialties. They were alone and face-to-face for the first time since high school. Just a table between them.

Stern fidgeted, drumming his fingers on the table. "How long have you been editor of the *Valley Voice*?"

"Eight years in August."

"Enjoy your work?" He unfolded the cloth napkin, placed it neatly on his lap, and reached for a piece of bread.

"It's a dream come true. I worked as a journalist for about ten years, then as assistant editor for six years. It's personally very rewarding, and I can impact people's lives."

"Where'd you go to college?"

"Syracuse University—right after high school."

"Yeah." Stern sighed. "I don't remember seeing you after the summer of '68."

"I graduated from Syracuse in '72, took a job with the *Voice* that summer, and have been there ever since." Amber rummaged in her purse for a business card, and handed it to Stern. He scrutinized it carefully.

"And you uh, got married after college?"

Amber rolled her eyes. "Not a happy time, Stern. I met Jeff at S.U. and was married for ten years. He was a decent guy, but we just never clicked, you know? I married mostly to fill a void."

"The one left by Heath's death?" Stern cringed, wishing he hadn't asked.

"Yeah, I felt I was ready for a relationship, but it turned out to be more of an emotionally sterile arrangement." Amber cast her eyes down and picked at the fringe on the tablecloth. "It really wasn't Jeff's fault. I think he tried the best he could, but *I* shut him out. Eventually he fell in love with someone else and we divorced a short time later."

"And the kids?"

"Two daughters." Amber brightened. "Heather and Heidi, both

in college. They're good kids and we manage to stay in touch frequently. I think they stay in touch with Jeff too. He and I get along better now, after the divorce—we're actually friends."

Stern took note of Heather's name, figuring it wasn't a coincidence. "So you took your maiden name back, huh?"

"Yeah, I wanted a new start. Greene sounds better than Stovall, don't you think?"

Stern nodded. His own last name was odd enough, but it could have been worse. Wiley Smouse from college came to mind—a geek with a personality to match his name. The name "Stern" wasn't so hot either, but it was his mother's maiden name. He felt honored by it and never considered changing it, though it was the source of some taunting as a child. He was very comfortable with it now, and thought it fitting.

"It's kind of a coincidence that we've both tried to influence other people through writing, don't you think?" She pulled her chair closer to the table and leaned forward, engaging his eyes.

"I guess you're right, in different ways though."

"How long have *you* been writing?"

"I started in college, but never pursued it seriously until I was about thirty. I worked professionally in the mental health field for several years but got burned out. It seemed that people never got much help. It was extremely frustrating at times."

"It's quite a leap from mental health to writing novels, isn't it?"

"Not in some ways. You get an insight into people's psyches and it makes for good material for the books. You know, some mentally deranged guy stalking a hapless woman and…"

"And you *enjoy* that kind of writing?"

Stern took a slow sip from his water glass. "I enjoy telling a story, and the genre because it affords the opportunity to express my desire for justice. The perpetrator always gets caught and suitably punished. The stories deal with possible real life scenarios. I think that's why people read them."

Amber gently touched his arm and smiled. "Do you remember, Stern, when we used to have discussions in school about our *mutual* desire for justice?"

"Yeah, now that you mention it, we were quite committed to our personal campaigns against all the evils of the world."

They both laughed at the thought of their impassioned and naive adolescence.

"And what about our discussions on the Romantic poets? Weren't you a Coleridge fan?" Amber continued.

Stern took a breath, glanced around to make sure no one was looking, straightened his shoulders like an orator, and quoted Coleridge,

"In Xanadu did Kubla Kahn
A stately pleasure dome decree:
Where Alph, the sacred river, ran
Through caverns measureless to man
 Down to a sunless sea."

Amber faked applause. "Bravo!"

"Well, do you remember it?" he asked, aware that his face felt hot.

"Oh, my! Vaguely. But I was more into Shelley and Keats."

"Ozymandias?"

"Yeah, I remember it."

"And what about the *Ode: Intimations of Immortality from Recollections of Early Childhood?*"

"I can't believe you can quote the title. That was Wordsworth, right? I've thought about that recently, believe it or not. It makes more sense to me the older I get. 'The child *is* the father of the man.'"

"Good memory," he said.

"And you liked Poe, too, didn't you?"

"I've read all his stuff. You can't deny his genius, but what a messed up mind he must have had—very morbid.

"Nothing like *The Pit and the Pendulum* for a bedtime story." Amber shuddered and screwed her face up in disgust. "Okay, so that was then and this is now. How has your world view changed, Stern?"

"The world is by and large tragic. I don't hold out much hope for mankind, and there's still too much injustice."

"Whoa! Sounds like you're still on the same campaign, huh?"

"Well, less idealized though. I mean what can I or anyone really do about it?" Stern swished the ice in his glass just as the young waiter came to refill it. "Thanks," he said, without looking up.

"And what about the inherent goodness of man?" Amber asked.

"What about it? I'm a realist, and don't see much evidence for *inherent goodness.*"

She paused in thought. "And, uh, still an atheist?"

Stern chewed slowly on a mouthful of bread and swallowed. "I guess maybe I'm more agnostic now—like you used to be, remember?"

"You've grown then, haven't you, Stern?" Amber's voice softened.

"Do you call that growth? Toward what?"

"Well, let me just say that I think you're making progress."

Stern thought for a moment. "Well, life does have a way of tempering us, doesn't it? If you call that progress. And reality often flies in the face of philosophy."

"And don't you think that prejudice perverts reason even in the greatest of minds? And sometimes the brightest people don't have a clue when it comes to simple truth."

Stern let her words sink in for a moment before commenting, "So then, what's *your* world view? *You've* obviously been tempered along the way."

Quick Boy interrupted Amber's response, as he swooped upon

them with their orders. He snorted the obligatory "Enjoy!" then, scurried off like a rabbit chased by a beagle, oblivious to their thank yous.

"Let's eat. I'll tell you later," she said, leaning forward and catching the aroma of the souvlaki.

Stern was curious, considering the change he'd noticed in her. He would continue matching wits with her later. The salad tasted unusually good in her company.

They left Aladdin's a little before nine with a promise to meet Thursday night at Amber's for dinner. The evening had gone much better than he'd expected, but neither dared broach the subject of *the accident*.

Amber was busy the following evening. That would give Stern time to reacquaint himself with Hollister, visit the site of the accident, and spend some time in town, at the library, incognito if possible. He needed to kick back and relax, too, but the urgency of the story pressed his mind beyond relaxation.

On the drive from Pittsford to the Hampton Inn just outside Hollister, he allowed his thoughts to run at liberty about Amber. He'd enjoyed the conversation with her and felt reconnected in spite of its brevity. She was every bit as beautiful as he remembered her in high school, but the softening of her manner made her even more appealing.

He snapped the radio on to distract him when his inner equilibrium teetered too much. Unfortunately, the "oldies" station played a Roy Orbison song about unrequited love.

"Room 213. Elevator's down the hall to the left." The night auditor motioned mechanically. Stern checked into his room a little after ten, dead tired, and thankful for a king-sized bed for his six-foot-four frame. He would sleep in if he could, maybe until eight, then head to town for breakfast and a quick tour. He checked the baseball scores before he went to bed. The Yankees had beaten the Red Sox, again.

Time for a mid-season swoon for the Sox.

His last thoughts before he drifted off to sleep were of Amber. Her voice, her hair, and, most poignantly, her eyes. Seven o'clock, Thursday night. Less than forty-eight hours and he would see her again.

CHAPTER 3

Carla Fletcher always picked Amber up at precisely seven-fifteen on Wednesday mornings to go to Costa's diner for breakfast on the way to the *Valley Voice*, and discuss details of work. If they had time, they'd catch up on their social lives. They were close, like sisters, and could share their most intimate thoughts. Amber was grateful for Carla's true friendship. Even when they disagreed, they always got things out in the open and never let things fester.

Today there would be little talk of work.

"What's he like?" Carla slid onto the booth's vinyl seat, plunked her purse on the table, and began pressing Amber. "He's not married, is he?"

"Coffees?" the waitress interrupted.

"Please," they both spoke and nodded together.

"He's never been married, though I certainly don't know why. Maybe he's too involved with his books," Amber said.

"Married to writing novels, huh? Is he a bore?" Carla frowned and wrinkled her nose.

"Not in the least. Hey, I only saw him for a couple of hours. We had a nice chat over dinner, reminiscing. You know—old stuff from high school."

"Two hours, hon? That's plenty enough time to get an impression. What's his real reason for coming to New York?"

"To get information for his new book. You know that, Carla."

"He obviously knows you're not married, right?"

"I told him over the phone and we discussed it last night. For heaven's sake, the guy's here to research a novel and he thinks I can help him. I have no other interest in him, and I'm sure he doesn't in me. It's purely professional." Amber grabbed the menu from between the sugar canister and napkin holder and began scanning for breakfast specials.

"So, you know *his* thoughts?"

"Would you quit it? He's a decent guy, successful, well kept, and isn't a dork. I'm not blind, but neither am I foolish."

"Jeez! Sounds like a pretty good option to me. When do you see him again to discuss the, uh, novel?"

Amber paused, folded the menu, and put it back in place. "Tomorrow night at my house for dinner. I'm not looking forward to rehashing the accident."

"Do you really think he's going to write a book about Heath?"

"That's what he says, so yeah, I believe him. It's fiction of course, but based on what happened. Or might have happened."

"You sure you want in on this, hon?" Carla eyes narrowed.

Amber nodded. "I've already consented and really have nothing to lose. He said I could beg off at any time. I might even have something to gain."

"Like what?"

"Closure."

"Closure?"

"Yeah, even after all these years, some things are still hanging in my mind. Maybe this will put them in place—finally."

Carla sighed and looked at her friend. "Whew, girl, I hope so. You want me to pray for you tomorrow night?"

"I'd be a fool to decline that." Amber dumped two packets of sugar substitute in her coffee and stirred it aimlessly. "Did you tell anyone else about Stern?"

Carla cleared her throat. "Uh—*hardly* anyone."

"And what is that supposed to mean? *Hardly* anyone?"

"I mean, I only told Zelda."

"Carla, you didn't, did you?"

"We-ell, you know Zelda. She has a way of finding out anyway."

Amber rolled her eyes. "And now the world will know." She could have kicked herself for letting on about Stern in spite of her friendship with Carla, knowing that she had a hard time keeping quiet. Zelda would use the information to launch a power crusade at the *Voice*, vying to elevate herself, and she'd try to hunt Stern down to write an article, something that Amber would have to veto.

"Why don't *you* do a personal interview with him, Amber? It would look good for the *Voice* and sell a lot of papers," Carla said, back-peddling.

"Stern doesn't want an interview. He said it would create too much distraction for him. Maybe on a return visit." Amber *had* secretly relished the idea of interviewing him and was slightly miffed at his reluctance. As editor, she wasn't about to be co-opted by Zelda Twigg. She despised Zelda's insolence partly because it reminded her of the way *she* used to be. Still, Zelda was a good, aggressive reporter, and an asset to the *Voice*. She would speak with her face-to-face in the morning.

Stern awoke at six forty-five, unable to sleep any longer. A road crew was already clattering and assembling not far from his second floor window, busily strategizing with their foreman over the day's labor. Stern marveled at the knack the workers had for standing around looking so official, while at the same time getting nothing done. Construction always seemed so slow and boring.

He dressed to remain as obscure as possible. Baggy jeans and sneakers, an oversized "I Love New York" T-shirt, baseball cap, and shades. Just a tourist spending a few days and moving on. After breakfast in Hollister, he'd get a feel for the people, and drive around town. Visit Sullivan Creek at the site of the accident and find a place to write. Back to his room by five-thirty for the evening. Eat a light dinner and write well into the night.

Before leaving for town, Stern checked with Frieda, his-live in housekeeper in Annapolis, where he'd lived for the last ten years.

"Leave it to me, Stern," she said. "You relax and get started on that book."

Frieda was a competent and capable woman, whom he could trust. Impeccable credentials with one exception—a bent for gossip. Still, she was a godsend for him and he had no qualms about leaving her in charge while he was away. He'd done it countless times before. During his absence, she was to oversee major renovations to his house.

At her office, Amber confronted her chief reporter.

"Zelda, Carla shouldn't have spoken to you about Stern Blankley being in town," Amber motioned Zelda to a chair opposite her desk. "It's not public knowledge, and we want to keep a lid on it, per his request."

"What? No interview?" Zelda scowled.

"None. Nada. Ain't going to happen."

"What a waste—"

"You mean to honor someone's privacy?"

"You know what I mean, how often do we get to do an interview with someone like him?" Zelda huffed and crossed her arms.

"He's on assignment and doesn't want to be distracted."

"On assignment for whom?"

"Himself. He has personal business to attend to."

"Like writing his latest novel, right?"

"Did Carla share *that* with you too?"

"No, but it's true, isn't it?"

"And just what *did* she share?"

"Just that he was coming and wanted to see you."

"That's all?"

"Yeah…"

"So you *assume* he's here to do a book?"

Zelda shrugged. "Hey, he's an author isn't he? It's a no-brainer when you stop and put the facts together."

"And what facts might they be?" Amber leaned forward on her desk and clasped her hands together tightly.

"Blankley's an author; everyone knows he's writing a new book. He's from here originally and just happens to be visiting for a few days. He's meeting with the editor of the largest newspaper in the area. He wants to remain anonymous—"

"Zelda!" Amber stood. "You know I have the highest regard for your skills, but I wish you'd pay more attention to your job instead of meddling. I don't want you poking your nose into Blankley's business. Is that clear?"

Zelda paused for a long moment and let the rebuke sink in. "You have my word, Amber. I won't approach him."

Amber calmed herself and sat down. "Thank you," she said. "And by the way…"

"Yeah?"

"If he *does* agree to an interview sometime in the future, I want you to do it."

"Really?"

"Of course, this wasn't personal; I just don't want you bugging him. He does have a right to privacy."

Zelda left Amber's office chastened but unbowed.

That girl reminds me so much of myself it's scary. Amber muttered to herself.

Chapter 4

Hollister had changed dramatically. It was more gentrified now through the influx of outsiders with money. Touristy and busy, it was a far cry from the rustic, working-class town Stern had known. Its transformation was largely due to its proximity to Wells Lake, and the burgeoning tourist industry. The population around the lake grew to about twenty-five thousand during the summer, up from ten thousand during the off-season. The local Chamber of Commerce was aggressive, exploiting the town's natural charisma for its commercial advantage.

Revenue flowed into the town in an uninterrupted stream for five months as zealous merchants waited anxiously to harvest the liberality of the vacationers. The locals often complained about inflated prices and seldom shopped at the tourist traps. Some said the town didn't exist for them, anyway.

Stern skirted the perimeter of the park in the village square on foot. It was as he remembered—timeless and unchanged. Maybe it was the true heart of the village in the midst of aimless materialistic bustle.

He sat on a dark-green, wrought-iron bench, scanning the park, amazed at the gaudy and scanty raiment of the tourists, convinced that America had lost its sense of shame and dignity. Three whining pre-schoolers brushed by him, tagging after exasperated parents, begging to go to the beach.

"Maybe later, if you behave," the mother said. The father glared at her, but said nothing.

The park itself provided a soothing refuge from the rabid clatter around him—plush and verdant, with rows of neat sidewalks extending like spokes from the park's central hub, where a Civil War statue of a nameless soldier stood erect, rifle in hand. Stern wondered how many would stop and reflect upon its symbolism. How many in the generations to come would have any understanding of its meaning? How long would the town tolerate its venerable presence?

The sidewalks were fashioned and lined with rows of vivid summer flowers: pansies, petunias, mums, and daisies all splendidly arranged in meticulous beds. Stately hardwood maples stood like sentinels keeping guard over the entire park. A thick, lacelike canopy of leaves provided a covering from the sun's scorching rays, which occasionally found openings, sending shafts of dazzling light to the ground. Here and there, pansies and petunias glowed iridescently with a splash of brilliance from the gleaming slivers of sunlight.

The ancient bandstand stood with quiet dignity at the north end of the park. Stern remembered the Hollister High School band playing there (a cacophony more than a concert) and he laughed at the thought of George Taft's pitiful trumpet solo before the snickering crowd. Stern had sat next to Jesse French, whose explosive laughter broke like a cloud burst, sending Stern into a seizure. Once, during eighth grade assembly featuring an opera, Jesse squealed hysterically when a full-grown man in a skin-tight leotard leaped onto the stage spinning and whirling like a crazed dervish. It was a set up for disaster. Ballet was as far removed from Jesse's appreciation as he was from mastering Chinese. Stern came unglued around Jesse.

He laughed aloud as he continued reminiscing about sixth grade music class with Mr. La Fond—a short, squatty man with thinning, reddish hair, whose love for music was only exceeded by his lack of the gift of song. Jesse couldn't sing a lick either, but his lack was more than compensated by his excessive mirth, and whenever Mr. La Fond would attempt to sing, Jesse would squeal like a pig.

"Mind if I join you?" A deep male voice interrupted, and Stern looked up to see a tall, lanky figure peering down at him.

"Uh, no, I guess not."

"Names Earl, Earl Teeter."

"Hi, my name's—Howie." Stern stared at the ground, wanting to remain anonymous.

"Howie?"

"Yes. Uh, Howie Short."

"I once knew a Howie." Earl sat down on the bench and stuck his hand out toward Stern. "Howie you doing!"

Stern looked around to see if anyone was watching. He managed a weak handshake, and a weaker smile, wishing Earl would just leave him alone.

"That's a joke." Earl grinned.

"Yeah, I know—it's uh, quite funny."

"You didn't laugh much, did you?"

"Sorry, I was lost in thought when you arrived."

"Well, I happened to notice you were laughing to yourself a few minutes ago."

How long have I been under observation? Stern wondered.

"Memories…just fond memories."

"You ain't from around here, are you?" Earl pulled a toothpick from his shirt pocket and stuck it in the corner of his mouth.

"No—from Maryland."

"What part?"

"Annapolis."

"Never been there. Been to Cleveland. Got relatives there. You been to Cleveland?'

"Many times." Stern shifted on the bench and slid several inches away from Earl, hoping that he wasn't some kind of weirdo.

"You must travel a lot, then."

"Quite a lot."

Earl paused for a moment and stroked his chin. "So, you're just a tourist, huh?'

"Yeah, just a tourist. Here for a few days. Gone by Friday."

"First time here?" Earl rotated the toothpick to the other side of his mouth with his tongue.

"Not exactly. I've been here before."

"Things ain't the same nowadays."

"How so?" Stern turned his head and looked at Earl.

"Last ten to fifteen years, things have changed is all. Outsiders come in, bought up all the stores and houses and stuff. It's a shame for us locals. We don't feel at home now."

"It *is* kind of sad, huh?" Stern said, warming to the odd stranger.

"More than sad, it's a down right pity. School's gone to pot—pun intended. There's no discipline. A lot of the old-timers quit teaching early. Kids run the school."

"That so?"

"Yep, and there ain't one graduate from Hollister on the school board. All outsiders—no local representation."

"Doesn't seem right, does it?" Stern shifted and leaned a little toward Earl.

"You got that right." Earl made a face as if he was trying to eliminate a bad taste from his mouth.

"Did you go to Hollister?"

"Yeah. Also took auto body at the Vo-Tech. Couldn't hack the academics, know what I mean?"

"Yeah, sort of." Stern shrugged and nodded, not surprised that Earl found academics of little interest.

"Did a stint in the Corps, too, then came back here to work. The little woman objected to the Marines though."

"The little woman?"

"Candy. She's my bride. Been married twenty years in August."

"Any kids?"

"Two boys." Earl beamed. "Earl, Jr.—we call him E.J., and Bubba—real name's Harold. Bubba plays football at Hollister. E.J.'s into mechanics."

"And Candy?"

"She works at Flo's Diner, and let me tell you, it's one of the few places owned and operated by us locals."

"Hmm." Stern nodded. "What's Candy do at Flo's?"

"Cook. Darn good one too."

"And what do you do for work, Earl?"

"Rathskeller's Auto Body, two miles out of town on Route 63. I'm the head body man. Been there since eleventh grade, except for the Corps. Worked nights and weekends while I was in school."

"Stern figured that Earl was around forty. Hair streaked with gray, dark piercing eyes, and deep furrows in his forehead. A ruggedly handsome face, slightly pitted from acne.

"That's a long time at one place," Stern said.

"Only thought of quitting once. I love the work and I'm good at it."

"Why did you think of quitting?'

"Old man Burlew sold the business to the Rathskellers about ten years ago. I thought of going elsewhere, you know, just making a change, but the little woman got scared, so I stayed."

Old man Burlew. Stern remembered Gus Burlew's Auto Body Repair Shop out on route sixty-three.

"Is old man Burlew still around?"

"Far's I know. He just got old and couldn't handle it anymore. Besides, he was an alcoholic. Someone said he dried out a few years back." Earl leaned toward Stern, "A legendary boozer, you know."

"No, I didn't."

"'Course you didn't, I mean, how could you?"

There was a brief, awkward pause and both men gazed out across the park.

Stern crossed his arms and leaned back against the bench. "Where do you live, Earl?"

"On the way to Bedford, six miles from here."

Amber lives in Bedford, Stern thought.

"You on break?"

"Come to town to pick up a few parts. Sometimes I take a break. If I'm in town, I come here and sit in the park, thinking about the old days."

"The old days?"

"You know, the way it was. It seemed more real then, you know what I mean?"

"Yes, I do," Stern said.

"You take that statue over there," Earl said, nodding his head in the direction of the soldier. "Ain't nobody stopping by there to look at him. Something special about that soldier though."

"I agree."

Earl glanced at his watch and rose suddenly from the bench.

"Well, I've got to get going. Randy's expecting these parts and I'm already late. Been nice talking with you, Howie." Earl offered his hand again to Stern.

Stern reached for it and shook it firmly.

"My pleasure, Earl."

"Probably never see you again, so best of luck. Hope you enjoy your stay here in Hollister." As Earl headed back toward the Rathskeller pickup parked along the square, Stern stood and called after him.

"Hey, Earl!"

Earl stopped and turned. "Yeah, Howie?"

"About Flo's Diner. Where's it located?"

"On South Main, next to the Laundromat, sort of off to the side and out of the way. Why do you ask?"

"Could you meet me there for breakfast tomorrow?"

"Could I meet you? Heck, I go there every morning. Candy fixes me up pretty good, you know. It's called 'blessing by association.'"

"What's a good time?" Stern asked.

"Six-thirty. I've got be at work by seven-thirty."

"I'll be there. I've got a few questions I want to ask you."

"Long's they ain't too hard."

"I'll go easy on you."

"Breakfast's on me, then. Okay, Howie?"

"Sure."

"See you tomorrow." Earl saluted like a soldier, whirled and strode briskly to his truck.

Stern watched him drive away; his thoughts returned to Amber. She was busy tonight. He wondered what she would be doing. *Probably has a date.* He couldn't imagine a woman with her brains and looks not having multiple suitors. But maybe men were intimidated by her intelligence. She'd never mentioned anyone, but then why should she? It wasn't any of his business. Still, he couldn't help but think about it with a hint of jealousy.

At six forty-five that evening, Carla stopped by Amber's house to pick her up for church. Something new for Amber, which she found awkward, though not unpleasant. Tonight a missionary from Guatemala would be speaking and showing slides. Amber had never met or heard a missionary speak.

Work had been brutal, and she was looking forward to the church meeting. Sitting with Carla made it much easier. She hadn't so much as given a thought to Stern the entire day until the drive home, and then she wondered what he had been up to and what *she* would plan for tomorrow night.

Actually, she thought, *what's to plan other than dinner? He's the one with all the questions.*

Chapter 5

Narrow and twisting, Back Valley Road followed Sullivan Creek out of town. The creek was one of numerous inlets to Wells Lake, noted for its excellent fishing. In the spring, rainbow, brown, and brook trout wound their way through the swollen rapids to lay their spawn along its banks. Stern recalled trekking through the cold water prior to opening day of fishing season, net in hand, while others flushed the trout downstream. The thrill of netting a three-pound rainbow illegally was still etched in his mind. The suckers ran at the same time as the trout, and outnumbered them ten-to-one. A rainbow was a real prize.

Several small tributaries fed the larger streams surrounding Sullivan Creek. Only two feet wide, but unhurried and deep, these provided ideal spawning sites for the trout. Legend had it that Roland Barnes, nemesis to the local game wardens, would lie on his stomach parallel to one of these rivulets and pluck the trout to land by hooking them in the gills with his fingers. Stern had never tried it or seen it done, but felt the legend was credible, and Roland always had a good supply of fish.

Stern remembered camping out on the banks of the creek in a parachute used as a tent, compliments of his older sister's boyfriend, who had been a paratrooper in the army. It was made of dark green, silk-like material, and the enormous, albeit flimsy, shelter leaked like a sieve if anyone touched it from the inside when it rained. It was large enough to hold eighteen neighborhood kids, and provided ample space for an indoor campfire.

When not used as a tent, the parachute provided endless hours of amusement as a wind trap. On blustery days, gusts of wind would inflate it like a sail dragging its hangers-on helter-skelter across Stern's front yard, at times nearly lifting them off their feet. Simple fun, a fragrant memory of childhood.

The fragrance faded rapidly as Stern approached the curve where Heath's car had plummeted twenty feet into the waters of the creek years earlier. Apart from the burgeoning undergrowth, the site was largely unchanged. Even the enormous, gnarled oak tree retained is dubious eminence as a marker for the tragic scene.

Stern pulled the Taurus to the right side of the road and shut the motor off. He sat for several minutes, envisioning what might have taken place on that late April night in 1968. If Heath had been going as fast as the police reports said, he had no chance of negotiating the curve. He had missed the oak tree, but his car had allegedly flipped several times before leaving the road and landing top down in the creek.

Stern climbed from his car and made his way to the edge of the road, now hedged in with concrete guardrails linked with thick, wound cables. Climbing over the rails, he found a place where he could descend to the creek, which flowed with less than a foot of water. Skidding partway down the embankment, he came to rest not far from where he surmised Heath's Plymouth must have landed, and made a mental note of the entire scene. He picked his way back up the bank to his car, grabbing whatever roots and saplings he could to pull himself up, and headed for the motel.

Amber arrived home at ten that night from the church meeting. She had no grasp of why anyone would want to be a missionary and live in some remote jungle in a third world country, but she found the presentation stirring anyway. And Phil Chambers was not what she expected. He seemed normal to her, articulate, pleasant—and he didn't whine for money.

She opened her newly purchased Bible and pulled the prayer card the missionary had given her from the inside cover. She studied the faces of his wife and three children intently. They all had smiles. Real ones too, not phony, liked they'd just posed for the shot. This was strange territory for her, but at least she had Carla to help her understand it all.

Before drifting off to sleep, she thought of Stern. Try as she may, she couldn't get him off her mind. She wanted tomorrow night to come quickly. *Would Carla remember to pray?*

Stern arrived at Flo's ten minutes early and found Earl already waiting.

"Howie!" Earl yelled as soon as Stern walked through the door. "How's it going?"

"Not bad," Stern said, turning aside and rolling his eyes.

"Hey, I want you to meet someone." Earl motioned for Stern to come with him as he strode toward the kitchen. "This here's Candy." Earl pointed to his wife with obvious pride and put his arm around her. "Candy, this is Howie."

Candy blushed at Earl's boisterous introduction, and Stern wondered how many times she had been embarrassed by her husband's public behavior. He offered her his hand.

"Nice to meet you." He smiled warmly at Candy, which put her at ease.

"Earl told me about you." She withdrew her hand quickly from Stern's and wiped it on her apron. "He said he met you yesterday in the park and had a good talk with you."

"And now here we are for breakfast, hon. I'll have my usual, but maybe Howie wants to see a menu."

"Good idea," Stern said. "Can we find a booth in the back?"

"Not a problem." Earl acted as if he owned the place. "We'll take the one opposite the ladies' room."

Stern didn't want to think about Earl's rationale, but followed him to the booth furthest back, away from the half-dozen other patrons who seemed oblivious to Earl's histrionics.

"She'll wait on us," Earl said. "Order what you want, and remember it's on me."

Stern scanned the menu and opted for eggs over easy, bacon, home fries, salt rising toast, with strawberry jam and black coffee.

Flo's was a typical, small town diner with a mundane atmosphere, and dated, tacky decor. A cheaply framed picture of a farm scene hung askew on the wall adjacent to the booth where they sat. Candy arrived shortly with their breakfasts, and Earl ate like a man possessed of a hunger demon. A mound of scrambled eggs, home fries, sausage, and bacon, with four pieces of burned toast.

"Why'd you want to have breakfast with me?" Earl asked between mouthfuls.

"I thought you might help me." Stern watched in awe as Earl continued feeding his unshaven face.

"With what?"

"I need information."

"What kind?"

"I'll tell you in a minute, but first I need to ask you a question."

"Shoot." Earl belched and patted his stomach.

"How are you at keeping things in confidence?"

"Depends."

"Depends on what?"

"What's the secret? You ain't killed nobody, have you?"

"Of course not." Stern flinched.

"They can pull my toenails out then, I won't tell a soul. Long's there's no crime."

"Trust me Earl, there's no crime."

"Let me guess, then. You ain't really Howie?"

Stern straightened, and put his hands on his thighs. "How did you know, Earl?"

"I have my ways. I can read a guy pretty good. A sixth sense, you know what I mean?"

"No, I don't."

"Well, I just had you figured as someone who was in disguise."

Stern frowned. "Well, you're right. I'm not Howie."

"Who are you then? Clark Kent?" Earl laughed, this time drawing stares from several patrons.

"Look, Earl, if I tell you, you've got to keep your mouth shut. I don't want attention."

"You must be important then?"

"People will know my name."

"That so?"

"Yeah."

"What's your name, Howie?"

"Stern. Stern Blankley."

Earl wrinkled his brow. "No name I've ever heard of."

Stern was not surprised. "I write books," he said.

"What kinda books?"

"Novels. Mystery novels."

"I don't read them," Earl said. "I do read *Road and Track* magazine and stuff like that. No mystery novels, tho." Candy approached with more coffee, and another serving of eggs, which Stern declined.

"I'm here in Hollister working on a new book."

"And that's a big secret?"

"It is for now, Earl. I just don't want people distracting me."

"People would know you, then?"

"I'm sure they would. I'm from here originally."

"Hey, you ain't *that* guy are you?" Earl stared hard at Stern.

"*That* guy?"

"Yeah, the guy from here that writes the books. The locals all read them."

"That's me."

"I'll be darned! I guess I do know you—I mean, I know who you are, just didn't recognize the name. What was it again?"

"Stern Blankley."

"Ster—" Earl started to blurt out, but Stern grabbed his arm to shush him. "Okay," Earl whispered. "Gotcha. Mum's the word."

"Can you keep your mouth shut, Earl? It'll help me get done what I need to without interruption the next couple of days."

"You got my word on it, How—uh, Stern. People around here know Earl's good on his word." Earl extended his thick, work-worn hand toward Stern. It was the third time he'd shaken it in less than twenty-four hours.

"Deal, Earl?"

"Deal."

"Now, here's where you come in." Stern leaned across the table lowering his voice to a whisper. "It's about old man Burlew."

"What about him?"

"You worked for him, right?"

"Yep. Eleven years in all. Gosh, he was a good boss. Taught me a lot, I'll tell you. I almost quit when he left."

"Yeah, you told me that yesterday."

"What you need to know about Gus?" Earl scrunched his eyebrows and narrowed his gaze at Stern.

"Are you still friends with him?"

"Don't see him much. Once in a while here in town, but I never visited him once he sold the business."

"What would he say if you visited him now?"

"Depends on what for."

"To ask some questions."

"Questions? About what?"

"About an accident twenty-eight years ago."

"What would he know about it, that's a long time ago." Earl stirred three packets of sugar in his coffee, and downed half a cup in one swallow.

"Well, I don't know what he might remember, if anything. Maybe alcohol ruined his memory."

"He drank for a long time, that's why he sold out." Earl shook his head. "What a shame, a real shame."

"It's worth a shot," Stern said. "If my memory serves me correctly, Gus was involved in hauling a wrecked car out of Sullivan Creek years ago."

"I'm not surprised. People always called on old man Burlew. Johnny-on-the-spot, he was, and reasonable too. Twenty-eight years ago, you said? I was ten."

"Then *you* may remember the accident, Earl."

"Maybe."

"Ever heard of Heath Proctor?"

Earl dropped his fork, and pushed himself away from the table. "You don't mean *the* Heath Proctor, do you?"

"Yes, Earl, *the* Heath Proctor."

"Ain't nobody's *not* heard of Heath around here, accept for the outsiders. He's a legend, you know. Football star—got killed in a terrible accident, and the town ain't been the same since."

"That's the accident I'm talking about, Earl."

Earl sat in silence, thinking. "Old man Burlew dragged the car out?"

"I think he did."

"He never mentioned it to me."

"There may have been a reason."

"Like what?"

"A secret, you know—a secret."

"There you go again with your stupid secrets. You going to fill me in on this one, too?"

"I would if I knew it, Earl. I've just got a hunch."

"Sixth sense, right?"

"Yeah, maybe it's rubbing off on me."

"I'll do what I can, but I can't promise nothing. It's been a long time, and he may not want to talk."

"It's worth a shot, right?" Stern said.

"Yeah, it's worth a shot, but what's the accident got to do with you being here?"

"The new book I'm writing is about Heath's life—and mysterious death."

"You making stuff up then, or writing the facts?"

"I'm trying to find out as much as I can about what happened, then piece it all together, add some new things, change names and places—make it into a mystery novel."

"Another disguise so no one will know it happened here, right?"

"Yeah, it's only fiction."

"Then why push things and pry into the past?"

"Just curious. I want to make it as real as possible."

"What do you want me to ask Gus?" Earl said, satisfied with Stern's explanation.

"Feel him out about what he remembers, what rumors might have been going around. Also, ask him if he thinks it was just an accident."

"You think he knows something he ain't never shared, right?"

"Maybe."

"Ain't no maybe to it."

"It's just a hunch."

"You got a bunch of hunches and you want me to ask Gus to prove them?" Earl frowned.

"Just see what he says, but don't come on too strong. Just casual, Earl, don't scare him off."

Earl paused. "You suppose that's why he drank?"

"What do you mean?"

"What he knows drove him to drink. You think so?"

"I hadn't thought of that, Earl."

"It's just a *hunch,* know what I mean?"

Stern laughed at Earl's wordplay and sensed a growing bond of affection for him.

"One more thing, Stern," Earl said.

"What's that?"

"Mind if I call you Howie? It sounds better than Stern."

"Fine with me, Earl. Safer too, don't you think?"

"Yeah, I got a big mouth, and my foot's been in it enough already."

Stern handed Earl a slip of paper with his phone number at the hotel and his personal number at his residence in Annapolis. "Call me, Earl, if you find out anything, okay?"

"If I do, am I going to be in the book?"

Stern thought for a moment, then smiled at Earl. "What's your name going to be if I write you into the story?"

"Howie!" Earl roared.

Stern joined his laughter, shaking his head as they left the diner together. Earl patted Stern's back with his beefy hand. Stern checked his shirt for stains the moment he got in his car.

CHAPTER 6

Zelda Twigg was true to her word. She would prove to Amber Greene that she had integrity. She would neither hunt Stern down, nor would she mention to another soul that he was in town. If she waited patiently, she knew her day would come.

Amber decided to knock off work two hours early to prepare for Stern's visit that night.

"You're in charge, Carla. I need time to get ready for tonight. And don't say anything flippant about him."

"Who? That dashing author friend?"

"You just can't resist, can you?"

"I'm teasing, hon. I'll bet you have stimulating, uh, conversation with him."

Amber ignored Carla's remarks and continued straightening her desk. "Call me if you need to, but don't call after six, unless you're dying or something."

"I'll be dying to know how it goes with Romeo. You suppose he quotes Shakespeare?"

"Coleridge."

"Huh?"

"He quotes Coleridge."

"You're serious, aren't you?" Carla put her hands to her mouth to conceal a smile.

"He likes poetry, okay?"

"Uh, huh. And you've become a sudden fan too?'

"I've always enjoyed, well—Wordsworth and Shelley. Keats too."

"'To be or not to be…that is the question.'"

"That's Shakespeare."

"I know, but it could apply to your situation. You could suffer the 'slings and arrows of outrageous fortune.'"

"I've already had enough of that. I don't need any more!" Amber slammed her desk chair into the front of her office desk and turned toward the window overlooking the parking lot. She fought off the tears.

"Look, hon, I'm sorry." Carla breezed toward her friend. "I was horribly insensitive. Me and my big mouth, you know…"

Amber turned and faced her, drying her eyes on a tissue. "It's okay, Carla. This whole thing carries a lot of emotional weight. I'll be alright."

"Forgive me?" Carla sniffled and hugged her.

"Don't be silly. Of course I do." Amber hugged her back, clinging for an extra moment.

Amber left her office at three-fifteen and stopped on her way home to pick up dessert for the dinner with Stern.

The drive home gave her time to reflect on the evening ahead. In some ways, it seemed like she'd been waiting for this evening most of her life—as if it were ordained. Then again, maybe her mind was playing tricks on her, blowing things way out of proportion. She would know soon enough.

Tonight would be more than a casual chitchat. While she prepared the meal, her thoughts focused more and more on the purpose of the visit: to discuss the tragedy so many years removed. There were still poignant memories triggered by certain scenes or locations she passed by in the area. She never traveled Back Valley Road if possible. Something *had* troubled her acutely for a long time. Maybe she should share it with Stern. Then she caught herself. Why on earth would she open up to him?

She thought of him. Why hadn't he ever married? He was handsome, successful, and personable enough. She narrowed it down to three possibilities: either he had never found someone he was truly interested in, he was too absorbed in his writing to share his life with someone else, or he was nursing a deep wound from a previous relationship. There may have been other reasons, but these seemed most plausible. If she felt bold enough tonight, she would ask him. Actually, she reminded herself, those were the very reasons why *she* had never remarried after the divorce from Jeff.

The clock ticked past six, and Amber started pacing. She had done a number of interviews with visiting celebrities, but there was more at stake here. *She* was the one being interviewed, so to speak. Besides, something stirred within her—something she hadn't sensed in years. She tried to suppress it, but found she really didn't want to.

On a yellow legal pad, Stern dashed off several thoughts from the day's activities, including detailed descriptions of his encounter with Earl, and his surmising about Gus Burlew. He had just enough time to shower and shave before driving to Amber's. He'd successfully blocked her from his thoughts for the last twenty-four hours, but now, on the way to her house the door of his mind opened like a floodgate.

Evergreen Drive, five miles from Hollister, was named for the pine trees that flourished in the area. Amber lived two-and-a-half miles from the junction of Evergreen Drive and Bedford Road. Her nearest neighbor was more than a mile away.

The Wilburs, an old, farm couple whom she seldom saw, but with whom she was on good terms, occasionally dropped by with something from their garden, just to be neighborly. Effie Wilbur spun her own wool from the few sheep they kept on the farm. An expert knitter, she had presented Amber with a pair of hand-knitted, woolen mittens for Christmas in 1992. Amber still wore them gratefully, and in return had given the Wilburs a framed, color photograph of their farm taken by an aerial photographer who had worked on occasion for the *Valley Voice*.

The Wilburs were just the kind of people Amber liked to have as neighbors. New people had built a house another mile from the Wilburs, but Amber had never met them. They pretty much kept to themselves and their horses. She could see the house whenever she drove by, and had nearly hit one of the stallions when it bolted through an open fence.

Amber's house was a large, brick, colonial built in the mid 1800's. She spent her spare time refurbishing the interior and working in her elegant flower gardens that lined either side of the brick walkway leading to her front door. Waist-high and neatly trimmed, the hedgerows that bordered the walkway, together with the flower gardens, gave the colonial an impressive look. The exterior renovations had taken nearly two years to complete, and the windows, set against the red brick with crisp, brilliant white made for a simple, yet distinctive contrast. Dark green shutters adorned each of them. There was a bittersweet aura surrounding the house, which had once represented the hope of a failing marriage. Jeff's presence was still there in the shared projects and some of the collected artwork. Thinking about it always brought a nasty tension headache, so Amber blocked it out.

Inside, the floors were hardwood oak. The only coverings were handmade, hooked rag rugs which Amber purchased on her many trips to the Maine Coast during the summer. She always took the ferry from Rockland to Vinalhaven a few miles off the coast to visit some of the local shops and bike around the island. She found the rugs in a quaint boutique and became friends with the proprietor. Amber enjoyed the stories behind the rug, which told of local history. Each one was signed and braided into bucolic scenes from vivid, assorted rag remnants. Her favorite depicted Vinalhaven Harbor with several surrounding islands and lobster boats, complete with traps.

Stern arrived shortly after seven, carrying a briefcase with his notes and two of his latest novels, which he'd autographed for Amber. He pressed the doorbell and fidgeted like a schoolboy waiting for recess.

The twittering of birds searching for their evening meal played in his ears. No traffic, no noise—only birds. The breeze reminded him of the walk along the canal two nights ago, although it seemed like ages. He relaxed his shoulders and sighed, releasing the day's tension.

The raucous cawing of a distant crow pierced the harmony like a foreboding intruder, shattering the stillness. He pressed the bell again.

Amber answered the door, dressed in a pale green, cotton summer dress, hair in a ponytail.

Girlish, he thought.

"Hello, Stern," she said, "welcome to the estate."

"Hi, Amber." The schoolboy feeling returned. "I was just admiring it."

"Well, it's an escape for me, and I enjoy it. It helps me maintain focus for my work. I try to live a balanced life." She turned and drew him into the house by the arm. Was it the fifth or sixth time she'd touched him? He found himself counting.

Balance? Now that was different. He spent precious little time away from his work, which reinforced his introspection, and undermined his attempts at relationships. Amber could teach him something about *balance*.

"I'll take your case for you and put it in the study," Amber said. "We can meet there and talk after dinner." She returned form the study and offered to show Stern around the house.

"I usually give first time guests a complete tour. It's a matter of pride, I know, but not without justification."

A flash of the old Amber. Whatever she did, she did well, maintaining high personal standards. Not unlike himself.

She escorted Stern from room to room, detailing each one's design and decor, all the while giving a succinct history of the house. Pre-Civil War, the house had been part of a huge estate which was parceled and sold, leaving only the house and fifty-six acres of land. The renovations had been put on hold for several years while the marriage foundered, and she lost interest until about four years ago when she got tired of living in what she considered a major embarrassment for a newspaper editor. That was when she began to understand *balance.*

Stern was impressed, though the spacious rooms were not to his liking. He preferred something modern, and thought the countless hours of renovation appalling.

"Way too much work for me," he said. "But, I can tell you've maintained your normal standard of excellence here."

"Coming from you, that's a supreme compliment."

"Hey, I can recognize quality work no matter where I see it. Something I got from my father; you may remember, he was a cabinetmaker by trade."

Amber finished the tour, which ended in the dining room, and glanced at her watch. She had scheduled dinner for seven-thirty, and they both agreed not to discuss the accident over the meal. There would be plenty of time to talk afterward.

"You're leaving tomorrow night to return to Annapolis?" she asked, as she served a wholesome looking garden salad with freshly baked rolls.

"Yeah, my flight leaves Rochester at four-fifteen. I could actually use two or three more days here to reacquaint myself with the area."

"But you're planning on a second trip anyway, right?" Amber spoke hurriedly, looking directly at him.

"Probably in about a month," Stern said, nodding. "That will give me time to get things rolling on the book. I may stay here a week or so then, just to write."

Amber was striking in pale green, and the ponytail was a perfect compliment. Her spirited charisma came alive in her eyes and smile.

What is it about her eyes?

He broke the visual contact, yielding to her greater intensity.

"Is the salad okay?" she asked. "The dressing is homemade—sort of a vinaigrette. Balsamic vinegar, Dijon mustard, Worcestershire, plus a bunch of other ingredients."

Motor oil would have tasted okay at the moment.

"Excellent," he said.

"Tell me about your work. You're very successful, and popular."

"The money thing doesn't motivate me a whole lot; I just do what I enjoy, and success happens to follow. As for popularity, that *does* stimulate me to write."

"Nine so far, correct?"

"Yes."

"All mysteries?"

"So far."

"I have to be honest, I've only read a couple of your books. I'm not much for mysteries, more into nonfiction, which probably comes from working as a journalist and editor for so many years."

"I brought copies of my two latest novels. I autographed them for you."

"You did?" Amber said, pleased. "I'll definitely read them and treasure them, and who knows, I could become a serious fan."

Stern was glad he'd thought of the idea and would be sure to give her one of the first copies of his latest book once it was published. Maybe the first copy.

The meal consisted of chicken, baked with fresh zucchini, onions and peppers from the Wilburs' garden, topped with tomato sauce and grated Parmesan. For dessert, Amber had purchased a sumptuous cheesecake covered with slivered, dark chocolate and served with freshly ground coffee. It was the best meal Stern could ever remember.

For the next half hour, they relaxed, exchanging memories from bygone years.

CHAPTER 7

"Do you know a man by the name of Earl Teeter?" Stern asked Amber as they headed for the study.

"Never heard of him. Why?"

"I met him yesterday in the park on the square in Hollister. He works at Rathskeller's Collision & Auto Body. About ten years younger than us."

"I've heard of the Teeter name; it's local, but I don't know anyone from the family." Amber directed Stern to a leather chair opposite a neatly polished maple desk. She drew her chair from behind the desk so that they were facing each other about five feet apart.

"Earl's an interesting man," Stern continued. "He claims to have a sixth sense."

"Clairvoyant?"

"Whatever you want to call it. I had breakfast with him this morning and he knew I was using an assumed name to hide my identity."

"Just like that?"

"Just like that. I was using the name *Howie Short* and he saw right through it. I can't explain it, the guy's just different."

"Sounds a little hokey, Stern. A sixth sense? Kind of runs contrary to your way of thinking, doesn't it?"

"You might say."

"So what's with this Earl guy, anyway?"

"He's on assignment for me."

"Assignment?"

"Yeah, he's been working at the body shop for years. Started back when Gus Burlew owned it. You remember Gus?"

"Of course, everyone around here knows him. Alcoholic, isn't he?"

"He's dried out, or so I hear. Sold the business years ago because he couldn't handle it along with the drinking."

"So, Earl worked for Gus. Is there some kind of psychic connection?"

"Gus pulled Heath's car out of Sullivan Creek after the accident."

Amber paused in thought. "Yeah, I guess I remember, but that was long before Earl worked for him."

"True, but Earl was good friends with Gus—like a son to him. Gus never mentioned the accident to Earl, so he's going to visit him to see what he remembers."

"Does Earl remember the accident?" Amber shifted anxiously in her chair.

"Yeah, he was about ten years old. He says Heath is a legend here with the locals. Earl's got a son that plays football for Hollister, so football is a big thing with him."

There had been near apotheoses of Heath following his death. The eulogy at the memorial service given by Tony Frieberg, the football coach, would have made the angels jealous. Heath was not forgotten; he lived on in peoples' hearts. The football field was named, *Proctor Field*, and every local kid knew about him and secretly aspired to be the next Heath Proctor.

It was all a distressing memory to Amber, a very painful chapter in her life that had never truly been closed.

"So what is Earl going to ask Gus? What does he expect to find out?" she asked.

"You know, Amber, I don't think Heath's death was an accident."

"The reason for the book, huh?" She drew her lips tightly shut and set her chin.

"The motivating force, yes."

"Aren't you exploiting it for personal gain?"

"That's *not* the way I see it. I told you I don't write for money. There's something unfinished here, and it's worth searching out."

"And *you* get to write a new book."

Stern stood, blood rushing to his face.

"Look, Amber, if it'll please you, I'll donate half the proceeds to the town. Without the book idea, I wouldn't be here at all!"

She rose to face him. "And what am I? An afterthought? Chopped liver?"

"A partner, I hope!"

Amber stood silent for a moment. "Please sit down," she said, "you're making me tense."

"Sorry, I guess I was a little defensive."

Another pause. "And just what *do* you think will turn up?" Amber asked.

"I'm not sure, but Earl is going to see if Gus will talk about the accident. He may know more than we think. Apparently Burlew started drinking at the time of Heath's death because he knew too much and wouldn't talk."

"So now he's going to talk, just like that? All those years of alcohol to drown obscure memories of what might have happened?"

"It's a stretch, I know."

"Look, Stern, if you're writing a mystery novel, why don't you leave it at that? Why do you want to uncover something so dead?" She had not intended the pun.

"Because I want to know. The town deserves to know, and quite frankly, Amber, you want to know too." He stood, again.

But he was right and she knew it. She wanted to lash out at him as she had done so often in secret—at no one in particular. *Yes*, she never thought it was an accident. *Yes*, she did want to know what had happened. And *no*, she wouldn't lash out at him. She took a deep breath, sighed, and slouched in her chair, shoulders falling forward.

"You're right. I do want to know."

Stern sat opposite her again, troubled by his own brazenness and the pained look on her face. "I'm sorry, Amber. I was terribly insensitive I don't want to hurt—"

"No, it's okay—really. You just hit a raw nerve is all. Some things I need to face again. I'm with you on it—all the way."

Neither spoke for what seemed like several minutes. The only sound was the wind outside, whistling through the shutters on the study windows. Stern studied the wood grain patterns on the floor and Amber sat huddled and motionless.

Finally, he spoke, directing his eyes upward toward her.

"I visited the sight of the accident yesterday. Some weird feelings..."

"I've been by it a few times, only out of necessity, but never stopped." Amber leaned forward toward Stern, her eyes met his.

"I had no trouble finding the spot," he said, "the oak tree is still there. A lot of undergrowth made it a little difficult getting over the bank."

"People claimed there were other skid marks at the scene, but I never went to check it out afterward. I was so upset after hearing of Heath's death. Tell me, why don't you think it was an accident?"

"I checked the skid marks, with a bunch of guys from our class. It was too hard to tell. So many cars had left marks there, including the guys I was with. We all felt invincible behind the wheel. But, it was certainly possible another car was involved—one that forced him off the road. So much didn't add up. Why would he speed like that with no one with him?"

"He never drove fast when I was with him," Amber said, "*never*. And he promised me he wouldn't speed when he was alone. But who knows—he was a teenage boy. I know he didn't drink or do any drugs; they weren't even around then, except for marijuana. He was too conscious of his football career to be that stupid. In the nine months we were together, he never had one drink in my presence. When he left my house that night at around eleven, we left on good terms, and he wasn't angry about anything to my knowledge."

"Let's suppose for a moment," Stern said, rising from his chair and pacing, "that someone *did* force him off the road. Suppose he did speed up to try to distance himself from whoever was behind him. Let's also suppose he was hit from behind or from the side enough to cause him to lose control of the car. It doesn't take much of a bump to cause a car to skid. The question is who, and why? Who would have had a motive?"

"No one I know," Amber said. "Heath had people who didn't like him, but no one who would want him dead."

"As far as we know, right?"

"Yeah, as far as we know."

"Did you have any other suitors at the time?" Stern asked, fishing.

"Only you."

"Oh, but I was history at that point. Remember?"

"Yeah, but maybe you were just crazed with jealousy, and now—now you're back because of unresolved guilt, trying to exorcise the demon by writing a book."

"Sounds like a weak motive to me."

"Depends on how much you loved me."

"Believe me, Amber, it wasn't *that* much."

Slightly stung by Stern's comment, she continued, "It would make a good novel though, don't you think? Maybe I should write one about you. Novelist hides secret past—seeks atonement after twenty-eight years."

"I'm sure it would be a best seller." Stern faked a yawn. "But tell me more about Heath. What was he like?"

Amber took a deep breath and paused, breaking eye contact with Stern.

"The accident floored me for months. I was wasted, with raging anger at times. Just lonely and empty at other times."

Stern nodded without saying anything.

"We were planning on getting married after college. You know, there was more to him than people thought. Sure he was a jock, but you had to get to know him. He had a good mind and was tender and caring underneath the façade.

"Outrageously protective of me too. And a jerk at times. I remember he crushed some poor sap into a locker once when the guy showed some interest in me—wrote a lurid poem or something."

"Hmm," Stern said, and continued to listen.

"He was abandoned at a very young age, but it didn't make him bitter. He drove himself mercilessly, and had no fears except that of failing, but he wouldn't allow himself to fail. I have no doubts that he would have become a pro athlete. He had the skills and talent—and a relentless will."

Amber sighed and bit her lip.

"Heath was the only person I ever truly loved, and I had no one to help me deal with the crush of it all. Mom and Dad didn't know what to say, and I was too proud to seek counseling like so many others did. I carried on the best I could and people marveled at how well I took it. But, I was one hurting teenage girl."

Tears welled in her eyes, and she blotted them gently with a tissue she had taken from a box on her desk.

"It's okay to cry," Stern said, nearly stuttering.

He sat stock-still and watched her. She was real now. More real than he'd ever known. And vulnerable. Like a person of high estate condescending in front of a subordinate, casting aside all pretense. He was acutely aware of his own vulnerability in her presence. He reached for her hand and placed it in his own. She squeezed back with a firmness he hadn't expected.

"It was evil," she said. "The whole thing was evil. Why did it happen? Heath had so much to give, so much going for him. Do you believe in evil, Stern?"

He released her hand. The question caught him off guard.

"I'm not sure what you mean?"

"Do you believe in the reality of evil? You know, a force against good."

"Of course. Don't most people?"

"I mean evil personified, not abstract. Something planned and purposed."

"Evil personified?"

"Yes. I'm convinced that not only was Heath's death not accidental, but there was a deliberate evil plot against him."

This was new stuff for Stern. In all the novels he'd written, he'd always employed human agents acting on their own behalf, but never engaged in the realm of evil as Amber was now presenting it.

"Do you mean evil agents influencing people to commit certain acts?"

"Call it what you will—the Devil, demons, evil spirits, whatever. I've been very troubled with those thoughts through the years."

Stern arched his eyebrows.

"You're suggesting that *this* was behind Heath's death?"

"I know it sounds strange but…"

"That's an understatement for sure, have you shared this with anyone else?"

"You know, the odd thing is I haven't, but Heath spoke of it weeks before his death. He sensed something evil against him. It haunted him at times. I thought he was being weird, but he said it was real. I never believed him until after his death, and I've lived with the thoughts for a long time—you're the first one I've ever discussed it with. Maybe I could have helped him in some way if I'd only believed him."

Stern groped for words.

"Maybe it was just a self-fulfilling prophecy, like a subconscious fear of failure producing a conjecture about an evil force and, uh… "

"Are you suggesting he *deliberately* drove himself off the road by some subconscious impulse?" Amber's face twisted in unbelief.

"Sorry, Amber," Stern said, "I guess it's just the psychologist in me. I'm not accustomed to this evil force stuff."

Amber shook her head.

"I'm telling you, the way he described it was so real to him. He would wake in the night with a cold sweat and sense a presence in his room. It was frightening to hear him describe it, and I can't for the life of me understand why I'm talking with you about it."

"You're sure you've never discussed this with anyone—not even a close friend like what's her name?"

"Carla?"

"Yeah, her."

"I swear you're the first; don't ask me why. I've just blocked it out. It frightens me."

Stern sat silent for a moment, letting her words sink in.

"So, uh—why *are* you sharing it with me now?"

"I'm not sure. All I know is that when you contacted me about coming to New York, I leaped at the idea after the initial shock, hoping the whole thing might be resolved somehow. I feel safe in telling you."

Stern rubbed his chin with his hand, baffled by her comments, but determined to hear her out—to be a friend and ally. The account was taking an unusual twist, and he knew he had to refrain from trivializing. If this had stayed with Amber for so long, it was no time to lecture her.

The only thing he knew about the paranormal was from a college class. The professor recommended a series of books by an author who had contacted the spirit world via psychedelically induced, trance-like states. Stern just never took the realm of the supernatural too seriously.

"You know, Stern, it forced me to seek answers. I've never found any plausible explanation; never believed in the supernatural. I know a lot of people believe in spirit guides and poltergeists, contacting the dead—all of that wacky stuff, but only recently has my mind been changing."

"What caused the change?"

"I read a book on it. There's another reality we can't see, maybe more real that what we do see." Amber raised her head, focusing her eyes on a Monet print on the opposite wall.

"More real than what we see?"

"It said that some scientists believe there are as many as ten dimensions." She looked back at him. "If that's so, that leaves six that we know nothing of, if you take away the three we live in, plus the dimension of time. What exists in those other dimensions? Don't you find that fascinating?"

"If it's true, it's intriguing. Why do they speculate about the other six?"

"I'm not sure. Something about the laws of mathematics can only be true if there are other dimensions. I love math, but haven't studied it that far."

"And you suppose that these uh, evil forces, or beings, live in these other dimensions?"

"Just speculation at this point."

"What about the good guys?" Stern fought off a smile. "Are they there too, in these other dimensions? Or is it just for the evil ones?"

"There must be both. I couldn't imagine it being one without the other."

"And what would you call the good spirits?"

"Angels, maybe. Who knows? I'm new at this, but don't you find it compelling, Stern?" Amber's voice rose with excitement.

"Quite, but who wins the battle?"

"The battles, or the war?"

"Both."

"Obviously, the evil ones win some battles, but I think the good ones win the war."

"Sounds like *Star Wars* to me, Amber, but I can tell you're convinced. Do you mind if I'm not?"

"Of course. I want you to be honest," she said. "No point in faking."

"I have another question, Amber."

"What's that?"

"Assuming these evil beings exist, were they responsible for the accident, or did they influence someone to commit a crime?"

"Good question. I don't know the answer to that. Either way, I believe they were involved."

"And you're sure, aren't you?" Stern sat back in his chair and crossed his arms.

"I'm sure—based on Heath's statements and behavior."

He shook his head. "That's not a lot of evidence, is it? Have you ever experienced anything like that yourself, Amber?"

"No." She shuddered. "And God knows I hope I never do."

"I'm with you on that, but quite frankly, I do think someone else was involved in the accident. Someone in another car, and I'm hoping Earl can flush it out from Gus Burlew. He'll call me if he does."

"Earl seems like a long shot to me," Amber said, settling back in her chair.

"He's got a sixth sense, remember?"

"And you believe *that*?" She screwed up her face in phony surprise.

"Yeah, maybe it's one of those 'good guys' helping him out."

"I don't think were so very far apart, Stern, you believing in a sixth sense, and me believing in the supernatural."

"I didn't say I believed in Earl's so called sixth sense, I just said it seems to work for him. But maybe you're right; we may be closer than we think. Anything else on your little theory?"

"I have some other thoughts on it, but now is not the time to share them."

Probably stranger than the ones I've just heard.

"Why not now?"

"I'm still working on it. I'll share it—in time."

That would have to suffice. Stern didn't feel he should push her, although she had made him curious. What could be stranger than ten dimensions? An unseen reality more real than what we see? He had food for thought and enjoyed plunging his mind into an occasional fantasy.

They left Amber's study for the more relaxed atmosphere of her living room. She directed Stern to a plush, dark blue, velvet sofa where they both sat a comfortable distance apart.

"Could I ask you a personal question, Stern?" Amber shifted and looked directly at him.

Stern thought for a moment. "There are two reasons I've never married."

"Well! Since you know my question, can I give your answer?"

"I like that quality, Amber. It reminds me of our discussions in high school."

"You started it!" she said, continuing the game.

They laughed together at their mock childishness, but their smiles caught each other off guard, and each sensed chemistry working.

"Okay, why do you think I never married?"

She wasted no time. "Number one, you're married to your work. And number two," she said, looking into his eyes, a demure smile playing at her lips, "you've never met the right woman."

Stern maintained eye contact with her, but said nothing. Then he crossed him arms, put one hand to his chin, and began nodding. "You, my dear friend, are absolutely right. I commend your perception."

"Have you ever thought of divorcing your work someday?" Amber sharpened her gaze.

"If I find the right woman."

Neither broke eye contact.

Then she grinned. "I like *that* quality, Stern. Such discriminating taste. I'm sure it will be worth your wait."

"I'm sure it will be," he said.

Stern punched the snooze button on the alarm and fell back asleep. It was close to eight when he finally awoke. He planned to write in the morning, then work his way to Rochester for his four-fifteen flight into BWI. He had promised to call Amber before leaving to let her know about his return trip in a month. That would give him time to piece together his thoughts and the details of the last three days. He needed to put some distance between them to focus on writing. She had occupied too much of his thoughts, and maybe time would release him from the sweet, but entangling captivity he found so transfixing. He would call a few times, just to keep in touch.

In his absence, Amber would do her own research, and contact anyone who may have had knowledge about the accident. Maybe even hook up with Earl—he probably believed in the supernatural, and maybe that sixth sense of his would lend itself to her theory.

The return flight into BWI was just as uneventful as the flight up four days ago, with the exception of the passengers on either side of Stern. To his left sat an affable woman who ran a small shop in Lexington Market in Baltimore. For the duration of the flight, she never stopped talking to him about her business. To his right was a young seminary student, polite and clean-cut. Except for introducing himself and sharing where he was going to college, the student never spoke a word. Stern noticed how peaceful and relaxed the young man appeared.

Such a contrast, with me in the middle.

He was thankful it was a short flight.

When the flight ended, the seminary student handed Stern a small sheet of paper and asked him to read it when he had a chance.

"Nice to meet you," he said with a smile.

Stern assured him that he would read it, folded the paper in two, and stuck it in his shirt pocket.

The woman had mercifully struck up a conversation with another hapless traveler as the passengers began to file off the plane. Stern glanced at the bewildered face of the woman's victim, who was nodding aimlessly as he struggled toward the exit.

Chapter 8

White Marsh, Maryland is a suburb of Baltimore on the northeast side, just outside of the Beltway. In recent years, burgeoning commercial growth with a large mall, restaurants, and businesses transformed the landscape. A variety of condominiums, row homes, and apartment complexes provide ample and comfortable housing for the expanding population.

Julie Fisher was a resident of White Marsh.

"Hi Mitch!"

Julie quickened her jog to catch up with her neighbor, a twenty-one year old business major in his last year at Towson.

"Oh, hi Jules. Out for your daily rounds?"

"I'm up to three miles, five days a week."

She huffed and puffed to keep up with Mitch, who, at six feet-eight played starting power forward for the Towson University Tigers.

"Hey, not bad for a girl with such short legs." Mitch grinned.

Julie was dwarfed by Mitch's hulking frame, and for every step he took, she took two. The racial mixture in the neighborhood was much to her liking, and she enjoyed the close proximity of others, taking time to get to know the names of all newcomers. She was especially attached to Mitch.

"There's no way I'm standing this pace for long," she said, wheezing, and Mitch slowed to her level, preferring her company to his workout.

"You're a true ambassador, Jules."

"Oh?"

"Yeah. I mean some people wouldn't take time to say 'hey' if they were paid to."

"The world's full of snobs, Mitch."

"But you've got to be careful too, you know. You're effervescence could get you in trouble. Some guys would take it the wrong way."

"I do use a measure of discretion big guy."

Julie jabbed at Mitch's ribs.

"Ow! Hey, we've got a scrimmage tomorrow; go easy on me, would you?"

"I don't suppose you're going to get beat up under the boards or anything like that are you, you weenie?"

"You don't know your own strength," he teased.

"Well, I do know some self-defense techniques—want to see?"

"I'm not about to attack *you*, little one!"

They bantered back and forth until Mitch made a turn and headed down Bel Air Road toward the city.

"Going to have to go single file here, traffic's too close."

"I'm afraid I'm fading anyway, Mitch, and you need to step up the pace. If I get a chance, I'd love to see some of the game. I have a crazy schedule though. See you."

"Bye, my friend."

Julie turned, slowed to a walk, and headed back toward her home. Thirty-two and divorced from an abusive, philandering husband, she kept most relationships with men on a superficial, but cordial level. She trusted Mitch implicitly, though, and valued his friendship. Plus, she appreciated that he lived nearby and would flatten anyone who gave her a hard time. It felt good that a man cared for her and was interested in her as a person, not just her body.

Her marriage to Erik revolved mainly around the physical, and he got tired of her after a couple of years. She was tired of him shortly after the honeymoon, when the real Erik was revealed. After the divorce, he'd threatened to stalk her and make her pay. That was seven years ago, and she hadn't seen him since, other than in passing.

Pity the poor woman who's fallen for his sordid charm.

As she neared her front door, Julie fished in the pocket of her jogging shorts for her house key. Several neighborhood kids approached her.

"Hi, Miss Julie," they called to her and ran to her side.

Julie stooped and smiled warmly at their eager faces, taking time to hug each one, speaking their names. She had two hours before work—long enough to entertain five children with cookies and milk.

"Go ask your mothers if it's okay," she said, mentioning the treats.

That sent them all hurrying in different directions homeward. Julie slipped inside, leaving the door open, expecting their soon return. Less than five minutes later, the last one popped through the door beaming like the Cheshire Cat. Most mothers in the immediate vicinity knew and trusted Julie, and they were all too happy to have a free sitter for an hour.

Julie studied the happy and innocent faces of her guests, momentarily grieving that she would never bear children of her own. Cervical cancer at a young age had taken its toll, and the doctors said she could never get pregnant.

It's just as well. Who knows what might have happened if I had brought children into such a chaotic and violent marriage.

Still, it was an emptiness she found hard to overcome.

The kids loved the party and felt special in Julie's presence. She took time with each one, serving them milk and offering the plate of cookies, taking care to monitor the amount they took, and demanding politeness. It gave her immense satisfaction and, for a precious moment, it seemed like they were hers. But the hour passed and her little visitors had romped sufficiently for one day. She sent them away with a kiss and a wave, and then she closed the door. Bittersweet tears formed in her eyes.

The soothing shower washed away the tears and refreshed her body, and after a brief prayer of thanksgiving for a new start in life, her mind focused on work.

Ten minutes to get to the library. Hope traffic isn't bad.

Just getting across Bel Air Road could take that long in rush hour, but that was still a ways away.

She pulled a blue cotton dress over her head and hurriedly ran a brush through her wet, tangled hair. The party had set her back, and now she had to cut short her grooming. She could do some of her makeup in the car on the way to work—just like so many others in the rat race. It wasn't unusual seeing someone shaving, brushing their teeth, or putting on lipstick while trying to navigate the narrow corridor of Route 1 toward the city. It was a miracle that people weren't killed. Julie recalled one horrifying ride with a friend who was holding a Baltimore city map in one hand, eating a sandwich with the other, while steering with their knee.

"There!" she said aloud, as she snugged on her sneakers, ready for the miles she'd cover at the library.

She arrived with two minutes to spare, thankful that she'd found a parking space for her ten-year-old, maroon Subaru. She patted the car's hood like it was an old friend and headed into the building, greeting coworkers with a warm smile and "hello." The head librarian, Mildred Gear (nicknamed Mid), was relieved to see her assistant and spent a few minutes briefing her.

"A busy day," she said. "My feet feel like their ready to fall off. You're a welcome sight, hon."

"Fridays are always that way, Mid."

Julie nodded and punched her time card.

"Well, hon, this has been unusual, even for a Friday. I can hear my recliner calling to me." Mid uttered a perfunctory "goodbye" and scooted out the employee exit, anxious to rest her weary feet.

As assistant librarian, Julie worked at the White Marsh Library from three to nine, six nights a week. A few courses short of her Master's in library science, she spent as much time as she could attending college classes to fulfill her lifelong dream.

With work and college occupying the majority of her schedule, Julie had little free time. Though an extrovert, she often declined socializing in favor of her preferred hobby: books. She loved to read and spent countless hours lost in a novel, and sometimes, especially on Friday night, read into the wee hours of the morning.

Julie glanced at her watch—three thirty-five. She yawned, rubbed her bleary eyes, and put the book on top of a stack of other mysteries on her bed stand. She gazed at a picture of the author hanging on the wall opposite her bed, closed her eyes, and let her mind wander. The greatest thrill of her life was when she met him personally at a book signing at Barnes and Noble a year ago. It was shortly after the completion of his ninth novel. Stern Blankley had autographed the book jacket beneath his photograph, which Julie cut out and framed. He had seemed so shy and unassuming, but took time to speak with her. Shortly after that, Julie put a notice on the bulletin board at the library and started a book club at her home on Sunday afternoons.

This must be the third or fourth time I've read this one. And his latest isn't due until next summer. I wonder if he's married...

CHAPTER 9

G us Burlew was a firm believer in a higher power. He'd been attending meetings of Alcoholics Anonymous every Thursday night in the Hollister Presbyterian Church basement and faithfully practiced each of the *Twelve Steps*. Gus had been "on the wagon" now for several years, thanks to his close friend and AA sponsor, Lester Wilkinson, who'd been in recovery for close to fifteen years. Early on, it seemed like a hopeless struggle for Gus. He drank hard every night of the week at local taverns. Mostly beer, but he never refused any alcohol.

Though he enjoyed times with his buddies, Gus's objective was to dull his mind from events of the past. People thought it odd that he never started drinking until he was about forty, then he changed almost overnight. He'd always been a sensitive sort of guy, moody and prone to melancholy—not a good temperament for alcohol. It was remarkable that Gus never drank during the day, and his alcoholism had never interfered with his work—at least until it finally took its toll on his health. His doctor told him he was going to drink himself to death in a few years if he didn't dry out. That's when Gus contacted Lester. Lester was a good guy in Gus's mind.

His drinking finally precipitated the loss of the business, and the proceeds from the sale of the shop had gone to pay off creditors. There was precious little profit left after that. Just enough for a down payment on a sixty-foot doublewide trailer.

Gus and his wife, Nattie, received social security, but it was barely enough to make mortgage payments and keep food on the table. Nattie had worked for thirty years running drill presses in a local machine shop. Her pension was a woeful seventy-five dollars a month.

The effects of alcohol left Gus with rambling speech and scrambled thinking. One had to concentrate to follow the unpredictable flow. At times, depending on the subject matter, he made perfect sense and was able to have a clear focus. But for conversation, he was often quite scattered.

It had been six months since Earl had any contact with Gus, and then it was only in passing. Occasionally, he would see Gus around town and nod to him. Still, Earl respected his former boss, and loved him almost like a father. In his last few years at the body shop, the affects of Gus's alcoholism had caused a breach in his relationship with all of his employees. Earl missed the old Gus. Maybe things would be like they used to be. How he longed for the old days.

Earl rang Gus's doorbell at precisely seven on Tuesday evening. He waited a few seconds and pressed the button again, this time holding it down longer. He glanced around the front yard of the doublewide. No grass to speak of, just a couple of tacky wooden lawn ornaments stuck grotesquely in the barren space. A rusty Ford pickup was parked in the main driveway and the skeletons of several junk cars littered the field behind the sun-bleached garage—victims of the elements. The whole scene was one of neglect and the inevitable effect of wasted years. Earl's mobile home was no palace, but at least it was clean. He hated junk lying around. It made him feel uncomfortable.

Gus made his way to the door and peered through the smudged glass, fumbling for the doorknob.

"Earl! Well, I'll be… What brings you here?"

"Haven't seen you in a coon's age, Gus, and just wanted to drop by." Earl forced a grin at his former boss.

"Well, I didn't know what to think when you called, you know. I mean, I haven't seen you either, since oh—I can't remember when I saw you last. It may have been a year or so for all I know, and so forth. But, hey, good to see you, my boy!"

Gus thrust his hand out to Earl who grasped it and squeezed it like a vice. He couldn't stand a limp-wristed handshake and had developed his into a ritual, proving his manhood.

Nattie Burlew peered shyly from the living room as Gus invited Earl to come in. A homely woman with an angular jaw that made her appear almost masculine, Nattie had wide set brown eyes fixed deep within her prominent cheekbones. Her worry-worn face had seen years of heartache.

As a devout Pentecostal, she attended the local Apostolic Tabernacle three times a week—a habit she'd practiced since high school. Other than the AA meetings, Gus never set foot in the tabernacle, or any church for that matter, much to Nattie's disappointment. Still, she was proud of her husband for joining AA and sticking with it. At least he believed in a higher power.

Gus knew Nattie wanted him to become a Pentecostal and be filled with the Holy Ghost. Yet Gus, somewhat fearful of the Holy Ghost, had heard about some of the shenanigans at the tabernacle and cleverly steered clear of it.

Nattie hovered in the doorway, one hand twisting a button on the top of her shirtdress.

Earl nodded to her and removed his Dale Earnhardt cap.

"Nice to see you, Mrs. Burlew," he said. "It's been a long time since I seen you last."

"Yes, Earl, since Gus sold the business, I think I've only seen you a couple of times."

"My apologies, ma'am. I guess I should have kept track of you folks a little better. Suppose the Lord'll forgive me for that?" Earl looked down at the floor in mock humility.

"The Lord will forgive you for more than that, Earl; you just got to let him do it." Nattie was ready to preach. As she always said, "Pentecost was in her blood."

"Don't you go off on that stuff, now, you hear?" Gus had heard it a thousand times and was sick of it. "The Lord this, and the Lord that! The Lord gives! The Lord takes away! Please Lord, take her away!"

"Gus, he's got a right to hear it," Nattie insisted. "Lord knows he may be a step away from Gehenna."

"Don't the Bible say something about a woman submitting to her husband?" Gus countered, then, turned to Earl. "Seems as though maybe I do remember a little something about the Good Book myself. Praise the Lord! I think maybe I'll do some preaching. I remember Grammy Hoover used to run the old Presbyterian Church here in town years ago—ran it with an iron fist and a stubborn will to match, if you see what I mean. There were three women who sat on the Board of Trustees, and Grammy was the one in charge. They pulled the strings on the moneybag, and whatever they wanted, they got. Reverend Timkins got rode out of town one day because he was preaching the wrong thing, and they didn't like it. I think he was preaching on a wife submitting to her husband. Yes sir! That's what it was, and they were furious. They'd have none of that nonsense in their church. I think they must have torn that page from the Bible after he left town."

Gus laughed to himself, like he had been the only one present for his sermon. "Where was I?" he asked, looking at Earl.

"I think you were going to take the offering."

"Right! The offering! Where's the basket? Nattie get a basket, will you? We've got to take an offering here for the Lord!" Gus bowed his head as if to pray.

"You'll both be sorry for this someday!" Nattie screeched. "The Lord will not be mocked!" She retreated to the kitchen to finish the dishes.

"No, I don't suppose He will be." Gus turned serious. "Earl, what do you think? Do you believe in a higher power or no? I never did until AA, you see. But I don't know who or what He is. Nattie seems sure, but she's nuts half the time, so I can't go on what she says. Lots of hypocrisy, if you ask me. Why don't they ask me, anyway? I wasn't born yesterday, and I've seen a lot in my lifetime. People come and go, you know. The churches kick half the reverends out anyway. What kind of example is that? I mean, I can tinker on one of them wrecks out back and think about God." Gus sucked in a lung full of air and continued.

"You see why I don't go to church, Earl? I don't care if the wife goes, but I decided long ago that I ain't going. Can you see what I mean? I wish they'd ask me just once, but they won't. They don't really dare to anyway."

"Who are they?"

"Who are they? Anyone you want it to be. People in general. Sometimes I feel like I could preach as well as those monkeys in the robes."

"You ain't got a sermon, Gus."

"I just gave one, didn't I?"

"Yeah, but you don't believe in the Lord. Who'd listen to you?"

"Do those robed hypocrites believe in the Lord? You see where I'm coming from? Now I'm making sense, ain't I? Admit it, Earl. You know I'm right. I tinker on my cars and think about God. They tinker with people's minds and take their money in the name of the Lord. Who's right? How come you ain't saying anything Earl? You believe in the Lord, or no?"

"I believe in the man upstairs."

"What? You got someone living on your second floor, Earl? I thought you lived in a trailer too. I can't see it."

"You know, the big fella up there," Earl pointed up.

"So he ain't really upstairs then, is he? Why do people say that anyway? The man upstairs. The man upstairs. At least Nattie don't say that. She hadn't better be thinking about no other man anyway, whether upstairs or down."

Earl's brain was beginning to melt down with fatigue. This wasn't why he came. Somehow, he had to get Gus back to earth. Nattie came to a timely rescue, emerging from the kitchen with a peace offering: two large glasses of lemonade.

"Thought you might be thirsty after all the talking."

"Praise be to Jehovah." Gus continued the jibe, but retreated when he noticed Nattie's lowering gaze.

"Enough is enough!"

Gus knew the meaning of *enough*. He'd learned it through the years. Nattie had kicked him out of the house countless times in the past for drinking and other ungodly infractions. He quickly changed the subject.

"So why are you here, Earl, really? You got something on your mind, don't you?"

Earl fabricated a story. "Well, I was just thinking the other day... you know Bubba, my boy, plays football for the Hawks, right?"

"No, I can't say as I knew that, Earl, I quit following the game years ago."

"Well, he's a junior and plays on the defensive line. Pretty good player too. He was asking me what I knew about Heath Proctor. Maybe you remember him better than me. He's a legend around here. Bubba had been talking with some of the players, asking if their dads remembered him. I was only in grade school then and don't recall much."

Gus's face grew somber. He spoke carefully, measuring his words. "You came out here to ask me that?"

"I thought you might remember," Earl said, aware of Gus's mood change.

"What makes you think I know anything about Heath Proctor?"

Had he broached the subject too soon? There was no way out now.

"Did you know him, Gus?"

"Of course I've heard the legend. It was a long time ago. Can't say as I knew him though."

Earl sensed Gus was hiding something. He *knew* it, but how to proceed?

"Was he as good as everyone says?"

"Heath was good, but legends grow," he said, looking away from Earl. "Nattie, is there more of that lemonade?" He swallowed half his glass in two gulps. Nattie scurried in with a pitcher and refilled Gus's glass. He used the interruption to escape Earl's questioning. "You want to see my garden, Earl?"

Gus was back in space.

"Ain't much this year. No rain. Weeds grow though. Gosh, how the weeds grow.

"They'd grow out of boards, I swear it. Out of stone, anything. Pitiful. Thorns and thistles, that's what the Good Book says. Ain't that right, Nattie?"

Nattie wasn't listening. She was off somewhere, praying for the two lost souls in her living room.

Gus rose and plodded to the back door. As they descended the precarious wooden steps, Earl saw that Gus was right. The garden was pitiful—fighting for survival amongst an excess of weeds. It fit right in with everything else.

"Nothing to brag about, now is it, Earl?"

Earl nodded without interest. He'd lost any momentum with Gus and knew he'd have to wait for a later date, if ever, to talk with him again about Heath. At least his sixth sense had confirmed that Gus was covering something. He'd have something to report to "Howie."

CHAPTER 10

Amber discovered Josh Woodhouse to be, in her mind, an atypical pastor. She scrutinized him carefully, paying close attention to his appearance and style. She remembered attending church once with a college friend years ago, and the pastor wore shiny white patent leather shoes with a gaudy plaid three-piece polyester suit. She had no idea what he said, or was she even the slightest bit interested; his appearance had been too much of a distraction.

Josh was different. Neatly and tastefully dressed, he spoke with passion, and for the first time in her life, Amber listened intently to a sermon. The subject matter was strange to her. Something she'd never heard before and she jotted down a few notes as he spoke. Carla had encouraged her to bring a notebook on Wednesday nights. Amber had reluctantly complied, but was now glad she did.

Josh Woodhouse was speaking about "principalities and powers, spiritual wickedness in high places, the rulers of the darkness of this world." He carefully explained the existence of evil forces—personalities with rank and authority, with specific assignments, even against people. Amber's heart pounded as she listened spellbound.

Her thoughts raced backward—backward through years of memories. Sorting and sifting. A distinct picture began to form in her mind.

CHAPTER 11

Down in Annapolis, Stern's housekeeper sat filing her nails at her desk when the phone rang.

"Could I speak with Howie?" the voice on the line asked.

"I'm sorry, there is no Howie here, you must have the wrong number." Frieda Baker spoke curtly, ready to hang up.

"Is Stern Blankley there?" the voice shot back quickly.

"And who may I ask is calling?" Frieda said, annoyed. She was used to dealing with all kinds and was expert at intercepting, screening, and dispensing.

"Tell him it's Earl, Earl Teeter. He's expecting me to call."

"And who might Earl Teeter be?"

Earl couldn't help himself. "He might be Donald Duck or Jack the Ripper, ma'am, or he could just be someone from Hollister, New York that Howie—I mean Stern, just spoke with last week. Tell him I have information that might help him with his new book."

Frieda suddenly took note. *The guy must know something. Stern did have some strange ones call at times.* "Can you please hold? He's in his office. I'll see if he can take the call." She put Earl on hold and buzzed Stern.

"There's a man on the phone from New York by the name of Earl Teeter. He say's your expecting his call."

"Oh, Earl! Good! I am expecting his call. Thanks, Frieda, put him through."

Frieda punched the button and reconnected with Earl.

"Mr. Blankley say's he'll speak with you, Earl. I'll connect you."

"Thanks, ma'am, I sure do appreciate it. Know what I mean?"

Frieda shook her head. *Hollister must be quite a place.*

Stern picked up the phone. "Hi Earl, how's it going?"

"Not bad. I got some good news and bad news for you."

"What's that, Earl?"

"First, the good news. I spoke with old man Burlew last night..."

"And?"

"And I got a strong feeling he's covering something, Howie, a strong feeling. Actually, it don't take a rocket scientist to figure it out. He clammed up real tight when I asked him about Heath. Wouldn't talk. Changed the subject. Something's going on."

"Sort of confirms what we've been thinking, right Earl?"

"You ain't wrong, Howie. I just don't have a clue why he don't want to talk."

"I can't believe *you're* clueless, Earl."

"Actually, Howie, I ain't clueless. It's just a figure of speech, you know. I got some ideas."

"Like what?"

"Here's my theory. Old man Burlew knows there was another car involved, and he knows who drove Heath off the road. He's afraid to tell for some reason."

"Maybe he did it," Stern said.

"Possibly, but I think somebody told him to shut his mouth about it or else."

"Or else what?"

"Don't know that, got to work on some things yet. I'll keep in touch with you. If I find anything else out, I'll call."

"But you're convinced Gus knows who forced Heath off the road?"

"No doubt about it. Why else would he seize up like he did?"

"After twenty-eight years you think he's still afraid to say anything?" Stern asked.

"Maybe he did do it. Maybe he's guilty and is covering his own tail."

"Or maybe whoever threatened him is still alive and Burlew's still afraid. He's an odd duck, you know. But I don't see where he had any motive."

"How do you propose to find out, Earl?"

"Nattie may be the key."

"Who is Nattie?"

"Gus's wife."

"You think she knows something?"

"Maybe, or maybe she could get it out of Gus. That woman has her ways. She gives Gus the hairy eyeball, and he toes the mark."

The hairy eyeball? Stern hadn't heard that expression in a while, but then he was speaking with Earl Teeter.

"How are you going to approach Nattie without Gus knowing?"

"I could see her at the Pentecostal Church. The Apostolic Tabernacle."

"You? In a church, Earl?" Stern smirked. He rose from his plush, black leather office chair and strode toward the large bay window overlooking a section of harbor.

"Scary, ain't it?"

"So you'd pay your dues to speak with her, even if it meant suffering through church?"

"I'd be doing it for you—remember? You're writing the book."

"What do I owe you?"

"Nothing. Just being a friend to you."

"See what you can find out from, from—"

"Nattie."

"Yes, Nattie. And one other thing, Earl."

"Shoot."

"What do you think they'll say when they see you in a church?"

"No doubt they'll think it's the end of the world. Armageddon!" Earl laughed hysterically.

Yes, Armageddon. "By the way, do you know Amber Greene?"

"Nope. Who's she?"

"Editor of the *Valley Voice.* A friend of mine. She's helping me with some information too. Maybe I'll have her give you a call."

"Whatever you want, Howie. I'm with you."

"Thanks, Earl. I'll see you anyway in about a month. I think I'll spend about two weeks this time."

CHAPTER 12

Earl fidgeted like someone waiting for the dentist. He hadn't set foot in a church since he was a kid. He sneaked in just before service began and found a seat in the back. It was five minutes to ten, Sunday morning, and the bell rang four times to announce the beginning of church. The Hollister Apostolic Tabernacle was now in session.

Earl scanned the pews in front of him searching for Nattie Burlew. He spied her in the choir loft behind the organ with eight other women and two men, none of whom appeared to be under sixty years old. The organist began a lively opening hymn and the Reverend Roscoe Swartz bowed, leading the congregation in prayer, pleading for the Holy Ghost to fall afresh on them.

Soon the choir was in full sway, clapping their hands and singing loud praises to the Lord. Earl stood, but didn't sway. He mouthed some words, but no noise came from his vocal chords. He felt too embarrassed to clap his hands, and was thankful he was in the back row.

But he was noticed.

Visitors were quickly spotted and pointed out. After the singing, people were told by Reverend Swartz to greet any newcomers, and Earl was the only newcomer. All twenty-five members converged on him, including the Reverend, hugging, shaking hands, and patting him on the back. It seemed to Earl to last for an hour. He felt foolish, but tried to go with the flow. Nattie came last, hoping the good Lord had already answered her prayer for Earl's soul.

"I need to talk to you after the service, Mrs. Burlew," Earl whispered, as the members returned to their pews.

"Surely!" Nattie bounced on her heels with delight. "Right out front in the parking lot, after church."

"What time does it end?"

"Twelve-thirty."

"Twelve-thirty?" He raised his eyebrows.

"Yes, usually by then, though sometimes we go later. It just depends."

Earl had never done time in the county jail, but he felt he was about to see what it was like. He prayed that the man upstairs would be so kind as to cut it short today.

The sermon was endless, with a lot of dancing back-and-forth behind the pulpit. Shouts of "Amen!" and "Praise the Lord!" filled the tiny sanctuary. Roscoe Swartz was soaked with sweat, Earl noticed, and he hoped the Reverend didn't have a heat stroke.

Earl glanced at his watch: eleven forty-five. He had to alleviate himself from the three cups of coffee he'd had earlier. His bladder couldn't risk another forty-five minutes, but neither did he dare to exit during the Reverend's sermon.

What do normal people do? Do they have overflows from their bladders like a radiator?

He began to fidget again and cross his legs—*like a sissy*—but it seemed to help a little. The Reverend continued. The noon fire whistle sounded and still no end. Twelve-twenty. Would this be one of those days where it "just depends," as Nattie mentioned? What did that mean, anyway? Ten extra minutes, or an hour? He decided if he got up to leave, he wouldn't come back. Just apologize to Nattie later, tell her the truth. He was new at this church stuff and hoped the Lord would understand that he had a smaller bladder than the others.

With one ringing flurry, a tirade against sins of all kinds and an equally furious assault upon the devil, Reverend Swartz mercifully brought his sermon to a close. He was on schedule today.

Hallelujah!

It was twelve twenty-five, exactly one hour and fifteen minutes after the sermon had started. Earl had survived. He slipped out during the altar call and made his way to the men's room. A relief in more ways than one. He felt like a new man now. A man set free. Maybe that's why people went to church. You feel so good when it's over.

"I thought you'd left," a voice echoed from behind him. It was Nattie, looking slightly perplexed. "I didn't see you after dismissal."

"Well, ma'am, nature was calling real loud, you know what I mean?"

"Were you there for the sermon?" her tone had a pleading, hopeful edge.

"Didn't miss a word."

"What did you think?"

"'Bout what?"

"The sermon. What did you think about the sermon?"

Now he had to lie, she'd forced him. "He's quite a preacher, ain't he?"

"You think so?" Nattie beamed.

"No doubt about it, he's one of a kind."

"I didn't see you during the altar call," Nattie continued.

"Well, like I mentioned, Mrs. Burlew, I had another call right at that moment. The men's room was calling loud and clear."

Nattie frowned with disappointment. She was sure the devil had worked him over real good, filling his bladder and all.

"You wanted to see me about something, Earl?"

"Oh yes, that's right. I did."

She was expecting a spiritual discussion with him. This was her moment—and his too. She prayed for guidance.

"Well, Mrs. Burlew," Earl began slowly, "It's about Gus."

"Gus?" Nattie's jaw dropped.

"Yeah, Gus."

"What about him?"

"It's about the other day when I was there. I needed to talk to him about something real important, but he changed the subject and wouldn't talk."

Nattie was well aware of how evasive Gus was when she wanted to talk. "That's Gus for you. What did you want to talk to him about?"

"Heath Proctor. When I mentioned him, Gus clammed up. You have any idea why?"

Had the Lord let her down? Earl hadn't come to church to repent; he'd come for information.

"Why do you need to know about Heath Proctor?" she said, almost inaudibly.

"Gus pulled his car out of the creek after the wreck years ago, right?"

"Yes, Gus did—he always got the wrecks, wherever they were."

"Why didn't he want to tell me about him?"

"Why did you need to know?"

"My son plays football and wanted to know about him, like all the kids do."

Nattie was silent for a minute. People were filing to their cars; a few stragglers remained talking. As long as there were others around, she felt safe to talk, and Earl's manner made her comfortable. And she did have something to say—something she now felt compelled to share with him, though she hadn't shared it with anyone else before.

Must be the Lord. He often spoke to her with impressions.

"We knew him. Heath Proctor," she spoke.

"How well?" Earl asked.

"Quite well. He was like a son. Gus loved him and helped him out."

"Helped him out?"

"Yes, he helped coach Heath's football games." Then she thought some, "No, I guess he was just always there, near the bench, rooting for the kid."

"It must have hurt bad when he died."

Nattie looked at Earl. "Yes, it hurt real bad. It hurt Gus more than me."

"And Gus had to pull the wreck out too."

"He was called early the next day; it was all he could do to get that car out. You know, Earl, Gus gave that car to Heath as a gift."

"I didn't know, ma'am."

"For winning the first State Championship. Gus did the body-work on it and gave it to Heath—a powder blue Plymouth. Gus was very proud of it. He was very proud of Heath too. Heath's parents gave him up, you know. He was raised by his grandmother, but she wasn't all there, either. The kid didn't have much of a childhood. Gus wanted him to win so bad."

Earl had hit the jackpot, but he wasn't quite prepared for this. He didn't consider himself a counselor, although felt like one now.

"It was a tragedy, Mrs. Burlew."

"And so it was. Gus was never the same."

"Think it was an accident?" Earl blurted out without thinking.

"No—no, it wasn't an accident."

"And uh, you're sure?" Earl proceeded carefully, not wanting to offend her.

"Gus told me it wasn't, and said he could prove it."

"How did he know?"

"He said there was fresh paint of another color on the blue Plymouth. Paint he recognized—on the rear bumper."

"Someone pushed Heath's car?"

"Right."

"Who?"

"Gus won't say. He's never said, and vows he won't." Nattie crossed her arms and clutched her purse tightly to her chest.

"That why he, uh, started drinking?"

She stared aimlessly at the gravel-laden driveway, her voice quavered, "Yes."

"You've lived with it for all these years?"

"All these years."

Earl had a twinge in his stomach and felt a lump forming in his throat. "You have any idea who ran Heath off the road?"

"None."

"Why won't Gus tell?"

"He's afraid."

"Of what?"

"He won't say."

"Must be pretty serious if he's still afraid after all this time."

"Guilt too," Nattie said. "Not just fear."

"Guilt?"

She leaned toward Earl and whispered. "He knows he was an accessory to a crime by not reporting it. Someone didn't want it reported and threatened him. That's my guess. Somebody with power and money."

Everyone had left the church parking lot and Nattie grew nervous. She started fidgeting with her hands, and shifted her feet back and forth.

"I think it's time to go," she said.

"Who could that have been, Nattie?"

"I don't know."

She was not convincing, and Earl suspected she knew who it was.

"Look, Mrs. Burlew, the Lord knows who done it. You suppose He might reveal it to you?"

"The Lord could if He chose to."

"Hmm…you must have a good connection with the Lord after all these years, Nattie, now don't—"

"I have good connections! But He doesn't always see fit to reveal everything to us, you know."

"But, this seems pretty important, don't you think?" Earl kept pressing. "Doing justice and all that stuff?"

"Earl, I'd be pleased if you wouldn't ask any more questions. As I said, I have to go. Gus will be expecting Sunday dinner soon and I don't want to keep him waiting. I'm sure you understand." Nattie moved in the direction of her car.

"I understand, Mrs. Burlew." Earl followed. "Can't keep a man waiting for his dinner. He'd probably get mad at the Lord for that."

Nattie swung her legs into her battered Buick, slammed the door, and turned the engine over. "I hope you can attend church again real soon, Earl. It would do you a world of good, you know," she spoke from her car window as she backed out of the parking lot.

"Mrs. Burlew?" Earl called to her.

"Yes?"

"Would you pray and ask the Lord about that?"

"About you coming to church?"

"No—about telling you who drove Heath off the road."

Nattie hesitated for a moment, "I'll pray, Earl," she said, then rolled up her window, and drove away.

Hmm. Earl rubbed the back of his neck and stuffed the other hand in his blue jeans pocket, as he watched her drive off.

Can't ask for more than that.

CHAPTER 13

"I think this Earl guy is on to something." The voice on the phone was Amber's. Stern hadn't heard from her in over a week, and the sound of her voice jolted him out of the mental torpor he'd found himself in for the past several hours—a fit of melancholy he had on occasion.

"He says that Gus Burlew knows who drove Heath off the road, but he won't say who it was," Amber continued.

"He's sure Gus knows?" Stern refrained from letting Amber know of his conversation with Earl.

"That's not all. He says he's quite certain Mrs. Burlew knows, too, or has a strong suspicion."

"Earl's got a way with him, don't you think?"

"He's pretty unrefined."

"But, people seem to trust him instantly."

"Well, he had one encounter with Mrs. Burlew and she shared things with him she'd never shared with anyone else, according to Earl. And I don't think he was boasting."

"What else did she share?"

"She told Earl that Heath's car had fresh paint of another color on the left rear fender. Something Gus had discovered and apparently shared with her."

"What does Earl think it will take to get one of them to talk?" Stern's lethargy vanished as he pressed the phone closer to his ear.

"He suggested torture." Amber laughed. "Seriously, he thinks I could talk to Mrs. Burlew about it. 'Woman to woman', as Earl put it."

"What are these people so afraid of, the sky falling?" *Gus's silence may have made him an accessory after the fact. If someone had threatened him, he was still fearful of retaliation. That, along with the guilt about not having disclosed what he knew—and the consequences if he did, made him keep his mouth shut. Nattie was probably protecting him.*

"Whatever it is, it's very real to them," Amber said.

"Maybe we should just back off and let it go; if it's revealed, it changes the whole dynamics of the book. What do you think?"

"*You* can back off if you want, but I'm not. Not now, anyway. I'm determined to find out what happened. For the sake of justice, right Stern? Isn't that what you wanted to begin with?"

Stern paused. "You're right, of course, Amber. For the sake of justice."

Chapter 14

Julie Fisher's discussion group met every Sunday afternoon from two to four at her house. The current group consisted of herself, Sue Ellen Thiessen, Melissa Goudreau, Shelley Rank, Fenton Newman, Saul Karras, and Toppsy Gordon. They were close-knit and faithful to the meetings. For the last two years, the group had been discussing all of Stern Blankley's books in detail, along with other popular mystery novels.

Sue Ellen had a Masters Degree in English and Literature, and with a good literary mind, she often acted as a resource and mentor.

Melissa was Julie's closest friend and clerked at a clothing store in the White Marsh Mall, a couple miles from Julie's house. Whenever time allowed, they spent it together swimming and doing aerobics at a local health club.

Shelley was a library assistant whom Julie hired and trained two months prior and was the most tentative of the members, harboring a slight jealousy over Julie's relationship with Melissa.

Fenton, short and balding, was a charter member of the group. He and Julie had started an informal discussion at the library before the group took shape and changed venues. Fenton, single and self-employed as a computer technician, had a voracious appetite for mystery novels—especially Stern Blankley's. Of all the members, he was the most eager for Stern's newest book.

Saul ran a Greek restaurant near the inner harbor in Baltimore. He was a newcomer to the group, and sometimes brought pistachio baklava to everyone's delight. An affable, garrulous man of sixty, Saul was married, with a crew of children and grandchildren. He had an enormous black mustache adorning his upper lip, which appeared even longer when he smiled, spreading across his entire face like a patch of shag carpet. Everyone liked Saul. Almost.

Toppsy ran a daycare center in White Marsh. Twelve children from upper middle-class families made her life harried in spite of two full time assistants. She could be surly at times, especially if she'd had a bad day, which kept the group on edge whenever she spoke. Her husband was a dispatcher for a local transit company and worked as much overtime as possible—mostly to avoid his wife.

As head librarian at the White Marsh library, Mid Gear was somewhat enamored with her name. It had a nice sound to it. Nice and terse. Just the way she wanted to be known, friendly, but all business while at work. She felt like she was cruising at about half speed all the time. Not too slow and not too fast—just in mid gear.

Mid's counterpart in Annapolis (Erline Slicer) knew Blankley's housekeeper, Frieda Baker who shared just enough about Stern's life and itinerary to maintain some confidence, though around Erline, Frieda compromised her standards. Frieda felt very important, and Erline's sizeable ears had a passion for gossip. The two chatted frequently, sometimes for hours.

Everything that Erline knew about Stern was forwarded to Mid, who in turn—if she had time and was in the right mood—kept Julie informed. Julie shared discreetly with the group, but never let on about her connections. She liked being the one with the inside scoop. As leader of the group, Julie presented as much as she knew. The scant information wouldn't sustain two hours of conversation, but they'd find something to talk about. There were few quiet moments when the group met. They liked books, they liked each other, and they liked to talk. Today, everyone was present and accounted for.

"He's going back to New York next week," Julie announced to the group. "He's meeting with a woman named Amber who's helping him with the book. They're piecing together information about an accident involving a high school football star. From what I understand, neither thinks it was an accident, and Amber is on the trail of something. That's all I know."

That was enough for the group to be astir.

"How can you possibly know that?" Toppsy asked.

"Connections," Julie smiled, then turned and winked at Melissa.

Melissa was proud of her friend. Sue Ellen was impressed. Shelley was suspicious. Fenton was mesmerized, and Saul bellowed with delight. They all secretly thought what a privilege it was to be part of such a well-informed group. They were so on the cutting edge.

CHAPTER 15

Stern decided to drive to New York instead of flying. He planned his trip so he could catch a Yankees-Orioles game on Sunday afternoon, stay overnight in Baltimore, then proceed to New York the next day.

The trip from Annapolis to Camden Yards took less than an hour, and he arrived early to watch batting practice and relax for the afternoon. The heat and humidity were oppressive, and the proximity to the Chesapeake Bay guaranteed sultry weather in the Baltimore-Washington area for most of the summer. Baltimore itself pulsated with hot, moist air, and the playing field was over 100%. Stern ignored the heat and enjoyed the atmosphere at the classy ballpark. Predictably, the Yankees won.

Stern caught Route 83 off the Beltway and headed north to Harrisburg, Pennsylvania. From there he continued through Pennsylvania on Route 15, past Williamsport, and into the mountains of northern Pennsylvania. He looked forward to stretching out his Porsche a little, if the opportunity presented itself. It was a shame not to let a car like that loose on an occasion. He was banking on the troopers not being too active on a Monday morning.

The six-hour trip from Baltimore to Hollister gave him plenty of time to think. The Susquehanna was unusually low; the summer had yielded precious little rain and Stern judged he could almost walk across the river in places, piecing his way between the numerous small green patches of land that appeared throughout the riverbed. Driving provided a release for him—a sense of freedom from the sequestered lifestyle he'd lived for the past month, reading and working on the manuscript.

Frieda would take care of everything in his absence, though she'd been unusually distracted and nosy for the past couple of weeks. Stern had no reservations in sharing with her about his work, and valued her feedback. It wasn't like her to seek out information though. Maybe she was just getting a little too old for the job, but Stern didn't want to think of replacing her. She'd served him well for twelve years, and she would make sure the renovations he'd scheduled were handled in a timely manner. Frieda could ride herd if she needed to, and wouldn't tolerate any work that wasn't up to standard—something Stern demanded of himself and others.

His mind shifted from Frieda to Amber. He longed to see her again, and pictured her smile during the meeting at the airport, and the evening at her house. For the last month, she had often occupied his thoughts, and her memory threatened to sabotage his work. He began to question his motive for returning to New York. Was it to see her, or to work on the book? Either way it didn't matter; he was anxious to get there. He hoped she had been thinking about him too.

North of Williamsport, Stern found the opportunity he'd been waiting for. Traffic was light, road conditions good, and the challenge of open asphalt connected with the finely tuned machine at his command. The Porsche roared ahead, consuming the pavement as he pressed the accelerator deeper toward the floorboard. Eighty… ninety…one-hundred and climbing. Stern felt his body forced back into the seat. Other vehicles appeared to stand still. He noticed bewildered looks on peoples' faces as he pushed the Porsche to its limits. The feeling was indescribable. *Too bad it's illegal.* As he approached a curve, he backed off the accelerator. Immediately Heath Proctor flashed in his mind. How fast had he been going in that old

Plymouth? What was he thinking when he lost control of the car? What were his last thoughts before he died?

Life's too fragile—one minute you think you're invincible, the next minute you're dead.

He braked the Porsche and slowed it to a legal speed.

Chapter 16

Amber had been especially pressed at work lately. The joy sifted out of her job like sand through an hourglass. The more she tried to gain control of things, the less control she had. Personnel problems, time constraints, declining readership, competition, and a host of other troubles assailed her daily. She hadn't had a vacation in close to two years and it was showing. Carla insisted that she take time off.

"Let it correspond with Stern's time here," Carla told her. "He may need you to help him, and you're not fit to help anyone at the *Voice* the way you are now. I'm not being critical, just observant, Amber. You need some time away. Life here will go on without you."

Amber knew she was right. Carla always seemed to be right. Thank God, she had her as a friend. "Of course you're right, Carla. I think I've had tunnel vision for too long. I need some time away, even if I just stay in the area."

"I'll be in charge, okay?" Carla assured her. "Now why don't you sit down, book your calendar, and figure out when you'll be coming back. I think you should leave tomorrow and stay away for two weeks."

"Tomorrow? But I've got a million things to do just to get ready!"

"They can wait. Just get the heck out of here for a while. Go meditate or pray somewhere. Work on your house. Go to France, I don't know—do yourself a favor."

Amber thought for a minute. "You really want me out of here, don't you?"

"Yes, and soon."

"So you can take over? A coup, right? You want to take over, Carla?"

"Yes. I covet the headaches you've been having lately. And the drawn look on your face. The bags under your eyes are especially appealing."

"Do I really look that bad?"

"I'm being kind," Carla teased. "I could have said more."

"And if things fall apart while I'm gone?"

"I'm in charge, remember? What am I, chopped liver? After all, you trained me."

"And I did a good job, didn't I?"

"As always."

"I do have a few blind spots though. Sometimes I need other people's eyes."

"Well, I have to look out for you. You're my boss—and my best friend. A rare combination, don't you think?"

"Maybe ordained. After all, in some ways, you're my superior."

"In what ways?"

"You know, spiritually. You're so much more mature and knowledgeable than I am."

"I've been at it longer, Amber, that's all."

"And yet you're my mentor. I accept that."

"Well, for now anyway. You learn so fast, though—who knows where you'll be next year at this time?"

"I'd like to know Carla—where I will be. I hope I can get the fire back for the job."

"Maybe you need a new fire."

"For what?"

"Oh, I don't know, maybe it's not meant for you to be an editor all your life."

"You still planning the coup?"

"No. Just being your friend."

"I don't know anything other than what I'm doing."

"Well, just think about it in the next two weeks. Maybe God has a plan for you."

A plan?

Amber had never thought that her life could be planned in any way. She had always been in control, ordering her own world, doing it her own way, and trusting her own instincts. Ambitious. She was forty-six and had a lot of life ahead of her. She had planned to be successful, and would continue to be.

A plan? Something providential? It was a strange thought to her. But then, she'd had many strange thoughts lately.

"I'll give it some thought, Carla. You've steered me right so far. I admire your faith and uh, pray for me, would you?"

"You know I will—and have for some time."

Amber was certain of that. She had experienced the effects of Carla's prayers more than once.

"When is he due to arrive?" Carla asked, plunking down in the big, green, overstuffed chair in Amber's office.

"Who?" Amber feigned ignorance and shuffled a stack of papers on her desk.

"Stern, of course."

"Oh, Monday afternoon."

"Where's he staying?"

"Same place as before, the Hampton Inn."

"How long is he going to be here?"

"I don't know, he didn't say for sure."

"Are you in love with him?"

"Whoa!" Amber looked up. "For heavens sake, Carla. Why would you ask that? I hardly know him and I certainly haven't spent very much time with him."

"Just asking." Carla leaned forward and put her elbows on her knees, chin in hands.

"You know, for being my best friend, you have a way of getting under my skin."

"But I'm usually right. Right?"

"Usually."

"And this time?"

"You're *not* right."

"I'm not so sure," Carla said, shaking her head.

"And now you're speaking for me?"

"I'm your other eyes, remember?"

"And what do you see?"

"I see a sparkle in your eyes when you talk about him."

"Like I'm starstruck, right?" Amber rolled her eyes.

"You said it, hon."

"You idiot, Carla, I think you've let your brain go into its wishful thinking mode."

"But don't you really like him a lot?"

"I like him, so what?"

"A lot?"

"Okay, confession time. I like him a lot."

"I thought so."

"But I'm not in love with him. I'm a grown woman, Carla, and I'd like to feel I'm a bit more mature than that."

"So you've said."

"I don't know him well enough."

"Well, maybe you're on your way. Maybe you can spend time enough with him to get to know him."

"Is that the real reason you want me to have a vacation? So I can get to know him well enough to fall in love?"

"It sounds romantic to me." Carla looked away, dreamily.

"Well, why don't *you* get to know him." Amber turned her back and gazed out her office window. "Maybe *you'd* fall in love with him."

"I would never steal him from you, Amber."

"You are a complete idiot, Carla! A complete idiot!"

"I have a nose for these things."

"Yeah, like Zelda Twigg has a nose for trouble."

"I suppose mine is a romantic nose," Carla said, sighing.

"But it can't distinguish smells too well, can it?"

"What do you mean?"

"The difference between liking someone and being in love."

"Why are you so defensive?"

"I'm not!"

"You are!"

"I'm not!"

"You're in love!"

"I am *not!*"

"Yes, you are!"

"So what if I am!"

"I knew it!"

Amber swore under her breath. It wasn't so much that Carla knew her so well, but that she'd lost control. Carla had defined her feelings exactly, something that she'd tried desperately to hide. What was the sense now? Was that why she was losing her fire for work? It probably didn't matter anyway. Why would Stern, who'd never had a serious relationship with a woman, want anything to do with her?

Where is your sense of self-respect, girl? Of course he would have every reason in the world to be interested in you.

"You know me pretty well, don't you Carla?" Amber said with resignation.

"I'm your friend. Best friend."

"Thanks for being my friend."

"Can I say a few other things, Amber—as your friend?"

"Of course."

"You know I was partly teasing, but I don't want to see you hurt. It's true that you don't know him. Just keep your eyes open."

"I will. And you keep yours open for me too, will you?"

"I'm your eyes, Amber—your other eyes."

"I really need these two weeks."

"Are you glad I suggested it?"

"Very glad."

Amber couldn't believe the sermon on Sunday was about the nature of love. Did this guy know her thoughts? Maybe Carla had put him up to it. No, she wouldn't do that. A love based on honor, dignity, and respect. Unconditional. Self-sacrificing. A redemptive love. God's love for the human soul. Josh Woodhouse's presentation was precise and heartfelt. It resonated within her. She was the object of God's personal love. Something to be received, believed, and experienced firsthand. She felt strangely compelled to open up to that kind of love. She sensed a deep inner need, an emptiness and lack of fulfillment, in spite of all of her outward success and accomplishments.

Something was lacking.

She focused on the message as if she were the only one there. God was indeed speaking to her, drawing her to Himself. She didn't feel unclean, or even unworthy, just empty, with an overwhelming poverty in her soul.

What followed was a simple transaction of faith. Nothing subjective. No lights going off. No fainting. Just a human response to a divine initiation. But just as sure as the emptiness was there five minutes ago, it was now gone. Something inexplicable, yet nonetheless real had transpired: a quiet peace permeated Amber's mind. Somehow, she had found God's love.

CHAPTER 17

Earl spent the night in sleepless agitation. He wanted something new to report when Stern arrived in New York. His mind simply wouldn't shut down. He was certain old man Burlew knew what had happened to Heath. Someone hated him, was jealous, demented, whatever. Or maybe it was some kind of macho thing. Two brash young fools racing, proving their bravado—then the unexpected. Some kid scared to death, running home telling his parents. A slick cover-up. Probably a well-to-do family.

Money and power. No, Heath would not have raced. Too risky. Back to square one. Earl was frustrated.

Next scenario. Someone intensely jealous of Heath's success. That's the most probable explanation. Now, to find out who was jealous. Still, the cover-up had to occur. Someone bought Burlew off and threatened him. Someone with *lots* of money and power. It was a hunch, but Earl's hunches so far had served him well. He had good sources in Hollister and would see what information he could get in the next few days.

I could be a detective.

Bodywork wasn't holding his attention the way it used to.

It would be good to see Howie again, and this Amber woman—well, she was a class act, and if Howie endorsed her, then Earl dittoed that. Would Howie really write him into the book?

Nah. Earl chastised himself for the thought.

The paint crew arrived at seven-thirty Monday morning. Frieda Baker disarmed the security system, opened the front door, and stood face-to-face with Flanner Crosby, the crew foreman. Frieda noticed the white paneled van with bold blue letters, ARCO Interior/Exterior Painting, Annapolis, Maryland.

"Good morning, ma'am," Flanner said. "I hope we're not too early."

"Not at all, this is the time we agreed on." Frieda scanned Flanner carefully, admiring his crisp, professional appearance, new painter's whites, ARCO paint cap, and well tanned face and forearms.

"We'll have a full crew shortly."

"I've been expecting you." Frieda opened the door allowing him to enter the foyer.

"I have a few papers that need to be signed before we can begin work. Is Mr. Blankley at home?"

"No, but I'm authorized to sign for him. I'll be here for the duration of your work, should you need to ask questions."

Flanner briefly explained the work contract, which Frieda signed without question.

"Is it okay to park in the driveway? There are two other vehicles arriving in a few minutes. We'll have a crew of four to six on any given day."

"The driveway is fine. Just leave one side open for visitors. I have ladies dropping by now and then. What will your hours be?"

"Seven-thirty to four."

"Every day?"

"Till we're finished. Only Monday through Friday, though."

"How long will it take to complete the work?"

"Two weeks, maybe more. It's a major job."

Frieda smiled and assured Flanner that his crew could come and go as they pleased. She would be delighted to fix them coffee, and they could use the facilities whenever they needed. Flanner declined the coffee offer for his crew, but gladly accepted the offer for use of the facilities. Two other vehicles arrived and three men in similar garb assembled in front of the van, awaiting instructions from Flanner. Soon the men were busy carrying tarps, paint cans, stepladders, and an assortment of painter's supplies into the house.

Frieda retreated to her quarters where she would spend most of the next week or so reading, answering the phone, and "having it over with" Erline Slicer, her good librarian friend in Annapolis. It wasn't unusual for them to kill the better part of two hours at night on the phone. Erline would be stopping by on Wednesday afternoon for tea, hoping that Frieda would have up-to-date scuttlebutt on the happenings in New York. What a privilege to have such a strategic connection. Erline felt her social status greatly enhanced by her relationship with Frieda, and she was more than thrilled to pass along tidbits to Mid Gear up in White Marsh.

What pressed Stern's mind was not the book, it was Amber. The month apart had done nothing to dull his interest in her. If anything, it had enhanced it. He had no idea she had planned a two-week vacation corresponding with his time in New York. During his last phone conversation, she made no mention of it to him. He was aware, however, of her disenchantment with her work. She gave no reason why, and Stern was somewhat ashamed of his speculation about it.

He had called Earl at Rathskeller's from his cell phone before he arrived in Hollister. They arranged to meet at Flo's on Tuesday morning for breakfast. Earl assured him that Candy would treat them as royalty and, once again, breakfast was on him.

"Praise be to Jehovah!" Earl said to Candy. "He's here!"

Candy was mortified, hoping no customers had overheard her husband. Thankfully, they were in the kitchen behind closed doors. Still, Earl's voice had the force of a cannon, and some of the patrons were whispering to each other and snickering. It was not the first of Earl's unabashed outbursts. Nor would it be the last.

Stern entered the front door of the diner and Earl strode proudly to meet him.

"Welcome back, Howie, we've been expecting you." Earl stuck his calloused hand out to Stern who greeted him with less enthusiasm.

"Hello, Earl, it's good to see you again. And how is Candy?"

"She ain't bad. Come on in the kitchen and say hi to the missus."

Stern followed as Earl paced his way through the swinging doors into the already sweltering kitchen. The weather in New York didn't appear to be any cooler than Maryland. An oppressive heat wave had continued into the second week with humidity above seventy percent and daytime temperatures in the mid-nineties. At six-thirty, it was already seventy degrees.

Candy was trying to appear busy, but couldn't hide her eagerness to see Stern again, in spite of her husband's antics. "Hi, Mr. Blankley."

"Candy, it's so good to see you again."

"Candy will fix us up just fine like before," Earl said.

Before Stern could answer, Candy nodded and smiled again, this time more confidently. She was sure of her skills as a cook.

"How long will you stay this time?" Earl quizzed Stern as Candy brought two cups of steaming, mediocre coffee.

"At least two weeks, maybe more."

"Going to get down to business, huh?"

"Yes." But Stern wasn't sure at this point what the business was.

"How's the book coming?"

"I've written about ten chapters so far. Nothing in the last week."

"Hit a rut?"

"You might say."

"Got your mind on something else?"

"Yeah, a lot of things."

Earl didn't inquire about those "things."

"Maybe you can clear your head a little while you're here. Take some time to kick back and relax. Pretty crowded here, though. Outsiders, you know. They're like ants; the town's crawling with them." Earl shook his head. A furrowed wrinkle appeared between his eyebrows. "They'll leave soon enough, a lot of them after Labor Day, though the leaf-eaters hang on until late October."

"The lake sounds interesting to me. Maybe I'll rent a boat for a day of two," Stern said.

"Wait till it's cooler. You'll scald yourself out there, if you're not careful."

"I thought that was the purpose in getting out on the water—to cool off, I mean."

"Long as you keep moving, it's okay. But you sit and drift or drop anchor, and you'll fry like one of Candy's omelettes."

Not a pleasant way to spend a day, Stern convinced himself.

"Still and all," Earl continued, "you could practically walk across the lake bow to bow this time of year. Now me, I go early in the morning on the weekends. Fishing. I know right where to get the best lake trout and landlocked salmon. Maybe a bass or two. Nice large mouth."

"Maybe you can show me some time, Earl."

"You, the big time author?" Earl cackled. "I'd give you something to wink about. A nice fish story, only you wouldn't have to lie. I know how to fish."

Stern had no doubts about Earl's fishing prowess.

"Been thinking about that Amber woman?" Earl asked.

How in God's name could he know that? He'd never given Earl any indication that he was interested in Amber.

"I kinda figured maybe you two were a bigger item than the book."

"And why would you think that, Earl?" Stern felt his face redden with irritation.

"You know why, Howie."

"No, I don't, Earl."

"Sixth sense," Earl tapped a forefinger on his temple.

"You really believe that, don't you?"

"Don't you?" Earl grinned. "Besides, I got a clue that she's been thinking about you too."

"A clue?"

"Yeah, I could tell when she called me to ask about the Burlews."

Stern took a minute to think it through.

"You alright, Howie?"

"What have you found out from the Burlews? Anything new?"

"I ain't had no contact with either of them since I spoke with you last. But I've come to my own conclusions."

"What conclusions?" Stern said, still bristling at Earl's comments about Amber.

"Someone here in Hollister threatened Burlew and probably bought him off to keep his mouth shut."

"Who might that have been?"

"I'm working on it. I figured that you and Amber would have some thoughts on that. I mean, you two knew the town pretty well and what was going on back then."

"Someone with power and money," Stern said. "Okay, let's assume you are right. All we've got to do now is narrow it down to that. That should be easy after all these years."

"You forgot one important thing, Howie."

"What's that?"

"Who was hateful enough to do something like that? Someone with a real mean streak in him. An arrogant type."

"I'll have to give it some thought. No one comes to mind. Maybe Amber's got an idea. I'm seeing her tonight."

Stern felt that Earl's conjectures were flimsy, but he had no better explanation. He was growing weary of the whole thing, anyway, and just wanted to rest his mind from everything for a while. No plans to write until he felt like it. He still had plenty of time to finish the book. What did it matter whether they found out who ran the kid off the road, anyway? He didn't need to know. The story was losing momentum. His focus was seeing Amber again. Maybe they could spend time together. She could help him get a fresh perspective.

"I've got to go, Earl." Stern rose abruptly after finishing breakfast. "I'll catch up with you later in the week."

"Yeah, I've got to go too." Earl paid the bill, kissed Candy, and left for work.

CHAPTER 18

Amber had given no indication on the phone that she was looking forward to seeing Stern. If anything, she seemed indifferent and too busy to talk. She'd had a change in plans and couldn't keep their dinner date for Tuesday night. Stern however, was welcome to join her at church on Wednesday evening at seven.

"Church?" Stern frowned. "Why there?"

"Because that's where I'll be on Wednesday night, if you want to see me."

"Can I see you after church—say, nine-thirty?"

"No, I've got a big day Thursday and I plan on retiring early."

Stern mulled the idea over. She wanted to meet him at church. No opportunity to talk. Why would she want to meet him there anyway? *Why is she going there?*

"Something new, Amber? Uh, I don't remember you being too keen on church."

"I've been going with Carla Fletcher for a while now."

"Why?" He asked bluntly, stung by Amber's indifference—and already forming a dislike for Carla.

"It's a personal thing, Stern. I kind of like it."

"What kind of church is it?"

"I don't know what kind—it's just different."

"What's that supposed to mean—*different?*"

"Smaller, less formal."

"Where?"

"A few miles outside of town. Do you remember Hawthorne Hollow Road?"

"Sort of."

"That's where we meet."

"At seven o'clock?"

"Yes."

Stern paused in thought for a minute, trying to figure where she was coming from.

"What time is it over?"

"Eight-thirty."

"I'll go," Stern said, matter-of-factly, shocked at his own response.

"You will?"

"Why not?" *What do I have to lose?* "It will be a change for me." He could certainly suffer for an hour-and-a-half. No big deal to him. If those were Amber's terms, that was fine with him. If he didn't get to talk with her, that was okay too. She was too much of a distraction, anyway. He would go to her church and get it out of the way, then refocus on the book. If she wanted to help, fine. If not, he'd already written nine novels on his own. Something had changed in her, and he couldn't tell what it was.

"I'll be there at six forty-five. Can you meet me there then?" Amber interrupted his thoughts.

"And you will escort me in, so I don't feel like an idiot?"

"If you like."

"I'll pretend you brought me as a guest."

"People will probably recognize you. You have fans here, you know."

So that's it? She wants to drag me there to make some kind of spectacle out of me. Put me on display. Let everyone know she knows me, then write an article for the paper. Author Blankley attends church with newspaper editor. She'll smile and have her picture taken with me.

"Will you have a press camera?" he asked.

"Are you that vain?"

"Just wondering. It would make for good copy, don't you think?"

"Not a chance. You want out?"

"I would be too much of a distraction, wouldn't I? I mean, people would look at me and not the reverend."

"My, you *are* vain! I think the people are more intelligent than that. And certainly more spiritually discriminating."

"Make the introductions after church, okay? Maybe I can sign some Bibles. What do you think?"

"I think you're insecure and should stay home."

"No, I'm coming. Maybe I'll meet the Lord," Stern said, smiling derisively, and sensing his plans shattering by the moment.

"I don't know if He'd go out of his way to meet you."

"Apparently He did for you, didn't He?"

"You're hopeless."

"And you, my dear are one of God's angels, aren't you?"

The familiar click of the receiver told Stern the conversation was over. He sat in stunned silence, wondering why he had called her in the first place. Well, he wasn't about to back out now. He'd be there Wednesday night, whether she escorted him in or not. In fact, he'd arrive late, at seven-fifteen, just to make her wonder.

She sat in the third row from the front, beside a brunette whom he assumed was Carla, judging from the occasional whispering going on between them. They seemed like schoolgirls as they smiled at one another. Someone was droning on about a church project about to take place that would draw in others from the community. Stern wondered if this was the reverend.

Not too impressive. He took a seat as far back as he could.

So far, he was unnoticed, although the drone had eyed him suspiciously when he walked in. All other eyes were in rapt attention for the vision being set forth by Herr Drone: church attendance could double or triple over the next twelve months if everyone participated.

Drive 'em, drone, drive 'em!

Stern shut the speaker out, feeling his cynicism rising. He glanced around the modest church building. Probably fifty or sixty people of various ages. There were three men on the platform. The one in the middle suddenly spied Stern. Their eyes met momentarily, and the man in the middle smiled at Stern, who didn't return the smile. Amber hadn't noticed him. She wasn't looking for him either, and seemed perfectly content to listen along with the others as the vision came to a close.

There was applause.

For what?

He wanted to leave. Maybe he should have come earlier and sat with Amber. But in the third row? No, he'd made the right choice, now he was waiting for an opportunity to bolt. This time the man in the middle approached the pulpit, and Stern considered the slight interlude as his chance to escape.

Too late.

To his utter horror, the man looked directly at him, and with a knowing smile, asked all of the visitors to please stand. Three others stood.

Stern felt naked.

"Are there others?" The man asked, looking directly at Stern.

No, there are not others. I'm not here, you don't really see me. Stern's legs straightened and he found himself rising reluctantly with the other three. All eyes were on the visitors, especially the late riser.

He looked around, thankful he wasn't the only one standing. The horror show continued as the man began to ask the names of the visitors and where they were from. His heart was now rapping against his chest, and he found himself sweating.

Why so embarrassed? A man of his stature, in a nondescript church, on a back road in upstate New York.

Why am I here?

"And you, sir?" The man's eyes seemed to pierce Stern. "What is your name, and where are you from?"

"I—uh, my name is Stern Blankley. I'm from Annapolis, Maryland."

Now several eyes blinked with recognition and the whispers started. Stern knew that the man must have known that he was coming. Amber probably told him. Was this routine, or was it just done because he was there?

"Let's give our visitors a warm welcome." The man cut short the wondering as the entire congregation burst forth with enthusiastic and seemingly genuine applause.

Stern felt uncomfortable with the ovation, but noticed that the other three visitors were smiling as if they had one foot in heaven. Then his eyes met Amber's. She was smiling also, but there was something in her eyes that he'd never seen before. Though he couldn't quite explain it, he felt he knew why she wanted him there. She held his gaze for what seemed like a moment suspended in time.

The man thanked the visitors for coming and said, "Will everyone please be seated." Stern discovered the man was Josh Woodhouse, the pastor of the church. His only recollection of a man of the cloth was from his childhood. The Reverend Percy Towner, a wizened man in his seventies, with dark piercing eyes and a raspy voice, probably damaged from years of preaching. Reverend Towner was an obscure memory, and Stern had only one encounter with the preacher when he was rebuked for eating the remainder of the communion bread one Sunday after church. He had also quaffed a dozen or so communion cups full of grape juice before Reverend Towner pinched his arm and scolded him. The whole incident had left a bad taste in his mouth.

Woodhouse was coherent, and wasn't canned. Nothing singsongy; and he didn't read the sermon. Stern found his delivery interesting, although he paid little attention to what was said. He fidgeted with his hands, and occasionally glanced toward Amber, who seemed quite intent on listening. Stern hoped that since he'd paid his dues, she might consent to talking with him for a half-hour or so. The emotional turmoil had gained intensity over the last twenty-four hours, and he wanted to clear the air as much as possible. It was not a comfortable feeling.

The service ended at eight thirty-five with a closing hymn. There was a flurry of activity and happy chattering after dismissal as people moved slowly to the rear of the church to pay their compliments to Woodhouse. Amber was lost in dialogue with Carla. They both joined the march of the saints. Stern stood, but was soon mobbed by what he thought were several ardent fans, all gazing in obvious admiration—more interested in him than the pastor. He disliked crowds, and frowned on attention, but this was different. Hardly anyone spoke about his books. Rather, they welcomed him and thanked him for coming, hoping he enjoyed the service and asked if he would be able to come again? Stern lied and said he had enjoyed it, but probably wouldn't be able to make it again.

Definitely not, he said to himself.

His eyes scanned for Amber. She was approaching his row, now speaking with another woman, still oblivious to him. It was her turn with Woodhouse, and Stern could see their conversation was animated.

He's probably single and has an interest in her. After all, she was commanding more of his attention than anyone else was. On second thought, she was more than likely cluing him in on her guest.

The sanctuary was beginning to clear and Stern sauntered casually toward the exit hoping to escape unnoticed. It was not to be. Woodhouse saw him coming, and angled over toward him, trying not to be obvious; though to Stern he was *quite* obvious.

"Glad you could visit, Mr. Blankley," Josh Woodhouse said. He extended his hand to Stern.

"My pleasure." Stern lied again.

"Amber says you're a personal friend of hers."

"I guess you could say that."

"You're from Annapolis, Maryland?"

He already knows that. Why is he asking again? "Yes."

"I understand you are the author of several books."

Quite astute—apparently he's not a fan. "Yes. I've written several."

"We're honored to have you here, and hope you felt welcome." Woodhouse put his hand on Stern's shoulder, pumped his hand again briskly, and went on to the next person.

Stern guessed he felt welcome. Uncomfortably so, if that were possible.

"I'm glad you could make it." Her voice came from behind him.

She finally acknowledges my presence. Her highness has condescended to a man of low degree. "Oh. It's you."

"Yes, it's me. I knew you would be here."

"Oh, you did, did you?" Stern folded his arms.

"Yes."

"You seem pretty sure of yourself, don't you?"

"No, just sure of you."

"Meaning?"

"You said you would come. I took you at your word. You were late to prove a point, right?"

Did he really have feelings for this woman? If so, they seemed to be fading fast. But she was right. He had to prove the point that he, not she, was in control.

"I couldn't get here on time." His third lie.

"That's okay," she said, letting let it drop. "I'm just glad you came. Did you enjoy it?"

A temptation for a fourth lie. They seemed to come quite easily for him. "It was a blast."

"It really pleased me when I saw you. You know, when our eye's met."

Stern thought about that moment. He could still see her eyes and yes, he knew she had been pleased that he was there.

"I ignored you on purpose," she said.

"Thanks a lot, I thought you invited me."

"You could have gone in with me at six forty-five, you know."

"And sit in the front row?"

"The third row."

"Whatever. Frankly, it would have made me uncomfortable."

"I understand."

"Do you?"

"Yes, you're proud," she said, and turned toward the exit.

They left the church, and walked into the parking lot. He would have cursed had he not been near the church. No, he wasn't proud. He just wasn't a sycophant like the rest of them. He caught her by the arm and stopped her.

"And who are you now, Mother Teresa?"

"No, just perceptive."

"You women are all alike. Now I know why I've avoided any serious relationships."

"Who's talking about relationships? You're upset because I'm telling you the truth. You know you were too proud to come on time with me." Amber yanked her arm from his grasp.

"What can I say? Your omniscience makes you God."

"And your pride makes you the Devil."

What a pleasant exchange to have at a church. No wonder he hated anything to do with it. It seemed to bring out the worst in him—or maybe it was Amber who brought it out. *Why does she have to be so blunt and arrogant?* Some things were so different about her, and yet some things would never change. And neither would he.

Mother Teresa and the Devil himself.

Not a good match. Not now. Not ever!

Stern aimlessly kicked a loose stone on the paved surface of the parking lot, watching it hop and skip in the artificial light. He felt like that stone.

"Maybe it's best if we go," he said.

"Is that what you want?"

"For now. We can talk later. I need to get some things straight."

"I, uh, have two weeks off," Amber said, with a hint of conciliation.

"I'm sure you need it."

"I do. Carla practically forced me to take it."

"Is she your guru?"

"Just a close friend."

"It must be nice."

"Huh?"

"To have a close friend."

"You don't have any?" Her voice softened and she turned to face him.

"Maybe. Maybe they're more like acquaintances."

"That's a pity, Stern."

"Yeah, it's a pity."

"Can we meet tomorrow?" Amber started walking again toward her car.

"That soon?"

"Yeah."

"Where?"

"At the lake—in the morning."

"Is that what you want?"

"Yeah, I guess it is," she said, sighing and fumbling in her purse for her car keys.

"Then we're friends?"

"Friends." She offered her hand and smiled at him. The life in her eyes was back—the vibrancy he'd seen in church. "Tomorrow morning at seven, at Friendship Point. Don't be late," she said.

How ironic, given the conversation they just had, Friendship Point on Well's Lake.

"I'll be on time." Stern walked slowly to his car, started the engine, and drove out of the church parking lot.

What have I gotten myself into?

CHAPTER 19

The road to Friendship Point broke at a sharp angle from the main road along the lake. It descended steeply until it flattened out parallel to the shore. A narrow, paved road, it carried considerable summer traffic from the cottagers who swarmed along the lake for their yearly seasonal reprieve from city life. There was a public beach at the Point, complete with picnic tables, grills, a beach house, metal benches, and a sizeable dock that formed a "T" in the water. Enormous willow trees provided shade for the picnic area. The beach was populated with flocks of seagulls and scores of ducks on the lookout for leftovers from picnics. It was not uncommon to find visitors practically hand-feeding the ducks, which seemed unaware of all the comings and goings.

Stern made sure he was there at six forty-five. The beach was deserted except for the wildlife. The lake was mirror calm as the morning sun cast its dazzling rays like silver glitter over its surface. A Canadian cold front had brought in a storm overnight, cooling the weather, and blowing the humidity out. He immersed himself in the pristine atmosphere, and then strolled along the beach. A raft of mallards swam in formation toward the shore looking for a handout. They paddled out of the water and followed him Pied Piper style. He noticed that one of the ducks had a deformed foot drawn up under its body. Smaller than the other birds, it hopped along quite deftly on one foot. Stern wondered at its chances for survival, especially with the fall and winter ahead.

The sound of car tires crunching on the crushed stone parking lot broke his reverie. It was Amber. In spite of the previous night's exchange, Stern was looking forward to seeing her and being alone together. They had acted like teenagers instead of adults, for which he was still embarrassed. But he harbored no ill feelings toward her and hoped she felt the same about him. Any fears he had to the contrary quickly vanished as she approached him, smiling in her customary manner and greeting him warmly.

There were no hard feelings.

"It's an incredible day. Thank God for the cooler weather," she said. "Have you been here long?"

"About fifteen minutes. Just enjoying the quietness, watching the ducks."

"They're cute, aren't they?"

He nodded. "And quite unafraid—almost tame."

"You want to walk or sit?" Amber said.

"Let's walk first, then sit."

"Sounds good to me." She skipped two steps ahead and caught his eye. "Hey, sorry about last night."

"Yeah, me too."

"You're right about the pride thing, you know. I didn't need to be so blunt."

"Doesn't matter, it's behind us."

"A new day and a new start, right?"

"Right."

It took only a short time to cross the length of the beach and back. The discussion was casual, centering mostly on the change in the weather and the stunning scenery around the lake, which Stern had taken for granted growing up. At the far end of the picnic area was a dark green metal bench under a huge willow. They decided it would be the best place to talk, and the least likely place for interruptions. A modest breeze now blew in from the lake rippling the water and pushing little waves gently against the shore. The rhythmic lapping created a perfect cover for conversation. A few other vehicles began arriving at the beach, but no one ventured into their area.

"The Woodhouse guy—I assume he's the Reverend," Stern began.

"The Pastor," Amber corrected. "It's a better title than Reverend."

"You mean he's not holier than thou?" Stern felt the sarcasm rising and regretted not checking it.

"No, he's just a person like you and me, Stern. And very down-to-earth."

"He seemed okay."

"He's a friend, I like him."

Stern bent over and picked up a willow twig, bending it back and forth. "How long have you been going to his church?"

"Two months."

"You were going there when I was in New York a month ago?"

"Yes."

"I thought I'd noticed a change in you."

"What kind of change?"

"I don't know—hard to describe."

"I guess I have changed. I hope it's for the better."

"There's still a lot of the old Amber left." The twig snapped and Stern paused to observe both pieces before tossing them on the ground.

"I know, all too well—like last night." Amber drew her legs up under her on the bench, facing him.

"Well, that wasn't criticism. I like the old Amber too."

"And do you like the new?"

"Yeah, I guess. She's not as caustic as the old."

"That's a pleasant way of saying it." Amber pushed at Stern's knee and screwed her face up.

"Couldn't think of the right word."

"Caustic is fitting for the old. You can use it if you like."

Stern paused, measuring his words more carefully. He leaned

back against the bench, twisting so he could see her face. "So why church? What brought you to that?"

"Carla got me started."

"But what was *your* interest?"

"Just curious. I had nothing to lose. She's my friend so I wanted to honor her."

"And it stuck?"

"Apparently so. I haven't missed a Sunday since she first asked me to go."

"And Wednesdays, too?"

"I've missed a few."

"It's a far cry from where you were in high school, huh, girl?"

Amber grinned, not offended by his characterization. "Hey, that's what you called me back then, remember?"

Sterns' face reddened. He bent forward, picked up a stone, and tossed it into the water. "I think it was a Freudian slip."

"I'm not so sure," she teased.

"It was just in context with what I was saying—about high school."

"Oh. I see."

There was a moment of awkward silence. Stern spoke, "So, now you're a believer in..."

"God, Stern. Crazy isn't it?"

"I'm still not convinced. Probably never will be."

"You don't sound too sure."

"Well, I guess I'm not the hardcore atheist anymore. Time changes things."

"I've, uh, had an experience with God, too," Amber said.

"An experience?" Stern looked at her again and raised his eyebrows.

"Yes."

"What kind of experience?"

"I can't describe it. I just know He's real. I know He loves me."

"Just like that?"

"Well, no. It was a process, but there was a time I knew it was real. I made a choice."

Stern paused in thought. "And you're going to try to convince me, correct?"

"No, I'm not."

"Then, why did you ask me to go to church?"

"To test our friendship."

"A test? So now I'm on trial, qualifying for friendship?" The pride was rising again.

"I knew you didn't want to come. I figured if you did—you honored me as a friend, like I did with Carla."

The explanation made sense to him, but he didn't like the idea of being tested.

"And did I pass the test?"

"You came, didn't you?"

"What if my motives weren't right?"

"That's between you and God."

"The God you know is there?"

"Yes—*that* God."

Why was he having this conversation? He didn't drive over three-hundred miles to discuss God with her. The whole thing made him uncomfortable. Still, the book seemed remote and in some ways, insignificant. Stern again wondered if he'd ever finish it. Now God was entering the picture. How would he get around that?

Here he was, talking with a woman he thought he was having feelings for, discussing a God he didn't believe in, and needing to write a book in which he had flagging interest. The day had started well, but was rapidly deteriorating. Where was Earl? Maybe he'd take him up on his offer for fishing.

"Earl says someone with money threatened Burlew and bought him off." Stern left God with Amber, and abruptly changed the subject. "He also thinks that if we put our heads together, we can come up with a short list."

"After all this time?"

"You've got it. And maybe they are still in operation today. After all, Burlew is still not talking."

"It will take some time. I'll have to wrack my brain on it. No one comes to mind at the moment."

"Same thought I had, or didn't have. I don't have much interest in pursuing it now, anyway."

"We've had this conversation before, haven't we? I think we should go on his hunch. Give it a few days and see what we come up with. Earl has been right so far, hasn't he?"

"I can't deny it."

"You need to write your book," Amber said bluntly.

"Who said I wasn't?"

"You're distracted, I can tell. Get going on it again. It needs to be written. I'm still on the team, remember?"

Stern had dismissed the fact that Amber was in on it as a partner. *A good thing at this point. Reason enough to keep going.* She was a catalyst. He decided to refocus and start writing again. "Let's work on that short list," he said.

"I already have someone in mind. It's a long shot though. I'll tell you soon. I need to talk with Mrs. Burlew first."

"What's your schedule like this week?" Stern asked.

"I have no schedule, that's the beauty of it. I haven't planned anything for the next two weeks."

Stern stood and faced her. "Well, I need your help—really."

"For the book?"

"Yes."

"You've got it." She offered her hand and he clasped it with both of his, then, pulled her to her feet.

"We can get a lot done together, Amber."

"Sounds good to me. What's the next step?"

"Let's talk to Earl. I'll call him and see if we can meet him tomorrow for lunch."

"What about the rest of today?"

"I have no plans, why?"

"There's a tour boat leaving at noon for a two-hour cruise. How about lunch together on the boat?"

"Suits me. I'm sure it's just what I need."

"Can I pick you up?"

Stern nodded. "At the hotel. I need to make phone calls this morning. I'll be ready when you get there."

Stern left with a renewed, although measured enthusiasm. He was relieved that he was back on track with the book, although he had no idea where he stood personally with Amber—other than being partners for the next two weeks.

CHAPTER 20

The phone call to Frieda Baker was to see if the work crew had shown up and how things were progressing.

"No problems," she assured him. Everything was on schedule, although the house was in disarray. Painting would be completed in two weeks, followed by new carpeting.

"No, nothing new or unusual on this end, but how are things going in New York? How is the book progressing?" Frieda plied Stern for information.

He had never been particular about what he shared with Frieda in the past, nor was he now. Of course, he divulged nothing of his personal interest in Amber. He figured if he shared too much, Frieda would read between the lines. He thought she seemed a little too eager to know what was going on, but he dismissed the thought quickly. He would call again in a few days to assure her he was getting the rest he needed.

Frieda couldn't wait to pass along to Erline the tidbits she'd learned. Erline Slicer was a blessed woman, and all too eager to hear from her close friend. It was amazing how itching ears could be scratched by the right person.

Oh, the relief of gossip! It was almost like a drug: so soothing and satisfying, yet leaving one craving for more. To hear was one thing, to tell was another. Erline would certainly pass along whatever Frieda shared to her up-line in White Marsh. Mid Gear was more matter-of-fact than Erline, but no less curious to discover something new. Just like the Athenians in the days of the Apostle Paul.

The lunch cruise was perfect, though the cuisine was mediocre and tasted like institutional food: flat and waterlogged. Stern and Amber decided not to discuss the book, per his request. The day would prove to be a precious time of relaxing and unwinding for both of them, thoroughly enjoying one another's company.

The rhythmic humming of the diesel beneath the lower deck was oddly comforting as the tour boat pushed through the blue lake waters along the western shore. At five to seven knots, the world aboard the boat was not in a hurry. Wide-eyed children waited anxiously in line for their turn in the wheelhouse. The accommodating captain gave each of them a turn at the wheel, while parents stood proud and grinning, with cameras and video recorders poised to memorialize the event. A parade of screeching gulls followed overhead, anointing the air with distinctive cries. Their diligence was frequently rewarded by the passengers.

A cool breeze swept across the upper deck with a steady refreshing vigor. Stern and Amber leaned together against the railing on the bow of the boat, gazing at the waters ahead. Like the walk at the canal, the moment would imprint on Stern's mind forever. He was quite sure he had never been in love before—never made room in his life for a woman. This was different. There was something between them. A connection he couldn't explain, not superficial, not an infatuation.

Maybe it's just me. Maybe I'm imagining or wishing it to be more than it is. What did Amber think about it? Or had she given it any thought at all?

"I've never been in love with anyone since Heath's death," Amber said, breaking the silence, as if reading Stern's mind.

"No?" He felt his heart pound in response to her words. He continued looking straight ahead at the water.

"Until now." She pressed closer to him.

"What do you mean?" His heart beat faster, his face felt hot and flushed.

"I'm in love again."

"That so?" Stern forced himself to appear disinterested, but every fiber of his being betrayed his outward indifference.

"Yes."

There was silence for a moment. Did he dare ask her "with whom?" Was he just living in a self-induced fantasy? *Probably the Reverend. They seemed enamored with each other at church.* He had to ask her. No sense in being a phony. He was wildly interested in her response. One way or the other, it would have a profound effect on him.

"With whom?" he asked, his voice weak and quavering. "Josh Woodhouse?" He turned to look at her.

She stared back at him, puzzled. She hadn't expected his reply.

"Surely you are a dense man!" She laughed. "He's happily married with three children. I can't believe you'd think I'm in love with *him*."

"Well then, who is it, Amber? If you care to tell me."

She grabbed his arm and pulled him away from the railing, focusing her eyes on his. "Stern, for heaven's sake, it's *you*! Don't you understand—I'm in love with you."

Had his heart stopped? He couldn't tell for sure. Then it broke like thunder in his chest. He was forty-six years old, and had never heard those words before.

Can it be true? Maybe she's kidding. No, she wouldn't do that. He could tell by the look in her eyes, the sound in her voice. He was aware of nothing but her, the words still ringing in his ears: *It's you— I'm in love with you.* His face flushed again as he searched for the right words. His eyes still held her gaze. An emotional floodgate had opened, and he was being swept away by its torrent.

"I, uh, simply had no idea, Amber—I mean, we've known each other for such a short time, and we seem to argue a lot."

"Yes, but we go back a long way, don't we, Stern?"

"Yes, a long way," he agreed. But how could he tell her how he felt? She probably knew, or suspected anyway. He felt awkward; his tongue was like a fat balloon filling his mouth.

"I don't expect a response from you, you know. It doesn't require one," Amber said softly, sensing his unease, "but something just clicked in me, Stern, ever since I first saw you at the airport. I wrote it off as infatuation, but while you were back in Annapolis—and our phone conversations, and well, it's like..."

"High school, Amber?"

"Well, yes. And no. It's so much more, Stern—the way I feel." She positioned herself between him and the railing and took both his hands in hers.

"Do you believe in fate, Amber?" he said after a moment's reflection.

"No. But I do believe God has a plan for our lives."

"For *our* lives? Together, you mean?"

"Maybe."

"But, I don't embrace your God or your faith."

"You will someday, Stern."

"You seem so sure of that." Stern found himself wanting to believe what she did.

"I am, because I know you're seeking and want to know."

"Do you think God brought us together?"

"I don't think it's a coincidence."

"I'm beginning to think you're right. And by the way, I have a confession to make to you."

"Please don't make it unless you mean it." Her eyes searched his.

"I do mean it, Amber. Believe me, I do."

"Would it be easier for you if I made the confession for you, Stern?"

"Is it that obvious?"

"I'm going out on a limb here with something I want to be true, but I have good discernment."

"And what is my confession?"

"That you are in love with me too. I know it's hard for you to say it, but I hope I'm right."

"Yes." Stern blushed horribly. I think you're pretty safe out on your limb."

"Then go ahead with your confession."

The words caught in his throat, but he had no doubt about the truth of his feelings for her. "I love you, Amber."

The boat slowed, turning toward the east shore of the lake, and began its return trip.

"Maybe you'd better slow down a bit," Carla cautioned. "Catch your breath, if you know what I mean, hon."

"We've already decided to spend the rest of the day apart—a mutual agreement," Amber said.

"He's not as stiff as he seems, is he?"

"Not once you get to know him. He's very warm and caring, but, he's shy."

"So, he actually told you he was in love with you?"

"I had to coach him."

"You had to *coach* him?" Carla snickered.

"He doesn't have a way with words."

"He's an author for heaven's sake, and he doesn't have a way with words?"

"Can't express himself verbally, like most men."

"So you coached him?"

"Yes."

"You're too much! You sure he meant it?"

"Positive."

"And he's not just playing you?"

"Hey, I'm not stupid, Carla. Besides, I don't think he would know how."

"A man without guile—now *that's* a rarity."

"He's just what I need at this point in my life."

"Wouldn't a little guile be more interesting?"

"Are you my spiritual mentor or not? A little guile is still guile."

"Just teasing, but you need to be rational. Let your emotions quiet down a little."

"Of course."

"What's he think about God, now that he's in love with you? Guys can fake interest pretty easily. It could be dangerous ground for you spiritually."

"I'm convinced he wants to know the truth."

"I've heard that before." Carla winced.

"He's different."

"And I'm a monkey." Carla whirled and plopped onto the couch in Amber's office, stretching her body to its full length

"Darwin's favorite, no doubt."

"Look, hon, you could be deceived."

"Why are you such a killjoy? I thought you were all for this. Or are you jealous?"

"He's not my type."

"You could be deceived, too, you know, Carla."

"Just go slowly. I don't want to see you hurt," Carla's voice softened.

"And you'll pray, right?"

"You know I will."

"Thanks, Carla. You're the best thing I've got going for me."

"Next to God and Stern, right? Or is it Stern and God?"

"It's an odd thing," Amber said, "but I think God has ordained this whole thing for some reason."

CHAPTER 21

Earl informed Stern and Amber that Gus had sent Nattie Burlew to her mother's in Pennsylvania for two weeks. The proposed meeting between Amber and Nattie would have to wait. Gus felt that he needed some space from the little woman, and against her wishes and better judgment, she left him alone. Her fear was that he would go back to drinking, and just wanted her out of the way so he could binge. He'd been acting strange lately. He assured her he wasn't going to touch a drop—he'd just had enough of her religious ranting for a while and needed a break.

Earl also felt this was a good time for him and Candy to get away for a week or so. He'd been hankering to see a live NASCAR race and had vacation time coming. He hoped that Stern would still be around when he got back. He really had nothing new to report anyway.

For the next several days, Stern and Amber spent practically every waking moment together walking, talking, sightseeing, having dinner together, and attending church on Sunday. It was all new to Stern—an emotional whirlwind. Time and scheduling, of which he was so scrupulously conscious, suddenly meant nothing to him. The book took a backseat, and he had no energy for it. Amber was his focus, and for the first time he could remember, he was utterly carefree.

The weather was glorious, the days idyllic, the memories sweet. She was an angel—he was convinced. Her God had made her so, and that was perfectly okay with him. And yes, she could discuss God freely with him. He didn't care. He even found himself agreeing with her, intrigued by her forthrightness and simple faith. Sleep was difficult, if not unnecessary, as he awaited the coming of each new day—a day that he would be with her.

Julie Fisher's group engaged in serious discussion of the most recent events in New York, knowing that Stern and Amber were on to something, or someone, like two detectives. Amber would come forth with a disclosure of some sort in a few days.

Julie created a mental picture. She felt peculiarly destined to be a part of it, and was thinking more and more that she actually knew this man, Stern Blankley. She prayed that someday she could see him face-to-face again.

Each member of the group was asked to share their thoughts with the others, and one by one everyone stood and spoke, until it came to Fenton Newman.

Lacking any self-confidence and given to fits of anxiety, Fenton suddenly felt ill. He trembled. His face and hands grew cold, and his heart pounded like a kettledrum. He felt an overwhelming compulsion to flee, to get out of the room. To hide. To do something. He rose from the group to excuse himself.

"What on earth is wrong with you, Fenton?" Julie noticed that the color had flushed from his ruddy face.

"I'm sick—I have to leave immediately." Fenton started for the door without bothering to glance at the others in the group. They stared in amazement at his ashen countenance. In a moment, he was gone.

"Was it the coffee? Or the baklava?" Julie wondered aloud.

"My goodness, did you see his face?" Sue Ellen added. "The man looked like he'd just seen his own corpse. Maybe he's never spoken in public before. Some people just freeze when…"

"A look of fear," Saul interjected, "sheer terror."

"I hope he's okay," Shelley said, her concern obvious.

"Maybe someone should follow him home," Melissa said. But no one volunteered.

Fenton's Honda had disappeared from the complex parking lot within seconds.

Julie felt it best to cut the meeting short. No one dared eat any more of Saul's baklava, in spite of the fact that no one else suffered any ill effects.

What got into that man? Julie asked herself. Seemed like a full-blown panic attack. Maybe he's been under a lot of pressure at work. I'll call him later and check on him.

CHAPTER 22

It was Saturday, thirteen days since Stern had left Annapolis. His life had changed in such dramatic fashion—feelings he'd never felt, shyness vanishing in Amber's presence. There was little, if any progress on the book, and the prospects for resuming work seemed slim in spite of Amber's encouragement and pressing deadlines. He had gone through many periods where he lacked initiative or inspiration, and had shelved his work for weeks at a time, but this was different. His energy was given to a fledgling romance and Amber occupied his thought life.

It was the first day of rain since he had arrived in New York. The forecast called for intermittent showers all day, heavy at times, with possible thunderstorms. Stern reflected nostalgically on his childhood love for rain and how he had at one time considered becoming a meteorologist. He recalled a primitive weather station he had made, with a crude anemometer and rain gauge, and how he often would gaze in awe at a passing storm, mesmerized by the power and force of nature. He had just gone to work at a summer job during his college years in 1972 when the flood hit. Oddly enough, he and a friend had been assigned to paint the floor of the beachouse at Friendship Point. They had finished one day's work and by the next day, the floor was under several feet of water. The lake level had risen dramatically within a twenty-four hour period, as a horrific deluge dumped several inches of rain. The creek and riverbeds gave way, causing enormous damage to roads and houses. Several people had perished without warning in the middle of the night.

Stern looked away at the hazy, grey mist suspended in silence over the lake. It was a perfect day to take a ride around the lake and observe the storm. Amber agreed and thought it sounded romantic. They would finish the day with dinner at her house. Stern was making tentative plans to return to Annapolis shortly. With precious time slipping away, they wanted to live what was left to its fullest.

Amber's Lexus pushed its way through the rain along the east side of Wells Lake. The swish of the wipers harmonized with the soft hiss of the tires on the wet asphalt. An occasional clap of thunder was the perfect compliment to nature's symphony.

Stern studied her profile as she drove.

She caught his gaze and smiled. "The eyes have a language all their own, don't you think?"

Stern paused and shifted toward her. "What do you mean?"

"Oh, just something words can't express."

"Hmm." Stern nodded.

"And yet," she continued, "the eyes can be deceived so easily through evil and darkness."

Amber's melodramatic shift made him feel uneasy. "Deceived?"

"Yeah, perception infected with evil."

The thought of evil spoiled the moment. But it brought up a subject he had wanted to discuss with her further. *Maybe tonight after dinner. But, not now - not now!*

"Amber, can we table this evil stuff until later? Somehow it just doesn't seem to fit." She ignored his question and continued, "I'm more convinced than ever that God brought us together for a reason."

Why can't it be just us? Why does God have to factor into it? "What do you mean?"

"I can't explain it; it's just a powerful intuitive sense."

That's good. She can't explain it—a powerful intuitive sense.

"It relates to God's sovereign plan, His will for our lives."

"You're including me in this again. I'm still not totally onboard with God, you know."

"Maybe you are more than you think."

"Do I have a choice? God being sovereign like you say."

"Of course you do, Stern. That's the beauty of it. He is sovereign, but He honors your choice."

"And what if I choose to ignore God?"

"Do you truly love me?" Amber took her eyes off the road long enough to convey to him the seriousness of her question.

"You know I do, Amber."

"Then you won't ignore the God I love. Neither will He ignore you."

"He's part of the package, then?"

"Of necessity. And priority."

Maybe he *was* beginning to see it. Amber loved him, but he was not first; God was. To him, Amber was first, and God was barely in the picture.

"Love can be idolatry if God isn't first," she said.

Is she the idol of my life? Am I a third party in this whole thing? Does she truly love me, even though I don't love her God? Or am I now an obstacle to her, as God is to me? Why had something so marvelously simple become so bewilderingly complex? Either he was the problem or God was. Something had to give. It was beyond him.

She pulled the car abruptly to the side of the road and turned into a scenic overlook. "Look, Stern, do you remember this spot?"

"I don't think so."

"We've been here before, in high school. We had a debate here one night, remember?"

"A debate? One of our dates, huh?" Stern rolled his eyes.

"I guess we really never had a real date, did we?" She put the gearshift in park, turned toward him, and slid her hand across the seat.

"I think we've redeemed all of that, Amber." Stern took her hand in his and squeezed it tightly.

The ashen sky hung like a thick smoldering blanket over the twilight stillness. In the distance, the moaning of a fire siren drifted through the dead air with a haunting refrain. A single streak of lightning flashed jagged fire to the static waters of the lake below. Finally, the rumble of distant thunder gave way to the waning melodies of the evening songbirds, and the storm was over. Night was upon them. The two weeks had flashed by. Tomorrow was Sunday and Stern had again agreed to church in honor of Amber. He had even lost his sense of self-consciousness in being there. This would be his fourth time in attendance, but only his second Sunday.

They hadn't heard a word from Earl and suspected that he was still away on vacation. The dinner meal was leisurely, and they discussed resuming work on the book. Both Stern and Amber agreed that a short time apart was probably in their best interest. She was due back at the *Voice* on Monday morning, and he had told Frieda that he would be back in Annapolis no later than Monday night.

Amber still needed to contact Mrs. Burlew, per Earl's suggestion, and Stern would do his level best to spend the next several weeks getting back on track with the book. Neither he nor Amber relished the thought of being apart, but they were, after all, adults, and the relationship needed a breather. They promised to stay in close touch by phone and e-mail to collaborate on the book. Stern was well aware that he was under certain time constraints. He had obligations with the publisher, an enforced discipline, which he needed at this point in his life.

Amber had found herself having to fend off Zelda Twigg on more than one occasion during the two weeks that Stern was in town. Zelda was chomping at the bit for an interview, and had left several phone messages pressing Amber for access to Stern. It hadn't been a convenient time for an interview, given the relationship that Amber had with Stern, something she would guard with her life, as far as Zelda was concerned. Carla had vowed not to let on. Amber would deal with Zelda on Monday and assure her that her time would come.

"There is one major stumbling block that I can't get beyond," Stern admitted to Amber after dessert and coffee. "You mentioned it in the car, and when I had dinner the first time I was here." The conversation took what seemed to be an inevitable drift toward the theological.

"The issue of evil?"

"Yes."

"Why does God allow it?"

"Right. Innocent people dying. Murders, rapes, crimes—you name it."

"It was never His intention or desire."

"But He allows it."

"The choices are ours, but He arranges the consequences."

"Meaning?" Stern's face drew a puzzled look.

"We are free, volitional beings, but there are obvious consequences and ultimate justice."

"Certainly not in this life."

"Well, you're right, and that's why I believe there is justice in the next life."

"The hereafter."

"Exactly. There's a verse in the Bible where Abraham pleads with God, "Shall not the judge of all earth do right." You and I both have a strong desire for justice. Where do you think it comes from?"

Stern shrugged. "It's innate."

"More than that. It's transcendent. A moral lawgiver who shall someday see that justice is done."

"The judge of all the earth, right?"

"You catch on quickly, Stern." Amber smiled.

"So people continue to suffer evil while God waits?"

"Evil is real. Not one of us is exempt."

"And God is not to blame?"

"He is not the source of evil. It's more of a consequence than a creation."

"Where did it come from?"

"Well, He does have an adversary."

"Obviously the Devil."

"Yes," Amber said, nodding. "In active opposition to that which is good."

"Then the Devil is to blame, and not people?"

"Not exactly, evil is also in the heart of everyone. So we too have the potential, through free volition, to engage in active opposition to God—the same as His archenemy."

"In agreement with the Devil?"

"Yes."

Stern stood and paced for a moment, lost in thought. "Where do we fit in? You and I."

"By being on the right side."

"And continuing to plead for justice? As Abraham did?"

"Uh, huh."

"And if we don't see it in this life, we will see it in the next one?"

"Now you see it!"

"I'm still not sure I do."

"But you will," Amber said with certainty.

"So you've said."

It was nine-thirty when Stern left Amber's. They would say their final goodbyes after church tomorrow. Stern's mind and body were exhausted, and he longed for the comfort of the hotel bed. A good night's sleep would help him shift mental gears and refocus his energies. The discussion with Amber had made him uneasy. Although her answers were thought provoking and seemed plausible enough, he was filled with doubt—and he couldn't dismiss the apprehension that gripped him. It was not a pleasant way to end an otherwise blissful two weeks, but reality was pressing hard into his dream world.

He thought of her girlish ponytail, her winsome smile, her engaging eyes, and the tenderness in her voice. So much a part of him, and yet in some ways, she seemed so far away.

CHAPTER 23

He arrived at church ten minutes early and noticed that Amber was not there. Carla always stopped by on Sunday morning to pick her up. Stern figured they might be discussing Amber's relationship with him, at some length. He decided to sit midway back from the front row and reserve two seats for them. People were warm and friendly as usual, and he found himself fitting in rather comfortably. Even the music had a new appeal to him, although he did not intend to try to sing once the song service began.

Josh Woodhouse appeared on the platform with two men flanking him on the right and left. The service started promptly at ten-thirty. Amber and Carla still had not arrived. *Maybe one or the other is sick or they had a flat tire.* He felt slightly self-conscious without them, and kept glancing to the back of the church. The service progressed, and after a lengthy opening prayer by one of the men on the platform, the congregation stood to sing.

He fought off a twinge of anxiety. *Has something happened to them? Was she offended last night? Was this another test?* No. There was some obvious explanation and he needed to relax—but for some reason, he couldn't.

The soloist had just started singing when a woman, whom Stern recognized as the church secretary, entered the platform from a door leading out into the left wing of the church, where the church office and classrooms were. She approached the men and spoke directly to Josh Woodhouse, who immediately followed her back through the door—a look of horror on his suddenly pale face. The other two men were whispering, and one of them approached the pulpit before the soloist had finished. He announced an urgent need for prayer for something on which he wasn't able to elaborate.

Stern knew it had to do with Amber. A vice-like fear wrenched him, squeezing the life force from him. He rose instinctively and made for the rear of the church, compelled to intercept the pastor. His feet labored as he pushed one in front of the other, fear increasing with every step. He noticed no one as he opened the front door and headed for the side entrance of the left wing of the building.

The sound of a car engine firing was the first thing that caught his attention, and he turned to see Woodhouse backing from his parking space. The car jerked forward with the squeal of tires, and Stern broke into a wild run toward it. He waved frantically at its driver, who stopped just short of hitting him.

"It's Amber, isn't it?" Stern stumbled up against the driver's door, his voice erupting with the force of panic. "Tell me what happened!"

Josh motioned to him. "Just get in—I'm headed for her house."

Stern broke for the passenger side door and within seconds was seated beside Woodhouse as the car jerked onto the main highway, the church fading in the distance.

"What has happened to her?" Stern's voice quavered. His mouth dry, his heart pounding.

"She's been shot," Josh said, as he pressed the accelerator further.

"Is she okay?" Stern stiffened, fearing to ask.

Josh's face seemed drained of all color. "She's dead."

There was complete silence. The words pierced Stern's heart like a hot, poison arrow. He was dreaming. A nightmare! He would awake at any moment.

But no, it wasn't a nightmare, and the words echoed through his head again and again.

She's dead, she's dead, she's dead!

He tried to speak, but couldn't. The moment froze in time. Smothered by a sickening weakness, he slumped in his seat, his chin falling lifelessly to his chest.

"It can't be true, tell me it isn't true." He roused himself and directed a pleading gaze at Woodhouse.

"It's true," Josh said, simply. "Carla found her this morning a little after nine. Apparently, she was shot sometime in the night. The police and EMTs are already there."

"I was with her last night." Stern swallowed hard, fighting off a suffocating tightening in his throat. "I left sometime after nine. It happened after that—but who? Who in God's name would shoot her? And, why?"

"I have no answers, Stern," Josh said. "The church is praying even as we speak. God has His reasons for the things He allows."

No! That's too cheap an explanation.

If ever he was convinced there was no God, it was now. No God would allow it, especially a God of supreme goodness. The one Amber tried to convince him to believe in. It was definitely a sham.

There is no God. There is no God. And if there was, I would despise him.

"Carla is completely devastated. She wanted me to come," Josh continued. "I can't imagine what must be going through her mind right now. It was a miracle she reached anyone at the church. Usually there's no one in the office during service. Jan Foster just happened to be in there."

Stern remained still, stunned, not knowing what to say nor wishing to speak. He wondered why he was there, riding with the pastor of the church to Amber's house. What was his part in it now? He just wanted to flee, abhorring the thought of facing anyone. A wave of nausea swept him and he had to resist his body's impulse to vomit. A grisly scene played in his thoughts—horrible images, sharp blades stabbing his mind with relentless, punishing blows. He put his head between his legs and vomited on the floor of the car. Josh hit the electric button to lower the window on the passenger side, silently praying for the wretch of a man sitting next to him.

As the car approached Amber's house, the flashing lights of emergency vehicles and three state trooper cars betrayed the rustic surroundings of the stately colonial building. A ribbon of yellow crime scene tape cordoned off the area, and several troopers served as guards preventing anyone from entering the house.

Carla Fletcher stood crying and talking with a trooper beside his cruiser. When she saw Josh's car arrive she begged leave and rushed toward him, half-stumbling as he emerged from the vehicle. Her spiritual connection with Josh had been the source of encouragement on a number of occasions—but they had never faced a moment such as this.

"This can't be happening," she said, sobbing. "I just can't believe this has happened."

Josh held her head close to his chest, the wetness of her tears soaking his shirt. He said nothing for several minutes, fighting back his own tears. She clung to him—her body shook with intemperate and raw emotion.

Stern sat motionless in the car, wondering what to do next. He felt numb. It could have been ten minutes or two hours, he wasn't sure, but the same trooper who had spoken with Carla approached him.

"Mr. Blankley?" he spoke through the open window. "I'm officer Page with the New York State police. Do you mind if I ask you a few questions?"

"I need to get out of the car," Stern said, aware of the stench wafting upward from the floor.

"Surely," the trooper replied, repeating the need to ask questions.

"Give me just a minute. I'm not feeling well."

The trooper was accommodating and pleasant.

"What is it you need from me?" Stern said, lifting his eyes and looking squarely at the uniformed man.

"Just a few questions, Mr. Blankley. I understand from Ms. Fletcher that you were here at the Greene residence last night. Is that correct?"

Stern had nothing to hide. He was candid with no emotion in his voice. "That's correct."

"It appears, Mr. Blankley, that we may have a homicide here, and you may be able to help us with the investigation."

"If I can help, I will." He leaned against the hood of the car to keep his knees from buckling.

"At approximately what time were you here last night?"

"From about seven to nine-thirty."

"You left at about nine-thirty?"

"That's correct."

"Did you notice anything unusual during your visit last night with Ms. Greene?"

"No."

"Did she give any indication of being in possible danger?"

"No."

"Did you have any reason to believe that she was in danger?"

"None."

"It appears that she was shot at close range with a high caliber handgun."

A knot twisted in Stern's stomach and he braced himself against the car. His mouth filled with saliva and he vomited again.

The trooper waited for Stern to regain his composure.

"One other question, Mr. Blankley. Where did you go after you left the Greene residence last night?"

What, am I now on trial? Do I have to answer that? The thought of him being implicated in this became a sobering reality. "Home—I mean, to the hotel. Please, I'm not feeling well at all."

"Thank you, Mr. Blankley. We'll have to contact you for further questions. Where can we reach you?"

"I'm staying at the Hampton Inn outside of Hollister, but I'm due to leave for Annapolis tomorrow morning."

"I'd make plans to stay for a few more days, Mr. Blankley. As I said, we will need to ask you a few more questions."

The trooper turned and strode toward the house, leaving Stern drained and bewildered. Surely he was not a suspect? Or was he? He was the last known person to have had contact with Amber before she died. He would explain everything to the police when the time came. He would have to call Frieda and let her know he wasn't coming back to Annapolis for a few days. What would he do with himself during that time? He had no friends in New York other than Amber and Earl. Carla was an acquaintance, and Josh was still an unknown. He would need someone to talk with about what had happened, and wondered when Earl was due back.

Amber!

Last night rushed with a rage into his mind. He saw her standing in the doorway smiling, waving, and blowing a kiss. Then he heard a gunshot. And another. He saw her slump to the floor amidst a pool of blood—her life ebbing, calling for him, calling for him...

The thought nearly drove him mad.

He opened the car door and removed the floor mat from the passenger side, thankful that vomit hadn't seeped onto the floor. He tossed it in some nearby bushes, trusting that Josh would understand.

Stern never noticed the arrival of the coroner, crime scene photographer, and evidence techs. His mind was cordoned off like the crime scene. He sat, huddled and cold, in spite of the late summer's heat.

Alone.

The loneliness gave way to explosive anger. If *he* could find who did it, *he* would kill them. He knew at that moment he could murder someone in revenge—a monstrous idea, foreign to him, but a viable servant to his rage.

Josh and Carla caught Stern's attention as they slowly approached the car.

"We are going back to the church," Josh said. "I've called on my cell phone and instructed my assistant pastor to have as many people stay as can. We need support—all of us. And prayer. It's the best place to be."

Stern had no choice. Again, he had a desire to flee, but no place to go. His car was still at the church. Josh put his hand on Stern's shoulder. "It's going to be okay," he said. "Besides, I need you."

What on earth for? A psychological prop to lessen the blow?

There was genuineness in Josh's voice that touched the awful wound sliced into Stern's heart.

Carla was aloof and cold.

Suspicious.

CHAPTER 24

Josh's car pulled into the church parking lot where several other vehicles remained. A good portion of the members had stayed after service praying silently, awaiting his return. They had not expected to see Stern and Carla with him. The assistant pastor immediately brought the meeting to a close as Josh assumed the pulpit to bring an updated report. Carla took a seat next to Rachel Woodhouse, Josh's wife. Stern chose to remain in the lobby of the church. He thought of leaving and returning to his hotel room, but something made him stay.

The news of the murder spread like wildfire. Several area television stations dispatched reporters and camera crews to the scene, and all the major regional newspapers and radio stations were equally represented.

The staff at the *Valley Voice* was numb. Amber was well liked and respected, having paid a price to gain her position as editor through integrity and a fierce work ethic. The entire town of Hollister was abuzz within a few hours and local gossip mills were cranking out wild and embellished accounts of what had happened. Some said it was suicide, although there was no gun found at the crime scene, and the fact that she was shot twice made it logistically impossible.

Others were speculating about possible suspects. It was largely known that Stern Blankley had been in the area recently, and his name was being cast about as a suspect. Some said she'd been shot with a shotgun, others claimed it was a high-powered rifle. Some said there was a terrific struggle involved. Still others maintained she was shot while sleeping. On and on it went.

There hadn't been a murder in Hollister since Casey McGrady shot his wife in a domestic dispute seven years ago, and certainly nothing this high-profile since Judge Wagner Whitcomb was found murdered in his home in 1957, the victim of a shotgun blast from the deranged brother of a man sentenced to thirty-five years for armed robbery.

It was well after noon when the church group was finally dismissed. Stern declined a lunch invitation at the Woodhouses' in favor of the solitude of his hotel room. He had no appetite anyway, and wanted to be left alone. He had to call Frieda and let her know he would be staying indefinitely in Hollister. He doubted that any major news wires had picked up the story yet, so she would still be in the dark regarding the murder. He was hoping any delay would be short lived and that he could return to Annapolis for a couple of days prior to the funeral.

Funeral!

He reflected upon the enormity of the events of the last two weeks. He couldn't dismiss the plaguing notion that his involvement had something to do with Amber's murder, but what the connection was, if there indeed was one, was a complete mystery to him. The guilt seemed to increase by the hour.

Stern returned to his room exhausted and phoned Frieda. She was dumbstruck, but more concerned for Stern's well-being and what she could do to help. He spoke with little conviction that he was okay, thankful that she didn't know how deeply he was involved with Amber. Frieda would place several calls for him and would manage affairs on that end until he returned.

He switched on the television to get his mind off the murder—to no avail. He flipped aimlessly through the channels, and settled on a baseball game between the Braves and the Mets, neither of whom he liked. After about a half-hour, he drifted into a fitful sleep. The game was interrupted as local channels broke away to cover the developing story of the murder.

Frieda called Erline Slicer, who called Mid Gear, who called Julie Fisher. Julie's group had just begun assembling for their Sunday afternoon meeting. Within forty-five minutes of Stern's call, the information line had been activated. The group sat in stunned silence for what seem like an hour contemplating the events in New York. Everyone was present and accounted for. How would this affect Stern's new book? It was eerily ironic that Amber had been murdered while researching the death of her teenage boyfriend of twenty-eight years ago. There had to be a link somehow, they all thought. And how was Blankley doing? Julie especially wondered—and more deeply than she let on. Others were shocked, but more curious, even casual at times.

But not Julie. She sensed he was suffering and needed prayer. The meeting—already three hours old—went on and on with endless speculation until everyone was played out. The whole group fell silent again for several minutes.

"He could be implicated," Saul announced.

"That's highly unlikely," Sue Ellen said. "What possible motive could he have had?"

"No one knows anyone's motives," Fenton piped in, to which everyone seemed to agree, except for Julie and Melissa.

"He had nothing to do with it," Julie said sharply, almost defensively.

"And you're so sure?" Shelley said, and then backed off, remembering that she had just been hired by Julie.

Toppsy was her usual abrasive self, and spewed her opinion like exhaling bad air. "I think he's the likely suspect. Probably all these murder mysteries took him over the edge. He can't distinguish fiction from reality."

"I agree with Julie," Melissa said, rather timidly, after Toppsy's outburst. Melissa wasn't a toady and remained an independent thinker. It just happened that she and Julie usually thought alike, and both women had good instincts. Then she added, "None of us knows anything at this point."

That brought the meeting to a close, and everyone was anxious to leave. When the house was empty, Julie and Melissa made grilled cheese sandwiches and tomato soup, and hunkered down for an evening of intimate conversation.

CHAPTER 25

Stern jolted awake. The words of the trooper assailed him. He would be "needed for further questioning."

When? Where? And for how long?

He just wanted to leave and go home. The whole nightmare rushed back to his mind like a blast of hot scorching air. He glanced at his watch. It was four-thirty in the afternoon. He'd slept two-and-a-half hours but felt miserable. His eyes burned and his head ached from the back of his neck to the top of his skull, a relentless pounding that grew worse when he stood.

The knock on the door startled him. As far as he knew, no one was aware of his room number except Amber and Frieda. His first thought was that it was the state troopers again, which irked him.

Just a few more questions. He was in no mood for answering any more questions as he made his way to the door. Peering through the security lens brought a strange and welcome sense of relief when he saw it was Earl Teeter. Unpretentious and nonthreatening—just the person he could talk to.

"How did you get my room number?" Stern asked, as he unbolted the door and beckoned Earl to come in.

"I have my ways, Howie. Maybe I've got connections, maybe I don't. And maybe I just figured it out myself. Anyway, it's good to see you, and, well...you ain't looking so good though."

"I suppose you've heard about Amber."

"It's all over town. Ain't no one's not heard of it. Candy and I got back this afternoon from our vacation. We heard it on the radio coming in. It's a terrible thing, Howie. You must be feeling real bad."

Stern wasn't about to cry in front of another man, but he felt he could have. He forced back the tears.

"What can I say, Earl? It's all happened so fast. It's like it's not real. I was just with her last night…before it happened."

"You a suspect?"

"Probably."

"Holy smoke! It ain't in you to do something like that, Howie."

"Thanks for saying so. The police want to question me further though."

"Better get a lawyer just in case."

It was a sobering thought, but made perfect sense. Something Stern would take care of in the morning.

"I guess Amber ain't gonna be meeting with Mrs. Burlew," Earl said, ruefully.

"That goes without saying, Earl."

"No, I mean she's not coming back from Pennsylvania—Mrs. Burlew."

"How do you know that?"

"I spoke with Gus on the phone a few days ago, and he said she wasn't coming home."

"Why's that?" Stern motioned Earl toward a chair.

"He's back on the bottle, big time. Told me he didn't care if he lived or died. She's had it with him. One of her friends from church called her and said she'd seen Gus in town drunk out of his mind."

"Guess her fears weren't unfounded, huh?"

"Yeah, and he's pretty hurt right now."

"Do you think *he* had anything to do with Amber's death?"

"Possible, but who knows. It'll probably push him over the edge anyway. He knew she wanted to meet with Nattie. Guess he won't have to worry about her disclosing anything now."

"He must have a tortured mind. No wonder he drinks."

"He'll wind up in the detox unit sooner or later—unless he dies first. Things could get nasty, Howie, you know that. You'd better buckle your seatbelt for a long ride. If you wind up being a prime suspect, it'll go big time, you know. I mean national media and all."

Things were happening way too fast. Surely no sane person would think he'd had anything to do with Amber's murder. But then, no one but Carla knew they were in love, and she had seemed unusually aloof and suspicious around him. Stern was confident the investigation would clear him of any implication. He was innocent and had nothing to hide. Still, he sensed an urgency to cover himself and obtain the services of a lawyer. He had good connections in Annapolis with some high profile lawyers. He'd make calls tomorrow and run the whole thing by them. Then he would be on his way back home—within a few days, he hoped.

He needed time to grieve, to get his mind straight, and think it all through. Inside the hurt was unbearable, and he ached at the thought of never seeing her again. It just couldn't be true, he kept repeating to himself. It was all too abrupt, too unreal. This couldn't be happening to him. His heart, so in love one day, and so utterly shattered the next.

The anger he felt toward her killer and toward God seized him with such a cruel force that he feared what he might do. He wanted her back, if only for a moment. Just to see her again, face-to-face, one more time. To see her smile and hear her voice. To watch her move so gracefully.

But it was not to be. Stern excused himself from Earl and went into the bathroom and wept bitterly.

Earl sat, silently hurting for his friend, hoping the man upstairs had some answers.

In contrast to the mood in the motel, the meeting that night at the church was given totally to prayer. At the request of Josh Woodhouse, Stern was the major subject.

"I've got a theory, Howie," Earl said when Stern returned from the bathroom. "My sixth sense has been hyperactive while you were in the john. Maybe this ain't such a good time to share it though. You want to be alone?"

"No, Earl, I would prefer you staying for awhile. What's your theory?"

"Well, it's just a hunch, no evidence."

"Your hunches are usually right."

"Well, I was just thinking, and I'd bet money on it that whoever killed Amber also killed that Proctor kid...uh..."

"Heath."

"Yeah, that's my take on it. Same person."

"Twenty-eight years apart?"

"Why not? Makes sense, don't it? You know, finish the job. She was getting too close to vital information, digging around with you and all."

"So maybe I'm next. You think so, Earl?" Stern raised his eyebrows.

"You never know. I'd be careful if I were you. Cover your backside. You got a gun?"

"At home."

"No good to you here. I'd keep it handy when you get home, if I were you."

Stern thought Earl was just "red necking," but then his voice had an ominous and sobering tone—something Stern found difficult to disregard.

"Alright, suppose you're correct. It must be someone local."

"So it would seem, but I don't assume nothin'."

"I think Nattie might talk. Now that she's away from Gus," Stern said.

"Who would approach her?"

"Amber's friend, Carla."

"It's worth a try. We can have our own little investigation going on, as long as we don't get in the way of the law."

"I know Amber wanted to speak to Nattie about it. She wouldn't say what it was about though."

"It makes sense then that someone got to her."

Stern's stomach constricted at Earl's statement. Again, a wave of guilt swept over him. If he hadn't reentered Amber's life, he was sure she'd still be alive today. Everything seemed like such an absurd and cruel hoax. Life mocked him. For a moment, he wished he had died with her. She was the victim of a hideous crime. He was a living victim of his own excruciating guilt. He was convinced there was no crueler tormentor than guilt.

What had his life come to? Losing the only woman he'd ever loved, gripped with unrelenting remorse, and driven with a burning rage to seek revenge. Hating even the thought of the God that Amber loved—apparently even more than she loved him.

And Earl, of all people, on the planet. Sitting in a hotel room with a man devoid of culture, whose claim to fame was a nebulous sixth sense and a knack for restoring dented fenders. At that moment, Stern understood why Gus Burlew drank. Henceforth he would be careful never to judge again a man given to the bottle.

Earl sensed it was time to go. The sight of his friend in such a wretched state was more than he could handle. He guessed his role as a counselor was short-lived. One thing he was sure of, he was committed to getting to the bottom of all of this. He owed it to Howie.

It seemed impossible it was still only Sunday night. Stern decided to find the nearest supermarket and buy some over the counter sleep aids. He would take enough to knock him out for twenty-four hours. Maybe for good. He couldn't decide. At that moment, it didn't matter. While he was away from his hotel room, his phone rang every five minutes. It was Josh Woodhouse. Earl had called Carla, who in turn had called Josh.

Chapter 26

The distant pounding was like hammer blows inside Stern's head. He struggled to regain consciousness, but the dead weight of his body fought against any effort to rise from his bed. The pounding continued. He heard voices—his name. Someone was calling his name.

The voices of strangers.

"Mr. Blankley, open the door. It's the police!"

The words pierced him. *They're back, to ask more questions.*

What time was it? He glanced at his watch. It was eight-fifty in the morning. What day was it? He'd lost track.

"It's the police!" the voice was more distinct and forbidding.

"I'm coming, I'm coming," Stern managed to get his lips to move, but his mouth was dry as cotton, and his voice croaked in a pitiful whisper. He staggered, almost stumbling to the door, and peered through the safety lens. Two state troopers stood, looking impatient. Neither of them gave any indication the visit was going to be pleasant. Stern slid the safety chain and turned the deadbolt to let them in.

"Mr. Blankley?" One of the troopers spoke with solemn authority, holding an arrest warrant in his hand.

"Yes."

"You are under arrest." The trooper reached for a set of handcuffs.

There was a moment of silence as the words cut through the mental fog and registered with Stern. The click of the cuffs echoed in

Stern's ears, amplified by an ominous reality that, in an instant, had changed his world.

"There must be some mistake," he said weakly, his knees nearly buckling under him and his head still pulsating with the effects of his stupor. But he offered no resistance. "Why…what?" he asked, as if he hadn't heard them, but knowing why they were there.

"For the murder of Amber Greene."

The reply was metallic, full of death itself; choking, pressing, and crushing with an unbelievable weight. His head sagged to his chest, and he needed help to stand. He felt like a victim of fate, moved along by a cruel force over which he had no control.

The news spread quickly. All the news wires picked it up, and the story had front-page coverage in many prominent newspapers across the country. All the major networks ran the story and the tabloids were in their glory: *Popular Author Prime Suspect in Grisly Murder.* A recent photo of Stern appeared in several papers, alongside Amber's. The *Valley Voice* ran an in depth feature article with a detailed account of Amber's history with the paper. Zelda Twigg was the prime mover. A special edition was forthcoming that would be entirely dedicated to Amber.

The most shocking news was the discovery of the murder weapon, hidden in some debris in one of the outbuildings at Amber's house. The serial number on the .38 caliber handgun had been traced, and matched the number on Stern Blankley's gun, which he'd kept locked in his bedroom in Annapolis. Finger prints on the barrel and back strap of the gun matched Stern's perfectly, and left little doubt in most people's mind as to the perpetrator of the crime.

The evidence seemed rock solid, but the motive was yet to be determined. Some speculated that Amber was going to divulge damaging evidence against him, perhaps related to the death of Heath Proctor. Some simply felt that he was deranged, his mind having been affected by all the murder mysteries that he had written. Perhaps the most bizarre, and yet most popular rendition with the tabloids was that Stern had perpetrated the murder to provide background for his upcoming book, which seemed to be floundering.

The town of Hollister was nigh into a lynching mood, with nearly everyone passing final judgment prior to the meeting of the grand jury. Although only a suspect with no indictment, the evidence was so blatant and few doubted his guilt—including Carla, who was being questioned intensely by the police.

There were, however, fierce supporters, notably Earl Teeter and Josh Woodhouse. There was not a fiber of doubt in their minds that Stern was innocent, and they would testify on his behalf.

The estimated time of Amber's death was between nine and midnight on Saturday. The only person known to have been with her that evening was Stern, by his own admission. It was widely assumed that his admission was a ploy, to make it seem implausible that he was the murderer in light of such an open and obvious disclosure.

Still, it seemed that the murder weapon was too poorly concealed, unless of course it had been concealed in haste by an amateur who had panicked. There was endless banter about the plausibility. The investigation would take weeks, but no one was denying the obvious. It would be pretty much routine.

Earl was on a one-man mission. He knew his friend was innocent, regardless of the damning evidence. He had his antennae extended full length wherever he went, and he was still betting on his earlier hunch. To him, it was an obvious setup. Why couldn't anyone else see it? *Besides, if Howie had done it, he wouldn't have been so stupid. He would have covered his bases better than that.* Earl was going to approach Gus Burlew and get the truth if he had to squeeze it out of him. He'd wait until the old man was drunk to approach him. Booze had a way of loosening the tongue.

Julie Fisher was shocked. She read and reread the *Baltimore Sun* and *USA Today* articles, as well as the *Washington Post* and *Times*. For a fleeting moment, she thought it might be true, but then she quickly renounced the thought. She felt as if she knew this man, and it was ridiculous that he could do such a thing.

For some reason, the picture of Amber in the *Sun* seemed hauntingly familiar; though Julie was sure she'd never met or seen her. Probably just a mental picture drawn over the past several weeks, she told herself. Anyway, Amber certainly was beautiful.

One thing Julie knew for certain, she would redouble her prayers for Stern. That much she could do, although it left her feeling frustrated, wishing she could do more.

The discussion group had decided to meet midweek instead of waiting until Sunday. There was just too much to talk about to wait. Her summer schedule allowed Julie to have two evenings off during the week. The group had rearranged their schedules to convene in what they considered an "emergency" session.

"I told you he could be implicated in all this," Saul Karras announced in his booming voice. "And now it appears to be a little more than an implication. I hope he's got good attorneys."

"I still wonder about his motive." Sue Ellen defended her earlier statement, mostly out of pride—but she doubted Stern's innocence.

"Since when has he been convicted?" Julie was sticking to her line of defense. "Do any of you really think he did it?"

"My gosh, woman, are you numb or what?" Toppsy Gordon's voice belched its customary ill-humor into the atmosphere. "What kind of evidence do you want, a videotape?"

"Thank goodness you're not the judge or jury, Toppsy," Melissa said.

"You and Julie would have acquitted Hitler," Toppsy shot back, ready for an exchange, but Melissa had made her point.

"Well, somebody's probably going to be rich. She probably had a ton of insurance on her," Shelley spoke up. "My husband sells insurance and—"

"And somebody's going to make a ton of money on a book, but it's not going to be Stern Blankley," Fenton interrupted Shelley before she could finish.

"And who do you suggest should write the book Fenton, you?" Melissa entered the fray with a sarcastic reply.

"I could certainly do it, if I had any inclination."

"Your inclination has clearly swollen your head. Maybe you need to do a little brain defragging," Melissa continued. Her comment wounded Fenton's fragile ego; for his head *was* out of proportion to the rest of his body.

"Hear ye! Hear ye!" Saul now assumed the role of the town crier to get everyone's attention and restore order. "May I suggest that we continue this lighthearted discussion over coffee? And by the way, I have an ample supply of pistachio baklava, freshly baked by yours truly this morning."

No one complained, and the banter went on and on without animosity, except for Toppsy. Her voice would often rise to a crescendo, the veins in her forehead bulging as tight as guitar strings. Fenton nursed his wounds and soothed his ego by gorging himself on baklava alone in a corner of the living room. He sipped a mug of hot chocolate, which Julie had made especially for him.

Melissa and Julie withdrew from the rest of the group. Their heads nearly touched each other as they engaged in what they thought was the only rational and worthwhile conversation in the room. When the group finally left at ten, Julie quickly prepared for bed—and fell asleep at midnight praying for Stern.

What was she to do? Frieda Baker wondered. Stern hadn't prepared her for this. She'd held the fort for over two weeks and now he wasn't coming home. Not now, probably not ever. She was distraught. *Could it be true? What went on between those two up there?*

The phone call was urgent with a clear and simple directive. She was to check the nightstand beside his bed on the right hand side, where he kept his .38 caliber handgun. It had to be there. There must have been a mistake in matching the serial numbers. But fingerprints couldn't lie—or, could they?

The gun was missing. The numbers matched perfectly. The fingerprints were dead accurate. It was *his* gun that was found in the outbuilding, and so far, there was not a shred of evidence leading in any other direction but to him.

Chapter 27

Jud Tillston was a hard-nosed trial lawyer from D.C.—reputed to be one of the best defense attorneys in the Washington area and a personal friend of Stern's. Though busy, Jud figured he wasn't too busy for his friend, especially in view of the magnitude of the case. He'd rearrange his schedule somehow.

A man of fierce legal integrity, Jud was not averse to the notoriety and media attention the case would bring. On the contrary, he relished the spotlight and was ready for battle. He hated losing, and refused to let his mind entertain even the slightest notion of not winning, should it come to trial.

District Attorney Hiram Morton Fenley II was puzzled and somewhat disconcerted over a letter he had received postmarked from the Hollister Post Office two days prior to the murder of Amber Greene. It read, "I'm back." Only two words—no signature, no return address. Over the years as a prosecuting attorney, Hiram had dealt with scores of criminal cases. He was curious about any possible connection between the letter and those cases. He'd had threats before, and at times was wary, but had never been preoccupied with them, either. This certainly was not an overt threat, but it did have an ominous tone to it.

At sixty-eight and in his forth term as District Attorney, Hiram had endured nearly forty years of trial law—an amazing feat, accomplished primarily due to his irascible temperament and an inordinate consumption of scotch. His temper was legendary, and his intimidating appearance at six-foot-three, three hundred pounds worked well to his advantage in the courtroom.

Although his power and control in the community was known to everyone, it was also commonly felt that alcohol had taken its toll over the years, and Hiram's prowess was on the decline. It was also rumored that he was physically abusive to his wife, a frail and retiring creature seldom seen and never heard. No one dared to take him to task over the suspected abuse. Hiram was a man to be feared—and not a few had suffered the effects of his wrath.

He sat alone in his study, sipping straight scotch, thinking about the case before him. He swirled the ice in his glass and mused. This could be his day in the sun. Something this high profile came along only once in a lifetime. He would finally get his due after all the years of dedicated and sacrificial service. He'd finish out this term and retire. Money certainly was no concern to him. He had lots of it and planned to spend his retirement living just as sumptuously as he could. If only he didn't have to drag that skinny little excuse of a wife along with him. She was an embarrassment to him, a blemish to his image. Oh well, at least he'd kept her concealed as much as possible through the years. He didn't want anyone noticing the bruises, either. It was difficult explaining how clumsy the woman was, falling over everything.

Careless—very careless, he said, smiling to himself.

Then there was the issue of Hiram III, his only son—Morton, as he was called. What a pitiful case *he* was. Hiram's eyes glowered and his mouth twisted into an ugly sneer as he thought of him. Morton, with his mother's genes and no inclination for law. There would not be a third generation of lawyers in Hiram's family. His son had no presence, a weak stature, and an effeminate voice. Hiram hadn't seen him in years and had no idea as to his whereabouts. It was almost as if he never existed. Hiram took a deep and soothing draught from his glass.

Just like he never existed. That's the way I like it.

He chuckled, amused at the thought of nature's mistake. It was, after all, the survival of the fittest. And he, Hiram Morton Fenley II, was ample evidence of that maxim. But poor Morton, Hiram wondered whether he was even alive.

Hollister was the county seat, and the jail was located in a new complex of buildings about two miles from town. The jail where Stern was held was clean and sterile with air conditioning—a major plus for the inmates in the midst of the oppressive heat. There were one hundred and twenty-seven inmates, ranging from drug offenders to category one sex offenders, and everything in between.

The only other time Stern had seen the inside of a jail cell was during college when his social psychology class visited a local jail to get a feel for what incarceration felt like. Thankfully, their sentence had been only twenty minutes, as each student, locked behind bars, tried to identify with the inmates. *Silly*, Stern thought at the time. What would twenty minutes prove?

This was no college class, and the stark reality of being shut off from the outside world left a sinking feeling in the pit of Stern's stomach—a malignancy that ate away at him while he sat motionless, letting it devour the last of his hopes.

A tormenting fear pressed his mind as he fought to bring his thoughts under control. All of this was a hideous and evil plot; an egregious setup by someone who had a penchant for brutality. An experienced killer who apparently had access to Stern's bedroom. He would have every one of the painters and carpet installers investigated.

Jud Tillston had already spoken with Frieda Baker on several occasions, but she remained largely incoherent—still in hysteria over what happened, and feeling guilty that someone had taken the gun on her watch. Jud would have to wait until she calmed down before approaching her again. She insisted that no one had gone upstairs without her knowledge, and absolutely no one had the key to Stern's bedroom. He kept it locked when he was away. She hoped no one implicated her in all of this. Jud assured her that the police would have questions to ask and that she would be subpoenaed to testify. Frieda could not endure the thought of seeing Stern in jail, let alone having to testify in a murder trial. She just wasn't cut out for all of this, not at her age. Though not one to drink, she was tempted to deaden the emotional pain with alcohol. Instead, she opted for a good prescription drug from her doctor. She'd get on that the first thing in the morning. Something strong for her jangled nerves.

Amber's face haunted Julie. She knew she had seen it, but where? She was convinced it wasn't something she'd just imagined. While rummaging through her desk one day at the library, the mystery was solved, but it gave birth to a new and much more perplexing one. There, in the midst of jumbled memos and paperwork, she found the worn and faded picture of a woman. Julie instantly caught her breath, and then gave an audible cry as if she'd discovered a hidden treasure. In her hand, she held a photograph that, in spite of the abuse of time, was an obvious likeness of Amber Greene. She quickly pulled the copy of the *Baltimore Sun* with Amber's picture and compared the two. There similarities were striking. The two photos looked like the same person, though many years separated them. The smiles were identical, the eyes, the hair.

Julie's mind began to whirl as she scanned her memory trying to place where and when she'd obtained the picture. It finally dawned on her that she had pulled it from a book several weeks ago and placed it in her desk. Apparently, someone had been using it as a bookmark. She had saved it with the intent of locating the owner. Her memory quickened as she began to piece together the innocuous discovery of weeks ago. It hit her like a blinding flash of light—she had taken it from one of Stern Blankley's books! One of his latest novels, she was certain of it. But what did it mean?

Her gut instincts were usually right and she had an overwhelming sense that what she held in her hand was more than just a tattered photograph. Maybe it was a bombshell. Maybe there was a connection with Amber's murder. Maybe God wanted to reveal something to her. Hadn't she prayed and felt somehow involved in all of this? She believed in providence: this was not a coincidence.

The picture appeared to have been cut from a yearbook. It was about the size of a senior picture and had been glued to a white piece of card stock. Julie carefully separated the picture from its backing and her suspicions were confirmed even further. On the backside of Amber's photo, there was another picture with the face partially cut away. The glue had disfigured the image on the back, but that was of little consequence. She couldn't recall what book she'd found the picture in, but was almost certain it was one of his newer ones. By far, they had the largest circulation.

The night dragged on, and sleep was an indifferent stranger. The melancholy that he had battled all his life stalked Stern like a silent killer, waging a pitiless tyranny against what was left of his emotions.

He had never felt so alone, so sick and dead within. There was no hope. Suicide was not an option—only a coward's way out. But death would be a welcome guest if it came his way. If he was given to prayer, he would have prayed to die.

He wished that he had stayed with Amber the night she was murdered. He would have rather taken bullets in his own flesh than to think of her facing that kind of death. It would have been a severe mercy to die in her stead.

But then the absurdity of it all—it was *his* gun! He laughed pathetically. Success, wealth, doing what he loved to do. In love for the first time in his life with a woman he would have died for. And she was gone.

Gone!

What if they didn't find the shooter? What if he, himself, was convicted of murder? What if he rotted a way in some rat hole of a prison? Amber had been right about one thing; she'd spoken to him about the reality of hell. Stern knew it was real. Its fires were inside his head. And God, if there was one, was a charlatan, a huckster of the highest order. It was about three-thirty in the morning when out of sheer exhaustion, he fell asleep.

Earl came during visiting hours. The sight of his friend almost made him sick.

"You look like you've been to hell and back, Howie."

"I'm not back yet, sorry to say." Of all the people on the planet, Earl was one that Stern never minded seeing. He was utterly without pretense, and had no agenda.

"Bad night, huh, Howie? You up to a visit or no?"

"Up to it, no, but needing it? Yeah, please stay."

"I came to bring a perspective."

"A perspective?"

"Yeah, you know, a way of looking at things."

"And what might that be?"

"Well, I ain't what you'd call an optimist. Sometimes they're blind as bats. But I guess you'd call me a realist—a practical sort of guy. You know what I mean?"

Stern grunted, but didn't speak.

"Well, Howie," Earl continued, "You've got to look at it this way. You ain't spending no time behind bars other than between now and the trial, if there is one."

"And you're so sure?" Stern lifted his head and looked at his visitor.

"Sure as day. I mean, you're an innocent man. You didn't kill nobody."

"And you're sure of that, too?"

"Would I say it if I didn't believe it?"

"No, Earl, you wouldn't."

"It's just a matter of figuring out who killed your lady friend, and you're home free."

"We've got people working on it now. Good people."

"You need some high level investigating." Earl grinned and pulled at his chin.

"I have the best. I've got contacts and money. The police are working on it too."

"Plus you got me. I'm your friend, and I can get my nose into things around here."

"Yeah, Earl, I've got you. What are you charging?" Stern broke into a weak smile.

"Not a cent, my man, I'm a rank amateur. But you've got to include me in your book. I kinda like that thought." Earl winked. "I might even read it."

Stern wasn't sure whether anyone believed he didn't murder Amber after the discovery of the gun, except for his mother, Josh Woodhouse, and the man sitting opposite him. Had he seen a flicker of doubt in Jud Tillston's eye when he heard they'd discovered the weapon with Stern's fingerprints on it and no one else's?

Earl never wavered. There was no hint of doubt. Stern could see it in his eyes. This man completely believed in his innocence. If he wanted to poke his nose into things, Stern welcomed it. It seemed that a glimmer of hope was sparked by Earl's visit.

"Got to go, Howie, but I'll be back, rest assured. I'm on assignment; and I've got to keep my job. Candy doesn't know I'm a private eye." Earl bellowed without a shred of self-consciousness.

Stern smiled in spite of himself.

CHAPTER 28

Earl was concerned for his former boss. Gus Burlew wasn't talking and didn't plan on it. Whatever benevolence Gus had once felt toward Earl was gone. The alcohol was back and Gus's personality had changed dramatically. Short-tempered and violent at times, Gus's speech often made no sense at all. Nattie was gone without a promise to return. It was either her or the alcohol, and Gus had chosen the latter. It was, once again, his god.

No point in pursuing anything with him. Earl shook his head in disbelief. *The man is hopeless and is going to kill himself with booze. You can't talk to alcohol anyway—it don't make no sense.*

Maybe he could get in touch with Nattie. He'd connected pretty well with her the first time around. She might be more willing to talk, especially considering the sad state of her husband. She was somewhere in Pennsylvania, but where? Earl figured he could find out easy enough and pay her a visit. Maybe he could get in her good graces if he got a little more religious. That would soften her up a bit. He'd ply her for information and tell her it was for the Lord's sake. He was just doing the Lord's work and needed her help. It was somewhat deceitful, Earl thought to himself, though not entirely. After all, he believed in the man upstairs; he believed in Stern's innocence, and he believed that Nattie knew something important—something she'd been hiding, because she feared Gus. Now that she was not around him, she'd feel safer.

Maybe I ought to get a badge, or some cards printed up. It would give me a little more credibility. Earl Teeter, Private Investigator. Have sixth sense, will travel.

"Guess I'd need a license for that," Earl said aloud.

Earl showed up at Nattie's mother's house in Williamsport, Pennsylvania, Bible in hand. He'd shaved that morning and was wearing his best clothes. Appearance makes a difference, he thought to himself. It took him ten minutes of brutal scrubbing to get his hands and fingernails clean, but the cracks in his hands and fingers still bore ample evidence of a working man's trade. He'd shaped up the outside pretty good, but the Lord knew the inside needed a lot of work.

Miracles do happen, he reminded himself. Maybe someday he'd let the Lord shape up his thought life. Stranger things had happened. Gilbert Flange had done a one-eighty a few years back and was out preaching and acting foolhardy for the Lord. Gilbert's reputation would have embarrassed Al Capone.

"Who is it?" The voice came from inside. It wasn't Nattie's.

"Earl Teeter, a friend of Mrs. Burlew's—from Hollister, New York. Is she there?"

"Just a minute."

Earl checked his fingernails again. The cleanest they'd been in years—of course, the two-week vacation had helped a lot, but one day back at work would wreak havoc. It seemed like five minutes had passed before the same voice announced the next question.

"What do you want?" A wizened face peered through the drawn curtain at the door.

Earl flashed the Bible, hoping the woman was a religious as Nattie. He didn't want to mention Gus because he was sure it would create an unnecessary stir.

"I need to speak with Mrs. Burlew about a couple of real important matters." That was vague enough, and nonthreatening. Again, he made the Bible quite visible, but he felt like a hangdog, pretending to be religious to gain entrance. This was a challenge for him, and he just hoped the Lord understood and would cut him some slack. He could hear two voices now from within the house, then the sound of the door unlocking. Nattie appeared as the other wisp of a figure hobbled out of sight.

"What do you want, Earl?" Nattie asked, eyeing the Bible with some suspicion.

"Well, ma'am, I need your advice about a couple of things." Earl continued to be ambiguous, but smiled and nodded.

Nattie opened the door and beckoned him inside.

"Come in, Earl," she said. "What's on your mind?" Her eyes sparkled as she glanced at the Bible. "What can I help you with?"

Earl stepped into the tiny kitchen. "I've been doing a lot of thinking and I need the Lord's guidance. Naturally, I thought of you." *Earl, you devil! You've got one foot in hell already and the other's getting close.*

"I'm honored that you would seek me out," she said.

"You suppose the Lord could use a man such as me?" Earl asked.

"The Lord could use a rat if he chose to. No offense to you, Earl."

Earl was no genius, but neither was he stupid. To him, that certainly sounded like a poke at his character. "Well then, maybe I'm that rat." A grin stretched across his face.

Nettie flushed, embarrassed, but quickly regained her composure. "You've got to be right with the Lord first, Earl."

"Just how right can a rat be now, Nattie?" He continued grinning, and Nattie lost her composure again.

"I mean, you know—well, uh, it was a figure of speech."

"What was?"

"The rat."

"The rat was a figure of speech?"

"Yes."

"Then I'm not really the rat?"

"No, no, of course not."

"Then what am I?"

"Well, you're one of God's creations," Nattie was getting her footing.

"And so is a rat."

"But a rat is just an animal."

"And I'm not?"

"Oh, no! You're more than that!"

"Thank the Lord." Earl sighed.

"You were created in God's image." Nattie turned and motioned him to sit down at the table.

Earl had heard that before, but didn't understand it. It sounded good though.

"God wants you to be part of his family, one of his own."

Now Earl felt on the spot. She was getting too close. *I mean, I can stand a teaspoonful here, but not a grain sack.* The woman was ready to pounce and he knew it. *Time to gain control. Back off and shift gears. Head her in another direction.*

"That brings me to my point," he blurted out.

She was breathless, waiting for him to take the plunge. She would lead him—or maybe nudge him, over the edge.

Earl glanced at his watch. "I'm on a schedule."

"Behold, now is the time! Today is the day of salvation! Call upon the name of the Lord, Earl! She was almost shouting now.

Lord, help me. Deliver me from this woman.

Nattie's mother tottered into the room to see what the commotion was. "I thought the house was one fire," she said. "I almost called 911."

Earl figured the interruption was an answer to his cry for help. The momentum shifted and he was able to seize the moment and turn it his way.

"Nattie," he said, "are you aware of the murder of Amber Greene? The editor of the *Valley Voice*?"

Nattie had lost the battle but not the war. The look on her face was a mixture of perplexity and disappointment. Once again, she'd failed in her efforts to convert Earl.

"Yes, I've heard, Earl. What a sad thing. A horrible, horrible tragedy."

"Well, Nattie, that's one reason why I'm here. I think the man upstairs could help me figure out who did it."

"Seems to me like it was that author fellow—Blankley."

"You've judged him before a trial, Nattie? That don't seem Christian to me."

"Of course," she corrected herself, "only the Lord knows for sure. But the news—"

"Since when do you believe everything in the news?" Earl pulled on his chin.

"Well, I don't. Anyway, the Lord knows. How do you figure He's going to use you?"

"I'm sort of completing the mission that Amber Greene was on before she got killed."

"I'm not sure what you mean, Earl. I thought you were trying to figure out who killed Ms. Greene. That couldn't have been *her* mission. I mean—"

"No, no, Nattie. Now you have to hear me out, first. Then I'll explain everything. You see, I've got this idea, maybe from the Lord Himself. I've spoken with Mr. Blankley, too, and he said that Amber was going to speak to you when you got back to New York. She also had a gut feeling about something real important to her."

"A gut feeling?" Nattie furrowed her brow.

"She wanted to speak with you about it."

"What kind of gut feeling?"

"Well, she had this idea of who might have killed—I mean *run* that Heath Proctor kid off the road years ago. She and Mr. Blankley were writing a new book about it. She thought you might know something about it."

Nattie recoiled in defense, "You're just digging for information, aren't you. What does this have to do with Ms. Greene's death?"

It was time for Earl to unload and see what she would do. "Nattie," he said drawing closer to her and looking into her eyes, "my hunch is that it's the same person, know what I mean? Same person killed them both. Amber Greene *and* Heath Proctor."

Nattie looked aghast. Earl could see fear in her eyes. He thought her heart had quit beating and she was visibly trembling. Her mouth tried to form words but no sound was coming forth.

Earl waited before responding, letting the impact of his disclosure sink in. After several seconds, he said, "Are you with me, Nattie? Did you follow me?"

"It doesn't make sense," she said weakly. "Too many years apart."

Earl thought he sensed a hint of acknowledgment in her voice, as if her mind was searching the past and trying to make a connection with the present. "Nattie, what if Amber was getting too close to the truth and someone didn't like it?"

"Who?"

"That's the big question, if we knew who did the first crime, we'd know who did the second. You follow me?"

"I follow." She nodded.

"I mean, we got two people dead, now don't we? Could be more to follow. We wouldn't want that, would we?"

"The Blankley guy could have done both." Nattie wrung her hands and shifted in her chair.

"He's a suspect in Ms. Greene's death, but he's got a list of alibis a mile long for when Proctor died." Earl couldn't confirm that, but he figured he was safe saying it.

"Why are you so sure he didn't kill her?"

"I told you I have a feeling is all. Intuition, you know what I mean? Let me ask you something, do you suppose Ms. Greene's suspicion might have been right, too?"

"I have no idea."

"I think you do. I mean, you already said there was another car involved. Remember? Paint from another car—a different color."

"I don't know anymore than that, I told you that before. Besides, Gus said—" she caught herself and abruptly looked away.

"Said what, Nattie?"

"Nothing."

"Did he threaten you if you told anyone?"

"No."

"What did he say, Nattie? It's so important that you tell the truth. You think the Lord would have you to?"

"I can't say anymore," she said, tears welling up in her eyes.

"Why can't you, Nattie?"

"Because—I'm *afraid*."

"Of what?"

"Gus said he'd kill himself if I told anyone."

"So you know who forced Heath off the road?"

"Gus told me when he was drunk."

"And you won't say who?"

"I can't. I believe Gus is serious about killing himself."

"He will anyway, the way he's drinking," Earl said.

"I love him, but I can't go back. It's too much for me, Earl."

Earl reached over and put his hand on both of Nattie's. She was a pitiful sight. He figured her guilt had driven much of her religious behavior. Outwardly, she was a pillar of righteousness, but miserable inside—with a dark secret too. Eventually she'd tell it all. Now was not the time. He had pushed her far enough. God would have to do the rest. All these years she'd lived with horrible guilt—and a fear of her own husband.

God have mercy on her poor soul.

CHAPTER 29

I'm back! I'm back! I'm back!

I Hiram Morton Fenley II awoke from a nightmare with those words ringing in his ears. He thought he'd brushed the anonymous letter off, but apparently, it had a subconscious effect on him. It coincided with Amber Greene's death, and that began to trouble him. He redirected his thoughts to the pending trial. He had an inherent dislike for Stern Blankley, and there would be no trouble finding the energy to prosecute him. Hiram detested mystery novels and felt they were beneath his dignity to read. The District Attorney had no time for such silliness. He continued to savor the thought of his opportunity for notoriety, and felt like a new man—twenty years younger.

No longer able to sleep, he got up and paced the floor, devising his opening argument.

It was a meeting of the minds: Stern's and Jud Tillston's. Formulating a defense strategy in the light of a forthcoming indictment which the grand jury would likely hand down soon. The defense would center on Stern's relationship with Amber, his impeccable character, and lack of any plausible motive. Carla Fletcher could prove to be a very troublesome witness, and the existence of a gun, the timing of the murder, and lack of any alibis presented huge obstacles. The investigation in Annapolis would hopefully turn up a few leads regarding the theft of Stern's gun. Someone had to have information on which to follow up. The police were questioning Frieda.

The housekeeper had regained a measure of composure, but was still prone to spells of hysteria.

Jud had a couple of men working in Annapolis digging for whatever they could find. The crew of ARCO Painting Company had disclosed nothing so far, and none seemed likely suspects. The carpet layers were equally dead ends. Frieda insisted the security system was always activated at night, as well as whenever she left the house. It was a habit she'd practiced for years without fail, understanding that her job depended on it. The consensus was that whoever gained access either bypassed the security system or stole the gun in broad daylight without being noticed. A nighttime entry was ruled out. The lock to Stern's bedroom presented little challenge and could have easily been picked. Whoever heisted the gun knew what they were doing. There were no fingerprints anywhere in the room other than those belonging to Stern and Frieda.

The thought crossed Stern's mind that Frieda may have removed the gun for some unknown reason, but he dismissed it quickly. There had been no overnight guests during Stern's absence, although Frieda had invited several lady friends during the day for tea. They, too, would be questioned.

Stern and Jud mulled over Earl's idea. If the same person killed both Heath and Amber, then there was likely a Hollister connection. A person who had a motive to kill them both could have waited years to finish the job. Deadly motives could seethe for a long time awaiting fulfillment. Amber never shared with Stern about her premonition. It never became a topic of conversation during their romance.

Both Jud and Stern concluded that the premonition, whatever it was, was probably accurate and had gotten Amber killed. Someone knew she was digging for damning information and got to her before she disclosed it.

It struck Stern that *he* may have been the object of the killer too. For whatever reason, the ploy failed and the second best option was enacted with Stern set up as the perpetrator. He wished more than once that the first option had succeeded, but now he was driven by a desire to discover the killer and bring him or her to account.

A new hope was stirring within him. Not only did he want to be vindicated, he wanted justice, for Amber's sake. For the first time since her murder, he felt that somehow it would all come to a favorable end. The thought lifted his spirits a great deal.

Josh Woodhouse had been in continual prayer for Stern and his legal team. The church prayed for the upcoming trial whenever they assembled. When the timing was right, Josh would visit Stern in jail. For now, however, the timing wasn't right.

Julie Fisher had a decision to make. Was she going to share her discovery with the reading group or keep it to herself? She chose the latter. Maybe she was just living in a fantasy world and was too enamored with Stern Blankley. Still, she couldn't repress the growing notion that somehow she would be involved in his life. The woman's picture already made her feel connected. Was it a serendipitous discovery, or providence? Whatever it was, it motivated her to pray as never before.

The computer database at the library wouldn't contain any information about who had taken Stern's books out if they had been returned, so there was no use checking there. The only ones she knew for certain had read the books were members of her group, but she was certain that none of them would have had a picture of Amber Greene.

Keep it a secret. Keep it a secret, for now.

If the picture *was* a yearbook picture of Amber, then the person who owned it might be a former classmate or someone within a few years of her grade. It was still possible that the picture was not of Amber after all, maybe just a dead look-alike. The only way to prove it would be to obtain a copy of a yearbook from Amber's graduating class. That would necessitate a trip to New York to find a reliable contact there.

Maybe, she thought, just maybe she could write Stern a letter. The thought thrilled her and became a preoccupation in the days ahead. She wondered if her prayers were just an effort to fabricate the plan of God, or if God was even in it at all. She was not a woman prone to obsession, but neither could she dismiss the compelling nature of the events unfolding before her. So far, she had told no one of her plans.

Jud's meeting with Earl was a study in contrasts—the consummate, polished professional, and the unrefined redneck. But they quickly discovered that their common ground transcended any differences. Jud was actually impressed with Earl's perceptivity; a term he chose to use in contradistinction to Earl's "sixth sense."

"You think that both of the Burlews know who was involved in the death of Heath Proctor, and that whoever it was, was also involved in Amber Greene's murder. Is that correct?"

"That's the way I have it figured," Earl said.

"What's the motive in either case?" Jud asked.

"Vengeance in the first case, and self-preservation in the second, to cover the first case."

"Someone knew Ms. Greene was getting too close to the truth?"

"Makes sense, don't it?"

"Maybe. Why won't the Burlews talk?"

"Scared."

"Of what?"

"Or who."

"Okay, of whom?"

"She's scared he'll kill himself if she says anything, and he's afraid of the bogeyman. Whoever it is that done it, they ain't gonna let it out."

"You know a lot of people here in town, right?"

"Right."

"Just keep digging to see what you come up with. I want to know what you find out." Jud gave Earl his card, which had a local phone number printed on it. "Don't hesitate to call," he told Earl.

"What you gonna be doing?"

"I'm going to see Gus Burlew."

"Good luck," Earl said.

"I'm sure I'll need it."

Gus Burlew was drunk at midday and in a sour mood. The house reeked of cheap booze, and wine bottles were strewn everywhere. Jud Tillston was not a welcome guest, but was persistent enough to get Gus to open the door after repeated hammerings. Gus was belligerent, and almost incoherent, threatening to throw Jud out.

About the only thing that came through Gus's rambling was something about Nattie leaving him when he needed her, and why would she do that to him? It was a no-brainer for Jud, who marveled at the thought that any woman could have subjected herself to such a revolting man and hellish atmosphere. It was hard for Jud to muster any pity for this contemptible excuse of a man, though he did feel a twinge of sympathy for his wife.

When Jud stepped back onto the porch, the door slammed shut behind him with such a force that he could hear the glass in the panes shatter. Gus cursed and yelled from behind the door.

A dead end there. Jud cast a final glance behind him. *In more ways than one.*

Two days later, a neighbor found Gus slumped in an overstuffed chair in his living room, dead of an overdose of alcohol and prescription drugs.

In what seemed like a final commentary on his life, Gus's funeral took place on a sullen, overcast day with a wind-driven mist soaking the handful of mourners present. The pastor of the Apostolic Tabernacle conducted the graveside service with a scathing tirade about the evils of alcohol. The eulogy blanched under the force of the reverend's vituperation. Earl stood with his arm around Nattie. She was inconsolable—though with the rain, no one noticed.

Earl wept silently, grieving for his former boss, and praying as best he could for the broken woman at his side.

"I guess that eliminates that lead," Jud shared with Stern during their scheduled meeting. "No surprise to me at all and certainly no loss to the community. Too bad he didn't share something that could have redeemed his life a little."

"A wasted life," Stern agreed, "and his poor wife."

"Earl said she was, in his words, 'real overcome with it all'," Jud said. "She's headed back to Pennsylvania permanently. Probably not a good idea to approach her for a while. Let her grieve for a few weeks, and then maybe Earl can get her to talk. After all, with her husband dead she's got nothing to fear from him. It's sort of ironic—her not talking for fear he'd take his life, and then him taking it anyway. It's a crazy world, Stern."

"Yeah, it's a crazy world." Three people were now dead and it was all related. Stern wondered what would happen next. There was a deranged killer still at large and an innocent man in jail awaiting an indictment.

It had been a little over two months since he first thought of writing the book. Since then, his life had been turned inside out and his entrance into Hollister had set in motion a series of nasty events. When and how would it all end? There had to be some meaning to it all. It seemed like justice was standing far off, impotent and shattered—a casualty of an evil scheme.

"Earl may be wrong, you know," Jud continued. "Maybe there's no connection between the two events. For all we know, Gus could have murdered Amber, and then drank himself to death."

"I don't think he had the mental wherewithal to pull it off," Stern countered. "How would he have gotten the gun?"

"Maybe he sobered up enough to make a trip to Annapolis. After all, he conveniently sent his wife out of town for two weeks. Maybe he hired someone to do it; he seemed quite deranged when I saw him."

"He had no money for anything—other than booze."

"Maybe he saved it when he was sober."

"I guess we'll never know. I still say he wasn't smart enough to do it."

"Our investigation has turned up nothing so far," Jud admitted. "Whoever killed her must have been hiding out while you were there, or arrived just after you left. No tire tracks, no footprints in the shed. He covered himself very well. The thing was planned, that's for sure."

"And certainly not by Gus," Stern added.

"So we're back to Earl's theory."

CHAPTER 30

J ulie Fisher's body was exhausted, but the thought of writing Stern Blankley a personal letter kept her mind surging well into the night. She composed and edited what she would say a dozen different times and was still not satisfied. What would she say? How would she say it? Would he even read it? And if so, what would he think? What would *she* think if she were in his place? Receiving a letter from a complete stranger who had found a faded photograph that might have been cut from a yearbook some twenty years ago; the likeness of a woman who'd recently been murdered, and for whose murder Stern was the prime suspect.

I would think it was absurd, she thought. *Something from an innumerable number of nutcases who imagine themselves to be sent from God to liberate their hero.*

Yet, how many of the nutcases had an actual photograph in their hands that had been tucked between the pages of one of Blankley's books? A photograph that bore a striking resemblance to the woman he was accused of murdering.

Julie clung to the belief that it had to be providential, however remote it might otherwise seem. Why had that photograph landed in her hands? Why was she obsessed with the thought that it was a key to a door she hadn't yet discovered?

She was more convinced then ever that she needed to write the letter, whether it made sense to Stern or not. If it didn't, she would knock on another door. Sooner or later, one would open. She fell asleep praying for a man whose life had pressed into her reality, and with whom she sensed a destined connection.

And at that precise moment, Josh Woodhouse was praying, not able to sleep, moved to intercede for a man whose soul was in mortal jeopardy.

The letter arrived with a stack of other mail, mostly fan letters, mostly supportive, but with a smattering of hate mail from turncoat fans and local acquaintances of Amber. Stern paid it little regard and tossed the day's mail in a pile of other letters for the legal team to review. It would be several days before the letter was found for Jud's perusal.

"There was a letter dated ten days ago from a woman in White Marsh, Maryland," Jud said during their scheduled meeting. "Something about a look-alike photograph of Amber. What do you make of it?"

"Not much," Stern said, mumbling. "It sounds hokey."

"I've read it and re-read it. Give it some thought, Stern. Think with me for a minute."

"I'm all ears." Stern crossed his arms and rolled his head backwards, trying to release the tension in his neck.

"Suppose it *is* a high school photograph of Amber. Suppose someone from Amber's class cut it out years ago, and that someone had a fascination with her, you know, maybe even an obsession."

"And used it as a bookmark as part of the obsession? Talk about a shot in the dark. My guess is that if there even is a photograph, it's not of Amber. Somebody wants publicity. There are a lot of freaks out there."

"Maybe, and maybe not."

"Then what do you suggest, Jud?"

"Write her back and request the photograph. We could do a search to see if any of your old classmates live in the White Marsh area. Right now we don't have a lot to go on."

"And if she won't send it?"

"We could get it easy enough, but, I'd prefer just let her do her thing for now."

"Maybe you could write her, as my lawyer. Legal stationary would carry more weight."

Jud nodded. "I'll get it out this week. If it's a hoax, we haven't lost anything other than a little time."

"I think I'm going to have lots of *that*."

Carla Fletcher was called to testify before the grand jury. Hiram Fenley was brutal and aggressive, pressing the jury for a swift indictment.

"How well had you known Amber Greene?" Hiram glowered with menacing eyes.

"Like a sister."

"How long had you known her?"

"Eighteen years."

"Did she know Stern Blankley?"

"Yes."

"How well?"

"Not well."

"How long?"

"Two months."

"What was his relationship with Amber Greene?"

"Professional and—"

"And what?"

"Cordial."

"Were they romantically involved?"

"She was."

"How did you know this?"

"She told me."

"Did you have concerns for her?"

"Yes."

"What kind of concerns?"

"That she didn't truly know him. That she was going too fast." Carla shifted nervously in her seat.

"Too fast?"

"Yes, in the relationship. I didn't want to see her hurt."

"Physically? Emotionally?"

"In *any* way."

"Did you have reason to believe she would be hurt, Ms. Fletcher?"

"Nothing concrete, just concerned, being a friend. I mean, she didn't really know the guy." Carla broke into tears, still in shock and grieving over the loss of her friend.

"No more questions, Ms. Fletcher," Hiram feigned sympathy, trying to take the edge off his raspy, guttural voice.

There seemed little question in the minds of the grand jurors regarding sufficient evidence to indict. The only question that remained pertained to the charge. Hiram would see to it that they were well instructed as to their options. He had no doubt that he could intimidate most of the jurors. He was in his stride, the old juices flowing—the smell of fresh blood. A nurtured vehemence was working in his soul. He was looking ahead to a guilty verdict, and life without parole.

When the news of Gus Burlew's death reached Hiram, he had a perverse sense of satisfaction. *The community is better off without him. I can't say I'll miss him, either.* A sardonic smile appeared on Hiram's meaty face.

Earl had time to reflect. He was, after all, a thinker. He went to the park on the square in Hollister and sat on the bench where he'd first met Stern.

So much has happened since Howie first came to town.

Hollister was once again in a major turmoil. Some old players and some new ones. Earl couldn't help thinking that something evil was being unearthed. Something long hidden in the bowels of the town. Something that needed to be expunged.

Waiting was difficult. Time would tell and time would heal. But the process would be painful—like surgery. This was not elective surgery. The events that were unfolding appeared to be beyond anyone's control, and Earl's own life was in an upheaval. He was sure that when the dust finally settled, he would not be the same man. Was it chance or was it fate? Or was it the man upstairs trying to get his attention. Maybe he'd go back to see Nattie, but not now. The timing wasn't quite right.

Julie was impressed with the letterhead, but not the letter. She had no intention of sending the photograph so the lawyer could make a comparison. She was perfectly capable of that. *Besides*, she thought, *he would probably write it off as insignificant, and who knows what would happen with the picture.*

She had a counterplan. She would write Tillston back and have him get a copy of Amber's senior yearbook and send it to Maryland. Why hadn't Stern written her, anyway? She would have probably sent the picture to *him* if he requested. And what took the lawyer so long to get back to her? It had been over two weeks since she'd sent the letter. Two long and agonizing weeks! How long before she received a response to the next letter? She'd send it as certified mail to add some weight. Lawyers respected that kind of action. Julie was ready to join the fray and knew just what she'd say in the letter, *Dear Mr. Tillston...* her mind was already on a run. *In response to your letter...*

Jud recognized the return address and signed for the letter. Julie's strategy had worked. The letter had caught his attention and caused him to take it seriously. He decided that he liked this woman after all, and didn't find her to be a kook. A counterproposal in no uncertain terms. The first letter was tentative; this one was incisive, written by someone who had passion and resolve. How could he get his hands on a yearbook? It should be easy enough. He'd run it by Stern.

"Call Frieda and have her rummage through the trunks in the attic," Stern answered. "I'm sure there's one up there someplace. You're actually taking this woman seriously, aren't you?"

"Two things I like about her," Jud said, nodding. "Number one, she isn't intimidated, and number two, she believes she is on to something—and that's more than we can say at this time. Besides, she's working for nothing." He grinned.

"So the guys in Annapolis haven't turned up anything at all, huh."

"Not a thing. Every one of the painters, rug layers, and friends of Frieda's has been thoroughly questioned. So far there's not a shred to go on."

"Can we hire new investigators?"

"Sure, but you've got the best now. These aren't novices, Stern. We've got two men assigned to this end working day and night. Even meeting with Earl, and they've only come up with one thing."

"What's that?"

"The killer may have parked a half-mile down the road from Amber's at a turnoff where the local teens hang out at night. He could have walked to her house pretty much undetected, there's so little traffic on the road beyond the turnoff. Maybe one car every couple of hours. There are multiple tire tracks in and out of there. It shows nothing, really."

"Why'd you mention it?"

"We need some encouragement."

"So far it's looking like I'm the one, right?"

"I'll say one thing; whoever wanted to frame you knew what he was doing."

"Assuming it's a 'he'."

Jud shook his head. "I'd hate to think a woman would do that."

"Me too."

"Think of it. He lifted that gun from your bedroom without being noticed and without leaving a trace of evidence. Obviously must have done it in broad daylight. Then he drives to New York. He couldn't get by airport security with a gun, anyway, and it's too easy to trace. So, he drives to New York and plants himself here for a few days, or longer. You must have been under surveillance as well as Amber. He must have known your plans and hers; at least enough to know when she'd be home. The guy is clever, but the gun plant was too obvious; he must have thought you were a complete idiot to make it so obvious. Or maybe he thought the cops would think you panicked, being a rank amateur."

"The latter sounds more likely. If I had planned it, they would have never found the gun."

"A good point for the trial, Stern. You're not that stupid."

"Thanks for the vote of confidence."

"You need all you can get, pal."

CHAPTER 31

Searching for the yearbook gave Frieda a renewed sense of purpose, if only for a short time. If it would help Stern, it didn't matter how trivial the job was. Jud Tillston informed her that it could prove to be of great value, but he wouldn't elaborate beyond that. Frieda certainly couldn't get the correlation—and she didn't try. The police had questioned her thoroughly, and Jud informed her that she would be called as a witness for the defense.

Any conversation she had with Erline Slicer was devoid of gossip and usually ended in tears. Erline had been at Stern's house on two occasions during his absence, for tea on the patio with other Annapolis notables. It haunted Frieda that it might have been during one of these parties that the killer eased into the house unnoticed and made away with Stern's gun. But wouldn't the painters or carpet installers have noticed? They were there pretty much all the time during the day. There could have been gaps though. The thought tortured her mind. What if she'd been gossiping on the patio while an insane murderer was inside the house going through Stern's room? Frieda shuddered at the thought and again gave way to tears. The hysteria had diminished, but the guilt grew in intensity from day to day.

There it was!

Frieda discovered it amongst several other books stored in one of the musty trunks in the corner of the attic. A copy of the *Hollister High Banner 1968*. The year both Amber and Stern had graduated. She flipped it open and leafed through the first several pages until she found Stern's picture. It brought a huge wave of admiration to her as she gazed in fondness at the youthful face of her boss.

This man couldn't kill anyone. She cried and clutched the book to her chest. *Why have these things happened? Why, to such a nice man as Stern?*

Frieda quickly searched the next few pages for Amber. She was taken aback at the face before her. Such a striking resemblance to the photos in the newspapers! Younger, for sure, but remarkably unchanged except for hairstyle.

She was truly a beautiful woman—unusually beautiful.

Frieda wondered if Stern was more involved with this woman than he let on. The caption next to her name read: *To Stern, a friend my equal in so many ways. I will always remember you—Amber.* Frieda closed the book, hating to part with it, but knowing it was for some good, even if she didn't understand. She wept bitterly and slumped to the attic floor.

The Annapolis investigation finally hit what might have been pay dirt. Clifford Weeks had worked for the Arco painting contractor for two days during the time they had been at Stern's house. He disappeared without notice and left no trace as to his whereabouts. A phone call by Flanner Crosby, the crew leader, had revealed a disconnected phone. No one bothered to pursue Clifford beyond that, and no one had bothered to mention his name in the initial investigation. He was finally tracked down in a bar in Dundalk, Maryland, at ten o'clock on a Friday evening. For five hundred in cash, Clifford was willing to share what he knew. Or maybe he was just clever enough to feign having information in order to finance his habits.

Notwithstanding, it was something to go on. It seemed that Clifford, in an effort to avoid work, was loitering in the foyer of Stern's house one day when the doorbell rang. Frieda Baker was indisposed, engaged in a frivolous tea party on the patio, so Clifford had taken the liberty of opening the door. All Clifford could remember was a basic description of the visitor: short male, dark hair and a moustache, probably wearing glasses, though Clifford couldn't remember for sure. He carried a briefcase and said he was there to repair something, although this, too, was vague in Clifford's mind—which right now, was bathed in alcohol.

Could he remember anything else? Anything at all? Clifford scratched the side of his head, straining for recollection, when it dawned on him. Yes. There was something else, he remembered. The man had puffy hands and short fingers. Strangest hands he'd ever seen, like something a doll or toy would have. Certainly not a working man's hands, nothing at all like *his* hands.

"Would that be all?" he asked, itching for the cash.

"No further questions." The investigator slid an envelope across the table in Clifford's direction, five crisp bills inside. Clifford's plans for the evening had just taken an abrupt turn. He was headed for "the block" in downtown Baltimore.

The story was thought to be credible by Stern's legal team, primarily due to the description of the man's hands. Clifford didn't appear to be clever enough to invent something that odd just to make a few hundred bucks. With millions of people living in the metropolitan Baltimore-Washington D.C. area, finding a man to fit the description given by Clifford would be daunting. Assuming he'd disguised himself, the only distinguishing feature would be his hands. No one else in Stern's neighborhood witnessed the man come or go. No one else on the paint crew had seen the man. The knowledge that he had allegedly been there added several degrees of guilt to Frieda's suffering conscience.

"Anyone you remember from high school with puffy hands?" Jud asked Stern.

"What?"

"Puffy hands—and stubby fingers. Anyone come to mind?"

Stern thought for a moment. "I didn't pay that close attention to guy's hands."

"Yeah, I guess you were probably into other things, huh?"

Stern made no response, convinced that Jud was grasping at straws.

The Grand Jury, after a relatively short deliberation, returned an indictment of murder in the first degree. At the arraignment, Stern pleaded not guilty to the charge. Bail was denied.

Hiram Fenley could not have been a happier man.

The indictment came as no surprise. Public opinion was running at about ninety percent in favor of conviction, though the trial would likely be months away. Jury selection would be difficult due to the public attention the case drew, and because the people of Hollister were so dogmatic in their opinions.

Hiram was pressing for a quick trial. The more he learned of the collaboration between Stern and Amber regarding their research for the novel, the more it inflamed his zeal to get things in motion.

Every ounce of evidence pointed directly to Stern: the gun, the fingerprinting, the timing, his visit with Amber the night of her death—all hard evidence. The murder had taken place in her study and yes, Stern had been in her study that night. There was no doubt that the crime lab would provide hairs, clothing fibers, and a myriad of other convincing items of evidence.

But there were some inexplicable oddities incongruous with the assumptions regarding Stern's involvement. There were no matching footprints to the outbuilding. Footprints from size ten shoes had been lifted from the area rugs adorning the hardwood floors throughout Amber's house. The prints matched Stern's shoe size exactly. There were, however, indentations in the lawn between the house and the outbuilding that appeared to be from shoes that could have been covered with something to mask the prints. The indentations appeared to have been made by someone approximately one hundred and thirty pounds or less. Stern weighed one hundred and eighty. The lighter weight suggested a very small man—or perhaps, a woman. Certainly, this bit of information would be hammered by the defense.

Unfortunately, the prints didn't show up in the outbuilding where the gun was found, and Carla later confirmed that Amber hired a man about that size to tend the grounds. He had been there the day of Stern's visit to make sure everything was in order. He was questioned thoroughly by the police and released.

The ballistics unit determined that the two bullets that pierced Amber's body were fired from the weapon found in the outbuilding. There was no doubt that it was the murder weapon, but there were some questions relating to the trajectory of the slugs, and the height of the shooter.

The defense strategy had shifted somewhat, and would focus on an attempt to prove a cover-up related to the story Stern and Amber were writing. Someone—whoever, didn't want certain information disclosed. Damaging information could have possibly led to the solving of a previous crime. A lot of hypotheticals, but perhaps enough to sway a jury. That, along with lack of a true motive and the obvious incongruities would be exploited to the maximum.

Jud was developing a major dislike for the D.A.

Stern was exhausted from the crush of events. His mind wavered between hope and despair. The longer the wait for the trial, the greater the possibility that something would turn up in his favor. Just the thought of the wait and the onus of a lengthy trial activated his melancholy.

It was on a particularly somber day that Josh Woodhouse made his way to the county jail. He had been cleared for regular visitation years ago, and was accustomed to frequent contact with the inmates, providing spiritual encouragement and counseling. Josh was not the person Stern wanted to see, but he relented if only to break the excruciating loneliness of isolation.

Jail policy allowed for a one-hour visit by clergy on specified days. The visitation room was fairly large, open, and sterile with stools fixed on opposite sides of a dividing wall, allowing visitors and inmates to converse freely, but with little privacy. One of the clergy pressed the intercom button and a voice responded, requesting the purpose of the visit. All of them had been cleared for entry and the lock in the steel door clicked open with a corresponding buzz. Each one signed the log with date, time, and name of inmate.

A second door clicked open after the first had been secured, and the group found themselves in the visiting area. It took about ten minutes for each inmate to be escorted into the room, during which time the clergy discussed everything from the weather to the status of their respective churches. Most knew each other and were friends, although there was often a subtle jealousy relating to who had the highest attendance, the most new converts, the biggest church budget, or the nicest building. Josh thought it was a shame and a sad commentary on the state of the church in general that conversations usually tended toward comparison. He hated those thoughts within himself whenever they raised their ugly heads.

"Who is here to see Blankley?" the guard called without emotion as he escorted Stern into the visiting room.

"I am," Josh announced. He approached a stool opposite where Stern was to be seated, and extended his hand over the partition with a warm but not effusive greeting. Stern forced a weak smile and took Josh's hand.

"It's good to see you, Stern," Josh spoke with genuine concern.

"Thanks for coming," Stern said, mechanically. His eyes met Josh's and he sensed tenderness in them that struck at the ache in his heart.

"You've been on my mind a great deal lately," Josh said. "I've waited until things settled a little before coming to visit."

Stern silently hoped that Josh would not be preachy or sanctimonious. They were worlds apart in their respective beliefs, and the barrier that Stern had erected in his mind would remain unmoved.

"I'm not sure the dust has really been stirred up yet," Stern said. "I think that's yet to come."

"I've read about the indictment."

"Pretty clear, isn't it? The evidence is all there."

"Any word on the trial?"

"Who knows? It could be months for all I know—with a possible change of venue."

"It *would* be hard finding unbiased jurors in this county, wouldn't it?" Josh agreed.

"Or anywhere for that matter," Stern said.

"How are you doing…personally?"

The question caught Stern off guard and his expression betrayed his response. "Okay, considering the circumstances."

"Seriously though. How are you handling it all?" Josh pressed gently at the risk of offending.

"I've had better days. Jail isn't my idea of getting away from it all. And the cuisine. What I've heard about it is true. It's part of the punishment." The levity broke the tension for the moment.

Josh put his arms on the edge of the barrier and leaned forward. "I believe you're innocent."

Stern waited before responding, "You're in the minority."

"I often am."

"What about the evidence?"

"It can be misleading."

"Let's hope the jury thinks so. Why do you believe I'm innocent?"

"I got to know you during your visits at the church. I observed you and Amber together, and I was with you the day of the murder. I don't believe you did it, and for whatever reason, you were framed—by someone very clever and depraved."

"Any thoughts of whom?"

"None whatsoever. But God knows."

The inevitable God factor had emerged. Stern knew it was coming, but what could he expect? After all, this *was* a man of the cloth. "Why did He allow it to happen?" Stern asked, bluntly.

"I could give you a canned answer, but I won't."

"Well, give me something that isn't canned."

"I don't really have an answer, although I believe we will both know it someday."

"That sounds canned to me." Stern crossed his arms and leaned back on the stool.

"Would it make a difference to you if you understood why it happened?"

"Certainly."

"Then you will know."

"When?"

"Someday."

"Someday?"

"I'm not God."

"I had that figured out."

"You have good perception."

"It wasn't difficult."

The lively banter gave Stern no reason to dislike this man. Instead, he found him not canned at all. Maybe an ally. Maybe a friend. Too soon to tell.

Josh rocked back on his stool. "Can I come again?"

"I don't see why not."

"Does that mean yes?"

"Yes."

The hour was up. The public address interrupted the several conversations in the room. The clergy assembled at the door that led to the hallway. The buzzer sounded and the lock clicked open. Josh signed out and waited for the next door to open. Within a few minutes, he was outside the jail, thanking God for the visit and praying again for the innocent man being taken back to his cell.

Stern thought about the words Josh had spoken so dogmatically...*then you will know. Someday.*

Jud Tillston sent a letter to Julie thanking her for her quick response. He assured her that her request was being taken seriously and they were working on locating a yearbook.

Stern decided not to have his yearbook sent to Julie, but forwarded to him. He was curious to read the autographs and to see Amber's high school picture. Jud reluctantly agreed and had a paralegal working on purchasing an unused copy from the school archives. If that proved unsuccessful, they would have to scrounge around town for a copy. Either way, Jud would find a copy for the amateur detective in White Marsh. It certainly wasn't a priority, but he'd make sure it got to her. Though humored by her, his gut instinct told him not to totally disregard her.

CHAPTER 32

I t was all Julie could do to keep secret her discovery and subsequent investigation from the book group, but she decided it was not yet time. Once she got the yearbook and could make a clear determination regarding the photograph, she would consider pulling the group in on it. She wanted in on the action and wished she was in New York as part of Stern's legal team. She would do anything to help: run errands, do research, and serve coffee and donuts. But for now, her work would be done alone.

The up-line from Frieda Baker to Erline Slicer and on to Mid Gear hadn't produced anything that couldn't be gathered from the media. Everyone in the group was aware of the indictment and the charges, as well as Stern's pleading innocent. Julie avoided the tabloids, not wanting her mind tainted by hearsay or misinformation. It had already been close to two weeks since she'd sent her registered letter to Jud Tillston, and she was agitated that there had been no response. Though it was a priority in her mind, it obviously was not to those in New York. She fixed a deadline of two more weeks. If she hadn't heard by then, she'd go to New York herself. She was back on her college schedule and would have to miss classes for the trip. The sacrifice was worth it to her—college didn't seem to interest her much anyway and she had difficulty focusing.

Whenever the group met, there was endless speculation regarding the murder. Everyone believed Stern was guilty except for Julie and Melissa. Though Melissa maintained a degree of suspicion, she followed Julie's lead.

"The only thing that would have made it more obvious would have been a video tape," Toppsy ranted. "But he's got money, so he'll probably buy his way out of it. This guy is a real sleaze ball after all."

"Do you believe in due process?" Sue Ellen took the high road, but she was just as convinced of Stern's guilt as Toppsy.

"She thinks due process is a kind of cheese." Saul roared, and the entire group delighted in the opportunity to humble Toppsy.

Not to be outdone, Toppsy seized the chance for escalation. The blood rushed to her face like steam from a pressure cooker. She was boiling for an attack, and was quite accustomed to verbal warfare. She would make Saul suck his words down like a piece of his own baklava.

"You are an odious and fatheaded, bigoted, Greek buffoon and everyone in this room knows it!"

The words erupted like a volcano. Everyone in the group glanced at each other, then at Saul, and finally at Toppsy, waiting for the next move. The humor drained from Saul's face and he shifted nervously in his seat. An affable man, Saul was not one for confrontation. He calculated that to pursue an exchange with this bellicose woman would be disastrous.

"I meant nothing by it," he spoke with contrition, hoping to diffuse Toppsy.

"You apparently mean nothing whenever you speak," Toppsy replied.

"Can't you two just drop it?" Fenton didn't care for confrontation either.

The rest of the group agreed.

Toppsy backed off but continued to eye Saul warily, glowering at him on occasion. She had honed her aptitude for nurturing and holding grudges, and Saul Karras was her latest unlucky victim. Saul avoided any further eye contact with her, thanking God for Sophie, his precious wife of thirty-two years.

After the meeting, Julie felt unusually alone. Alone with her thoughts and alone with her secret. She prayed for guidance for the days ahead, and for protection—she had a gut feeling that she would need it.

Hiram was testy and headed for the liquor cabinet. Scotch, his greatest comforter in moods like these, often exacerbated his temper. This was not one of those times. Few people ever observed Hiram in these states, except his wife and his son. Mrs. Fenley knew when to steer clear of her husband, although it wasn't always possible. More than once, she'd feared for her life and that of her son, locking them both in her room until Hiram came to his senses.

Since Hiram Morton Fenley III, or Morton, as he was called, had left home years ago, Mrs. Fenley bore the brunt of her husband's wrath alone—a dirty little secret that no one outside of their house knew. Hiram could be as close to the devil as the demons themselves.

He hated that there would be no one to carry on the Fenley legacy, no third generation of lawyers. It wasn't his fault that his wife couldn't conceive after the birth of Morton. Nothing wrong with *his* manhood—she was to blame. A sterile woman in more ways than one. He lamented his curse and refilled his glass with scotch.

There was not a shred of doubt in his mind as to the guilt of Stern Blankley. He figured the defense would do everything in its power to stall, and time was not on his side. He had even sensed a few lapses in his otherwise brilliant memory. His doctor had instructed him to lose weight and cut back on the alcohol. Without his blood pressure medication, Hiram would have been dead by now.

Forty years in the courtroom had taken its toll too. Granted, he lived in a rinky-dink town and nothing of any import came his way except once in awhile. He knew he could have made it as a big time prosecutor elsewhere, but that would have meant a loss of influence and control, something he'd had a great deal of for a long time in Hollister. He had assembled a highly competent legal team of his own and had no fear of the hotshots from D.C.

Hiram closed his eyes; they appeared to retreat into the recesses of his fleshy face. He envisioned the courtroom, addressing the jury, calling the witnesses. He could almost hear the jury foreman delivering the verdict before a hushed and somber courtroom:

We find the defendant guilty…

Then victory and release!

The publicity, all the media attention, well deserved accolades—what a way to end a career. Must be something providential working on his behalf to bring his life of service to such an illustrious close (though Hiram had little regard for providence). His periodic appearance at the Presbyterian Church was only for show, to enhance his image as a fair and decent man. He had even written a check for two hundred dollars for the offertory the last time he went to church. He was pretty certain he had been the biggest giver of the day.

With Stern's permission, Josh Woodhouse made regular weekly visits to the jail. His visits were brief, always coming and going on a positive note, nothing heavy, just checking in. If there was anything he or the church could do, Stern could let him know. He always made it clear that he believed in Stern's innocence, and that a good portion of the church felt the same, though he couldn't speak for them.

Stern appreciated that Josh didn't preach or offer platitudes or advice. Little by little, he began to look forward to the visits and felt a curious bond growing. Josh would be subpoenaed as a witness and it wouldn't do any harm to have a local minister testify on your behalf, especially one who believed so strongly in your innocence. Stern reflected on the few times he'd been to church with Amber. He was thankful now that he'd been there, if only because he had one more ally in the Pastor of the church.

"You really think he's guilty, don't you?"

"That's not a new disclosure. I've said it all along."

"And what do you think his motive was—you've never said that."

"I'm not speculating on a motive, just evaluating the evidence."

"But you saw them together. You knew the relationship better than anyone else. Surely you must suspect something." Josh hadn't spoken at length with Carla Fletcher about Amber's death. He had kept his distance until the time was right.

Carla sat cross-legged on the worn leather chair in Josh's office. Her body was rigid and her voice tense. "She was my boss and my best friend, like a sister. Now she's dead. Murdered! I'm very angry." Carla's face tightened.

"And you need a place to direct your anger, right?"

"I don't need *you* to play psychologist with me!"

"Maybe your anger has compromised your judgment a little." Josh pressed further. "I don't think there was a motive for him to kill her. Furthermore, he was in love with her. I believe there *was* someone who had a motive and planted the evidence."

"Who?" Carla scowled at him.

"I have no idea."

"What about the gun—and the fingerprints?"

"Why wouldn't his gun have his own fingerprints on it? I'm sure he must have used it in target practice. Someone could have stolen it and used it, without ever leaving fingerprints."

"And you actually believe *that*?"

"As much as you believe he's guilty."

"We're miles apart, then."

"Apparently so."

Carla sat silent for a moment, breathing deeply, "And, how does the church feel about it?"

"It's split about fifty-fifty."

"Most of the town thinks he's guilty.

"The town doesn't know him, Carla."

"And you think you do?"

"Well enough."

"So you think he'll be acquitted?"

"It may never go to trial. At least as far as he's concerned."

"I'm still bitter," Carla spoke through her clenched teeth.

"I can understand the anger as part of grieving, but anger and bitterness together are a bad combination when it's directed at someone who may be innocent."

"It sustains me right now."

"But it will destroy your emotions, long term."

"I can't seem to help it. He deserves the death penalty."

"And if he's not guilty?"

"Somebody is—and I'd feel the same about them."

"You want justice, or revenge?"

"I want somebody to pay for her death! I can't say it any plainer!"

"Then you'd be released from your anger and bitterness?"

"Yes, I think I would be."

"Until then, you're still in prison."

"Huh?"

"To your anger and bitterness."

"You're so flippant and casual. Don't you have any feelings at all about what happened?"

The arrow struck him. "I'm deeply grieved."

"But no anger or bitterness?"

"I can't afford the bitterness. I'm angry at the injustice."

"And what does God have to say about it?" Carla asked.

"Amber had a verse she loved to quote."

"What's that?"

"From Genesis 18:25, 'Shall not the judge of all the earth do right?'"

Carla nodded slightly. "I remember her quoting it, now that you mention it."

"It's ultimately in His hands," Josh said

Carla sighed, shoulders sagging. "I know you're right, but I can't release it right now."

"Will you at least pray that He has His way?"

"It can't do any harm."

Josh took her hands in his and prayed for God's intervention. He also prayed for her and for Stern.

Carla's hands tightened firmly on his.

In White Marsh, Maryland, Julie Fisher also prayed for Stern, that somehow, no matter what the outcome of events, he would personally know the God who loved him. She fell asleep that night wondering where the yearbook was and why it hadn't arrived. If it wasn't in her hands within three days, she would be leaving for New York.

Earl was restless as a caged cat. It had been three weeks since the death of Gus Burlew. Surely Nattie had had some time to grieve. What harm would a little trip to Pennsylvania do? All she could do was tell him to get lost. She was sure he was lost anyway, so that was no big deal, although Earl figured that God was big enough to find him and save him. Even without Nattie's help.

He would go unannounced. She would have to refuse him face-to-face. That would give "old boy" Earl an opportunity to use his charm, something he had mastered while working for people on their auto bodies. The cars were like people, too, and he treated them with special care, putting a little bit of himself into each one. He never dreamed that he was being trained for something like this. The more he thought of it, the more he liked working with flesh and blood. At least that way he got a little feedback. The thought of hanging out that shingle kept playing with his mind. *It wouldn't cost no hundred dollars an hour, either.*

The thought was intriguing—and hilarious.

CHAPTER 33

It had taken her two days of on-again, off-again attempts, but the paralegal had scrounged up a copy of the 1968 *Hollister Banner*. The school had referred her to someone who had organized the last '68 class reunion, who in turn had referred her to a geeky man who collected scores of yearbooks over the years. He had three copies from that year. They were all in pristine condition, as the geek had made it a matter of pride to dust and polish his collectibles frequently. His house was a veritable museum with memorabilia from every year since 1965, including pennants, basketballs, baseballs, pom-poms, sports shorts, and jerseys—even a cheerleader's skirt from his *ex*-girlfriend. She'd been mortified when she found out he had paid someone fifty dollars to lift it from the school for his collection. The relationship ended immediately upon the disclosure.

Scotty Pomeroy, 'Suds' as he was called, was all too eager to part with the yearbook—for a hefty fee. He figured it must be pretty important to someone, and he had two extras anyway, which he kept secret from the paralegal.

"'68 was a good year," Scotty boasted. "Not unusual that you'd want a copy. I'm surprised others haven't been around. Amber Greene's in there, you know; so's that Blankley fella—the one that shot her."

"So they say." The paralegal hadn't given her name and Scotty didn't ask. "What are you asking for it?"

"I figure it'll go for a premium. Think about it; it could be a collector's item someday."

"So what do you think its worth?" She reached for her purse.

233

"To me or to you?"

"Or whomever."

Scotty's mind whirled with figures. He didn't want to lose the sale, but he wasn't about to give it away, either. "One hundred dollars, firm," he said, surprising even himself.

"For a yearbook?" The paralegal arched her eyebrows in mock surprise. She didn't care what the price was, and had five hundred with her if she needed it.

"They cost a lot today. And this is a collector's item."

"I'll give you fifty in cash." She fished out two twenties and a ten from her wallet.

"Can't do it. Not for that. That's robbery. I need eighty bucks."

"I'll give you sixty. Last offer." She folded the bills and started to replace them.

"Deal!" Scotty reached for the cash and the paralegal pulled an extra ten-dollar bill from her wallet. She placed the money in his hand.

"Thanks, Scotty. You've been a real help." She smiled and tucked the book under her arm.

"And thank you, Miss, er—uh..."

She had vanished before he could ask her name.

Sixty dollars for a twenty-eight-year-old yearbook with two in reserve? Heck, I could have held out for the hundred bucks. I knew she was bluffing.

The investigation for the defense was slow and miserable. Any lead, however promising initially, always led to a dead-end. The lack of any substantial progress was puzzling to Jud and his legal team, and disconcerting to Stern. There was nothing for him to do but wait.

Barring any radical discoveries, the case would go to trial and all would be in the hands of the lawyers and the jury. Stern imagined what kind of jury would be empanelled. People were never impartial. The thought of his life in prison made him shudder. The county jail was like a picnic compared to where he might wind up. His mind conjured up an array of horror stories, images of what he'd only read and heard about. *Attica or worse.*

Hope, a cruel prankster, appeared one day and disappeared the next, followed by the most difficult thing to deal with, encroaching fear. Fear of the unknown—that he had no control over his destiny.

Cold and alone, isolated from the world, locked in a surreal nightmare from which he never awoke. The dread and torment sapped him like a fever. He slumped in his cell—his body sagging pitifully with emotional pain.

The yearbook arrived by Fed Ex on a Tuesday afternoon. Julie was due to work at three, but had a premonition that she shouldn't leave her house. She phoned work to say she'd be late, and was home when the package arrived. The sight of the Fed Ex van made her tremble.

Maybe a false alarm.

No!

The driver approached with a package.

Julie frightened the poor man as she flung open the door before he could even ring the bell. He had never been thanked so profusely in his life and went away shaking his head thinking it was way too early for Christmas.

She clutched the treasure to her chest and thanked God for its arrival. She couldn't remember a time when she had been this excited. The return address bore Jud Tillston's name and that of his D.C. law firm. A letter was affixed to the front of the package, which she quickly opened.

Dear Julie,

Sorry this is late. I hope it is useful to you. Contact me if you need to.

Sincerely,

Judson A. Tillston, Esq.

She carried the bundle to her study. From her desk, she withdrew a white business-sized envelope that contained one item: the photograph. She removed it and placed it on the desk. She opened the package and withdrew a blue yearbook. The front cover bore an embossed image of a school building. Across the top of the book the words *Hollister Banner '68* appeared. She held in her hands what she hoped might be the key to a baffling crime.

She had been plagued with doubts and thoughts of sheer stupidity regarding her theory, but her gut feelings carried her beyond the doubts. Within seconds, she would know if the photograph that lay on her desk was the same as the one of Amber Greene in this blue book. If it was, a major piece of the puzzle would be in place. But there were so many more pieces. She wondered what it would look like completed. She opened the book.

You're a crass buzzard, Earl said to himself, en route to Pennsylvania. *Why can't you let the poor lady grieve on her own? Because it's for a greater good,* he answered his own question. *Besides, how long is she gonna grieve for a dead drunk? Probably she feels guilty more than anything else. Knowing Nattie, she's got to be gut wrenching guilty. Maybe I'll be a breath of fresh air. A knight in shining armor, riding in an orange pickup.*

The only one he'd ever seen of that color. He'd done the bodywork and paint job himself, just the way he liked it. A 1990 Ford F150. The paint was smooth as glass, a nice blend of red and yellow he'd perfected at Rathskeller's garage. *Man, it looks good!* It certainly turned heads, anyway. Not quite the color of a pumpkin—more like an evening sunset.

Julie opened the book. She could hear her heart pounding. The moment seemed almost sacred. The *Banner* had been dedicated to Heath Proctor. His elevation to hero status was amply documented.

His handsome face took nothing away from his stature. She thought for a moment on his death and wondered at his eternal destiny.

She began turning the pages and glanced casually at the unfamiliar faces before her. Though her mission was to compare the photos, she had another face in mind—Stern's. The autographed photo from the book jacket was also lying on her desk, and she had no trouble matching it with the one in the yearbook. With a girlish infatuation, she studied the details of his face for several minutes. She decided she liked the way he looked now, more mature and masculine, though his eyes retained a youthful sparkle. Both photos revealed the slightest hint of a smile, which hinted at impishness.

She drew a deep breath, putting her hand over her mouth. Amber Greene's photograph in the yearbook left no doubt about the identity of the one now in her hand. She released her breath as she studied the faces.

They were one and the same!

The puzzle was coming together. How likely was it that someone else in the book was the owner of the photo she'd found? *Quite likely*, she thought. However, there were four hundred and forty-three other senior pictures to choose from. She had already surmised it was more likely a male than a female. A male with a lingering fascination with Amber, or perhaps an obsession of some sort. Someone who may have frequented the library where Julie worked. A face in the crowd of hundreds who visited weekly.

It would be a daunting task to study so many strange faces in the book and try to match them with visitors to the library. Sure, she'd recognized Stern's picture immediately, and Amber was the exception. But years could do a lot to people's faces. When she had time, she would peruse the senior pictures for a familiar face, starting with the males. She would also match their names against recent computer records at the library to see if any had checked out any of Stern's books. And then there were the underclassmen…

It wasn't her style to stare at people, and she wished she could enlist others to help her. The more she thought of it, the more impossible the task seemed. What she needed was a little divine intervention. If God's hand was in it and He wanted to disclose an identity to her, He could easily do it.

She prayed. The thought came to her. What if she did find a familiar face—then what? Call Jud?

Not yet.

Chapter 34

"The night of Amber's death, we discussed the subject of evil. Evil forces, personalities, the devil and demons," Stern said. "It was almost as if she had a premonition about what was going to happen."

It was the first time Stern had broached the subject of the supernatural with Josh since Amber's murder. "She was trying to convince me of their existence, though I found it incredulous."

"They are real," Josh said bluntly.

"She said you'd taught about them."

"On several occasions."

"Why do you believe they are real?"

"The scriptures clearly reveal their existence."

Stern continued, ignoring Josh's comment, "She also told me some time ago that Heath Proctor had a strange preoccupation with evil before his death. What do you make of that?"

Josh took a moment before answering, carefully weighing what Stern had said. "In his case, it's hard to say. I didn't know him."

"Do you think that these so-called forces or personalities had anything to do with Amber's death?"

"It's possible; people can be driven to commit crimes or be influenced by them. In extreme cases, there can be demon possession."

Stern had read about such instances in magazines before, but chalked it up to primitive, tribal ignorance. Now he was challenged to reconsider.

"Assuming that to be true, I have a serious question." He shifted on his stool, leaned forward, and fixed his gaze on Josh.

"Why did God allow it, right?" Josh beat him to the punch.

"I guess you're used to being asked that."

"I am, and there's no easy answer, Stern."

"What does your theology tell you?"

"That God's people aren't exempt from the effects of evil."

The answer didn't jibe with Stern's idea of what God would be like. "Doesn't that diminish His power—if He can't protect His own?"

"I didn't say He *couldn't* protect them."

"Why wouldn't He, then?"

"You limit God's sovereign purpose by your concepts."

"I find it hard to believe that His purpose was Amber's murder," Stern objected. "That's a pretty hard sell."

"His purpose was *not* her murder, but He had a purpose *in it*. Evil is not a creation of God, but a consequence of free volition against Him. He allows evil to run its course. It ultimately serves an eternal purpose. A purpose we don't often see. Why was Lincoln shot? Or Martin Luther King, or Kennedy, or the Pope?"

"You sound exactly like Amber. She said the same things."

"God allowed the most monstrous of all evils against His own Son, and He didn't interfere," Josh continued, carefully selecting his words, conscious of Stern's skepticism, waiting for his response.

"Why?"

"So that justice could be done."

"*That's* justice?"

"He was guilty," Josh spoke simply.

"Who was?"

"Jesus Christ."

"Of *what*?"

"All sins ever committed—including yours."

Stern pushed back on his stool and thought for a moment. "Seems strange that God would judge His own son."

"That's the price of redemption. The just dying for the unjust. The guiltless for the guilty. You believe in justice, right, Stern?"

His whole life he'd believed in it. Wrote about it, desired it. He wanted to see Amber's killer brought to justice. "Right now, I want to see it more than anything else."

"But you're falsely accused, right?"

"Right."

"And so was He."

"Who?"

"Jesus Christ."

He'd heard the story before, but never gave it much thought. *The just dying for the unjust. A man falsely accused. Dying for something he didn't do.*

Would he go free and the killer be brought to justice? Or would he face a life in prison for something he didn't do? If forgiveness was a prerequisite for his own release in God's eyes, he hadn't, and would never forgive Amber's killer. He would kill the man himself, if he ever got his hands on him.

"To think about killing someone is the same as doing it in God's eyes." Josh appeared to read his thoughts. "The one who thinks it is no better than the one who does it. He just hasn't taken the thought far enough."

"That includes me," Stern admitted. "I don't deny it."

"That in itself is a type of prison. Locked into your own hatred and vindictiveness."

"But what about justice?"

"We both desire it. That's a God-given desire. Vengeance is another thing altogether."

"Then you're saying I'm no better than her killer?"

"In thought, no. In deed, yes."

"It's okay to want justice—just not vengeance?"

"Exactly."

"So in God's eyes, I'm just as guilty as Amber's killer?"

"God judges motive, Stern."

"So, in God's eyes I'm also worthy of the death penalty, even though I didn't actually commit a crime? Am I on the same page?"

"Without mercy you would *ultimately* be judged as a murderer, because of the intent of your heart," Josh explained, "even if there's no judicial penalty in this life, because no crime was committed."

Stern sat, silently pondering Josh's words, "And the real killer?"

"Should be found, convicted, and sentenced according to the law."

"And does he get mercy from God?"

"The crime is also a sin for which he, too, can be forgiven. It all depends on whether you want mercy and forgiveness or not. If you do, any sin can be forgiven. If not, then eternity will see that justice is done."

The conversation ended when the public address system again announced that visitation was over. It was an unusual visit, and it left Stern troubled in his conscience. There were issues he had to face, and for the first time in his life, he was forced to consider the possibility of the evil potential in his own heart.

Something was drawing him in a direction he'd never gone before. He saw Josh in an entirely new light. He saw himself in a new light, too, and his motives had been laid bare before God. He had been brought face-to-face with the ugliness of his own heart in such an unusual twist. In essence, he was no different than Amber's killer. He'd just never played out the intentions of his heart.

He felt torn between judgment and mercy.

It all depends on what you want.

Josh's words kept echoing in his ears.

CHAPTER 35

"It's me, Earl Teeter," Earl yelled through the door to Nattie Burlew.

"Earl?" Nattie hurried to let him in.

"Yes, it's me, Nattie. Can I come in?"

Nattie peered through the curtain to see Earl standing with his hands in his back pockets, looking quite innocent. This time she didn't hesitate to open the door. Much to Earl's surprise, she was glad to see him.

"Bless you, Earl," she said, greeting him warmly, "it's so good to see you again. You were so kind at the funeral, and I haven't had the chance to thank you."

Earl shrugged. "It was nothing, Nattie."

"Oh, it was more than you'll ever know. It meant so much to me. Not many were there, and you were a great comfort."

Earl felt sheepish. Her gushing left him at a loss for words. "Funerals are hard times," he said. "It was for me too. Gus meant a lot to me."

"His life was so sad, Earl, so sad." Tears came to Nattie's eyes. "I can't believe what he did to himself—and to his family."

"He must have felt no way out," Earl said.

"There was a way out, but he just never would receive it. Now he's gone and I fear for his soul, Earl." The tears came freely, and Nattie's frail body shook with emotion.

Earl had the foresight to put a clean handkerchief in his back pocket before he left New York. He plucked it out and offered it to her. "It's clean, Nattie. I put it in my pocket this morning."

"Oh Earl!" She sobbed, grabbing the hanky. "I'm sorry, I'm sorry. I didn't mean to cry so; it's just that I feel so bad about what happened. I didn't know what to do after he sent me away for those two weeks and went back bingeing. I just couldn't return to that, Earl. Do you understand?"

Her face looked miserably hurt and guilty. Earl wondered how much this woman had suffered through the years. "It wasn't your fault, Nattie. He made his own choices."

"But maybe if I'd been there, he—"

"Don't matter now, and wouldn't have mattered then. Nobody's responsible for another's choices."

"But maybe I badgered him too much, Earl. You think so?"

Earl coughed. He didn't need to agree with her on that one. "You just wanted the best for him. Can't fault you for that."

"And now he's gone on to who knows where, Earl. It's too much for me to think about." Nattie wiped her eyes and blew her nose on his handkerchief.

"You got coffee, Nattie?" Earl used her nose blowing as an opportunity to change the subject. "I ain't had a cup since I left New York and could sure use one."

Nattie collected herself. "I'll make some fresh, Earl. I could use a cup, myself."

Hiram busied himself in preparation for the weeks ahead. Pretrial maneuvering was extensive and time-consuming, and he found himself driven with an energy approaching revenge. The more he threw himself into the trial, the more focused he became and the less tolerant of those around him. His staff bore the brunt of his impatience, which was exacerbated by the increase in consumption of scotch. He ate very little and fed off his nervous drive. Recently he'd tipped the scales at three hundred and eight pounds and could easily afford to lose weight. He wanted to go to trial at a trim two hundred and eighty, if he could manage it. If he lost any more weight than that, he'd lose some of his intimidating presence. Not something he was willing to do.

Long ago, Hiram had sacrificed his sense of justice on the altar of retribution. He knew that's why he'd survived all these years as a prosecutor—fourteen years as Assistant District Attorney, the last fifteen as District Attorney. He was never more fulfilled than when he won a trial and heard the jury return a guilty verdict. His record to date revealed an astounding success rate.

The People of the State of New York versus Stern Blankley would be his crowning achievement.

Though not an advocate of the death penalty, Hiram could easily make an exception in this case. If ever there had been a man that deserved to die, Stern qualified. And Hiram had the town of Hollister behind him, a feeling he relished. Never a popular man with the locals, this was different. That, too, helped motivate him. He'd never cared a whit about anyone's opinion in the past and he didn't now. But what a rush it gave him to ride the wave of sentiment in the community. His only fear was a change of venue, but then it seemed like almost everyone was convinced that Blankley was guilty, no matter where he went. Juries were seldom unbiased, and he would do his best to see that this was one wasn't, either.

Mrs. Fenley often had nightmares and rarely slept all night. Insomnia had plagued her for years, and her face bore the look of one who was sleep deprived—sunken eyes, dark circles, and sallow skin. Gaunt and listless, she withdrew further and further from Hiram, spending hours in her room—which delighted him immensely.

Nattie's mood altered noticeably. She sat opposite Earl at the kitchen table, clutching her cup with both hands as if it provided security for her. Her grey hair hung in limp strands down to her diminutive shoulders. The warmth of the cup, the steam wafting upward toward her drawn face, and the first pungent sip of black coffee did wonders for her soul.

Earl was used to freeze-dried instant at home, or Candy's scorched brew at the diner, but this was the real deal. "It's very good coffee, Nattie," he said, smiling kindly.

"I've been living on it since Gus died. I think my nerves are shot."

Nattie is quite a wired little woman to begin with. The caffeine will probably make her nerves dance. I wonder if she ever sleeps.

It could be awkward to broach the subject of the dark secret she and Gus had kept over the years. Earl wracked his brain to think of a way to start. He decided if it never came up this trip, it was worth it; to share a cup of coffee with a dear lady whom he'd grown very fond of. *Maybe I'll just let her take the lead. If it comes up, fine, if not, I'll wait till later.*

"I didn't have the best relationship with him, you know, Earl."

"Sorry about that, Nattie."

"We didn't see eye to eye on a lot of things. Religion, as you know—and drinking."

"He was on the wagon for a long time." Earl nodded.

"And he would have stayed too."

"Why'd he fall off?"

"Memories."

"Memories?"

"From years ago. Things he'd hidden. Lots of guilt. Self-hatred, I suppose."

"Self hatred?" Earl frowned.

"Yeah, for what he'd done, or didn't do, I should say. You know, Earl, I share some of the guilt."

"You do?"

"Yes, for what I've hidden. But I was so afraid. Afraid he'd kill himself if I ever mentioned anything. God have mercy on me, Earl.

I've thrown myself into the Lord's work for years to cover my guilt, but it eats at me."

Earl could only nod again and say nothing, hoping she would have the courage to continue.

"And now he's dead anyway. I guess I have nothing to fear now. It's just the guilt that's so bad."

Earl felt like a priest at confessional, and very much under qualified. He'd had his share of guilt in his lifetime and never figured out how to deal with it.

"I honored *him*, Earl, but I figured I'd sinned against the Lord."

There's no way I could have ever been a priest, Earl thought. *The more she talks about her sin and guilt, the worse I feel about myself.* He could see that Nattie had a great burden to release. Despite his own inadequacies, he figured God must have had him there for a reason. There was not a sound to be heard anywhere in the house except for the lonely ticking of the dining room clock. The moment seemed suspended in time. Earl looked at his hands, now folded in front of him on the table.

Nattie broke the silence.

CHAPTER 36

Julie shared with the group about Amber's picture and how she had found it, but shared nothing about what the connection might be with the events in New York. Nor did she share about the yearbook. Then she immediately had second thoughts as if she'd betrayed her own investigation. Who knew what others might do with the information?

No one seemed to think it was any big deal, just a strange coincidence. Maybe it wasn't Amber after all. The picture could have belonged to anyone, they agreed, or, to no one in particular. Maybe somebody found it lying around someplace and started using it as a bookmark.

Why all the fuss, Julie?

Her ego was deflated that no one marveled at her discovery, but she was also relieved that no one seized upon its potential significance. The subject was dropped as quickly as it had started, and she vowed to share nothing further with anyone, except perhaps Melissa. She could be trusted, and Julie needed her input and feedback. It was difficult for her to keep everything to herself.

The group broke at four o'clock, but no one wanted to leave. Everyone continued milling about, chatting about a myriad of subjects. Melissa cornered Julie in the kitchen. "Why did you share that with the group before sharing it with me?"

"I shouldn't have shared it at all," Julie said, grumbling.

"You think it means something, don't you?"

"Possibly."

"I need to know what you think. You know you can trust me."

"Melissa, you'll probably think I'm nuts." Julie leaned heavily against the wall and let out a deep sigh.

"Maybe, but how do you know it's really her picture?"

"I've got a copy of the yearbook from which it was taken."

"You do?" Melissa put her hand to her mouth. "Where'd you get that?"

"From New York."

"Who got it for you?"

Julie lowered her voice. "Stern Blankley's lawyer."

"You're kidding!"

"Shush…no, I'm not." Julie quieted her friend. "Apparently he thought it was worth following up on."

"What has he said about it, Jules?"

"Nothing."

"But he still sent you a copy of the yearbook?"

"Yes."

"Where's the book?"

"At the library."

"And the pictures match?"

"Exactly."

"*And* you found it in one of Stern Blankley's books?"

"Yeah, probably a month ago."

"What's your take on it?"

"It's sheer speculation—a long shot. Better sit down for a minute." They both took chairs at the kitchen table.

"I'm all ears," Melissa said.

"I think there's a connection with Amber's murder."

Melissa put her hand to her mouth again. A connection?"

"Yeah, hon, there's something going on. I'm sure of it."

"Okay super sleuth, what's the scoop?"

"I think whoever owns the picture may have had something to do with her murder."

"You are putting me on, aren't you?"

Julie shook her head. "I'm dead serious."

"You really are, aren't you?"

"I've never thought it was a coincidence. More like a providential discovery."

"That's quite an extrapolation. Who do you think owns the picture?"

"I have no idea."

"And how are you going to find out?"

"I've narrowed it down."

"Narrowed it—to what?"

"About two hundred-plus males."

Melissa's brow furrowed as she pondered her friend's sanity. "Over two hundred male suspects?"

"Yes."

"They could be anywhere right now. Where did you get your short list, if that's what you call it?"

"From the Hollister yearbook—all the male seniors."

"You're right about one thing, Julie," Melissa said shaking her head.

"What's that?"

"It's a long shot."

"But someone who visited the library in the last month left that picture in one of Stern's books, probably wishing they hadn't. The picture is very worn, like it's been used for years. Most likely a male, wouldn't you say?"

"I don't want to think about what's going on in his mind, Jules." Melissa frowned.

"Someone who's had a thing for Amber, who she knew from high school. Quite possibly someone in her class, who's also in the yearbook."

"Have you searched the book for a familiar face?"

"Not yet, but I'm going to start. Probably tonight at the library."

"Have you checked the phonebook for numbers for these guys?"

"I haven't done that either, but I plan to."

"You think that this *someone* is, uh, living in this area?"

"Someone checked the book out, didn't they?"

"So it would seem," Melissa agreed, feeling a knot tighten in her stomach.

"Think about it, Melissa—what are the odds of me finding a photograph of Amber Greene one month before her murder, stuck in a book—the author of which is a prime suspect?"

"It would cause some suspicion, wouldn't it?"

"I initially matched it against the photo in the *Baltimore Sun* and it startled me. That's when I contacted Stern."

"And what did he say?"

"His lawyer, Jud Tillston wrote me a letter and requested the picture."

"And you said, *not on your life!*"

"Basically, in so many words. I mean he could get it if he wanted it for evidence, but—"

"You're gutsy, Jules."

"I sent Tillston a certified letter requesting a copy of the yearbook instead. I was surprised he sent it, but even if he hadn't, I was headed for New York to get one myself."

"You're really into this thing, aren't you?"

"I feel like I know him somehow."

"Tillston?"

"No, Stern."

"Sounds to me like you *want* to know him."

"I'm convinced that God is leading me in this, Melissa."

"And where is it leading?"

"I'm not sure."

"You want help?"

"Sure. I'll make a list of names and you can check the metropolitan Baltimore phonebook."

"Then what? Call them up and ask if they murdered Amber

Greene? There could be dozens of people having the same names as any one of your suspects. Think about it. What if there's a Joe Smith in the yearbook? What about underclassmen? That would expand your list quite a lot."

Melissa was right, the idea was a little absurd, but then they could narrow their search to the White Marsh/Perry Hall area. Whoever borrowed the book most likely lived there. There might only be a half-dozen "Joe Smiths" to sort through. And maybe only one "Melvin Granger," provided he was a suspect.

"Have you searched the database at the library to see who has his books out now?"

"I'm working on that too."

"Suppose you find a familiar face after searching the yearbook. That doesn't prove a thing."

"No, but it makes things much more intriguing, doesn't it?"

"What would you do then?"

"Call Tillston immediately."

"Does Stern Blankley know anything about you?"

"He must have read my letter."

"And gave it to his lawyer," Melissa added.

"Yes."

Their conversation was interrupted by Toppsy as she barged into the kitchen, looking for a refill for her coffee mug.

CHAPTER 37

*W*hat do I want, anyway? Stern asked himself. *I want out of this jail. I don't want a life in prison. I want to be acquitted and go back to a normal life.*

The sting of Amber's death still hurt him deeply with an intense inner aching. The anger had diminished, though it lashed at him when he least expected it. The last meeting with Josh had an unexpected impact on him. The greater prison was inward. In place of anger, he had bouts of unbearable, tormenting remorse, followed by despair and depression. A hopelessness from which there seemed no escape. He felt singularly responsible for Amber's death, though he was innocent. Maybe he *deserved* prison. Maybe that would be just punishment for entangling her in his life. Maybe that would assuage the guilt.

It had been over a month since her death, and he spent endless hours rehearsing that night: what she wore, how she looked, their conversation, their blossoming romance. It was probably less than an hour after he left that she was murdered in cold blood. He shuddered at the thought.

Depression immobilized him for days, and self-recrimination sapped his spirit. And there was nothing, nothing to prove his innocence. He would have to wait until the trial, trusting his lawyers and the jury. At least he wouldn't have to lie. But innocent men were convicted every day. And guilty ones went free.

"My dear Earl," Nattie began. "I've known you for a long time and though you've exasperated me at times, you're a decent and kind man. You've treated me better than a good share of the people at church. I don't think you're so far away from the Lord as you make out to be." She drew a deep breath and was silent for a moment. Then she said, "While you were here before, I told you I couldn't share with anyone what Gus told me that one night when he was drunk—for fear he would follow through on his threat. Now he's dead, Earl, and I have nothing to fear. Gus should never have hid what he did all these years. He would have been alive today if he hadn't. I'm sure of it." Nattie wrung her hands like a wet dishcloth.

Earl swallowed hard, almost afraid to breathe as he lifted his eyes from his folded hands to view Nattie's face. It was etched with pain and guilt. What he was about to hear would help explain the downward spiral in Gus's life, ending in his suicide. It would help explain the zealous behavior of the withered woman sitting opposite him. And most importantly, it would help explain a mystery of nearly three decades, confirming in his mind that his sixth sense was correct.

Hiram Morton Fenley II was a man possessed, driven by a wanton desire for acclaim.

Julie arrived at the library at five-fifteen in the afternoon, anxious to examine the male faces in the yearbook tucked safely in her desk. She fought the encroaching feelings that the search was absurd, a product of her fertile imagination. Even Melissa was skeptical, though without complaint, deferring to Julie's wishes. The rest of the group didn't know the whole story. At least she'd had the good sense not to share it. She figured she could also check the internet for the possible whereabouts of Amber and Stern's former classmates—this was just a start, which, for now, curiosity dictated.

There were many regulars at the library, several of whom Julie knew by name, and scores of other faces with which she was familiar. If there was someone in the book that frequented the library, with some diligence, she could match a picture to a live face, provided the years hadn't taken too heavy a toll. Any suspicion could quickly be confirmed by comparing names. Her plan for the night was to work her way through the letter G.

Amused, she gazed at all the outdated hairstyles and glasses. The plastic smiles of embarrassed adolescents showed hope that the camera would somehow work a miracle on their behalf. The *haves* were obvious, and the *have-nots* received no miracle. Stern and Amber stood out above the rest, along with Heath.

Her search had yielded nothing through the first four letters, although there were a couple of guys who looked vaguely familiar. She jotted their names down just in case and tried to imagine them twenty-eight years older. She glanced from the book to faces of men as they walked by. *Risky,* she thought, and decided not to stare or smile. Just a good solid look. Three letters to go and she would call it a night.

Nothing in the E's at all.

But there was a face in the F section that caused a double take. It *was* familiar, remarkably so. Round face, small mouth, prematurely receding hairline, almost square-framed black glasses hiding a studious face. Whose face was it? She studied it picturing a man of approximately forty-six with the same features, probably bald by now. The name was unfamiliar to her.

Then it struck her.

She knew that face! It emerged from the page and transformed before her incredulous eyes. A face she saw every week, sometimes more than once. Someone she spoke with, and had even struck up a friendship with. Someone who was a fanatic for Blankley's novels.

The face was Fenton Newman's. But the name beneath it read *Hiram Morton Fenley III.*

What did it mean? The names didn't match, but the faces did. Julie could see Fenton's face very clearly in the one before her. The mouth—so small. And a head that was nearly round. Fenton was bald now, with no glasses. She knew that he wore contacts. The ears matched too, almost no lobes. She'd noticed it on Fenton. Her heart raced with possibilities.

Had he changed his name? If so, why? Because he had something to hide. That was it! He was hiding from something. I can't believe it; he's in my book group!

He had to be the one with Amber's picture. It was all coming together. He'd left it in one of Stern's books. He'd had it for all those years.

A perverse preoccupation with Amber.

Who knows what went on in his head? Julie remembered him bolting one day from the group, apparently ill—or so they'd thought.

He was Amber's murderer! Julie was certain of it. But what was the motive?

There were four faces in the yearbook she now recognized: Stern, Amber, Fenton, and Heath Proctor. Her mind began piecing together a heinous scenario. The faces were all somehow connected. Fenton was jealous of Heath. Secretly in love with Amber. Had he been the one who drove Heath off the road? And killed Amber because she was getting close to the truth? And set Stern up somehow? Annapolis was only an hour away. Was there a psychopathic killer in her group?

Julie's heart froze with fear.

"It was Morton Fenley, Earl. Hiram Fenley's son." Nattie sighed heavily, shaking her head.

"The D.A.'s son?" Earl's jaw dropped.

"That's right. The D.A.'s son drove Heath Proctor off the road and down over the bank into Sullivan Creek."

"How do you know that?" Earl asked.

"Gus told me. Heath's car had red paint on it from Morton's Thunderbird."

"How did he know it was Morton's car?"

"Because Hiram had it in Gus's garage the next day for Gus to fix. He told him to make it a priority and not to let anyone else work on it. He also told Gus to keep his mouth shut about it. If Gus told anyone, Hiram threatened to close the business down—to ruin us financially. He also made threats about harming us in *other* ways."

And Morton murdered Amber Greene, Earl said to himself, but not to Nattie.

CHAPTER 38

S tern had bottomed out. His coping skills were beat, and outside support consisted of a faithful few whose visits helped sustain him. Hate mail continued to arrive on a regular basis, mixed with occasional letters of encouragement, mostly from longtime friends and hardcore fans.

He tried to write, but lacked motivation. The boredom was interminable.

Josh's words came back time and time again: *It all depends on what you want—some choose mercy and forgiveness—some don't.* Stern was in no position to reject either, but not quite sure what he needed to do to receive them. If there was hope, he hadn't found it. Something had to break. He was neither free in body nor soul, with the greater prison inside his head. He longed for release and sought it carefully—rationalizing, justifying his intentions, but to no avail.

He sagged on the jail cot, staring aimlessly at the ceiling. Now he understood how people went insane and broke with reality. His emotions were stripped bare, like open, festering wounds. The guilt pressed on every side crushing him further and further into despair. He shut his eyes and wept, turning his face into his pillow to muffle the sound.

The guards told Josh that Stern hadn't eaten in two days and that something had snapped in him. They would do their best to get him to come to the visiting area, but with no guarantees.

Stern went, almost against his will. He had no desire to see Josh, but grasped at the opportunity to leave his cell. He stumbled into the visiting room haggard and unshaven, gave a perfunctory nod to Josh, and sat on the stool behind the barrier.

How long, Josh wondered, *can this man resist God's mercy?* He couldn't remember seeing a man look more miserable than Stern. A wave of compassion swept over him, and he nearly broke into tears.

"Rough week, huh?" Josh asked.

"The worst," Stern said, looking aimlessly at his folded hands.

"The guards said you haven't been eating."

"No appetite."

"Any progress on the investigation?"

"None."

"What's your lawyer say?"

"Nothing's turned up."

"Any trial date?"

"Not yet."

"The church has been praying."

"I need it."

Enough of the small talk. This guy's hurting and needs more help than I can give him. "When are you going to open up to God?" Josh asked bluntly.

Stern said nothing for a couple of minutes, then, he quietly mouthed a question, "What do I have to do?"

"Be honest with Him about your need. Call out to Him."

"No magic formula?"

"None."

"That simple?"

"Simple, but profound." Josh refrained from preaching, letting Stern take the lead.

"The thing you said last time—about mercy and forgiveness..."

"I remember."

"Well, I, uh, guess that's what I need."

"It's free."

"For the asking?" Stern lifted his eyes and looked at the man who'd become his friend.

"Yes."

"I think the only other option is insanity."

"Not a good option." Josh's lips tightened and he shook his head.

"One I can't afford."

"It's a gracious transaction, Stern. Faith is the only requirement."

"How much faith?"

"Faith enough to acknowledge that Christ is the answer to your need."

"I have so many doubts."

"We all do at times."

"It's a big step for me. I've always been such a skeptic."

"You have everything to gain and nothing to lose."

"So, say I open my heart to God and receive forgiveness. What about the impending trial and prospect of a guilty verdict?"

"No guarantees on that," Josh said, "but you'd have infinite resources to face whatever happened."

Stern cast his eyes to the floor for a long moment. "I guess I can't bargain with God on that, can I?"

"Not a good idea to bargain with Him. But we can earnestly pray for a favorable result. First things first."

"I need time to think on it."

Haven't had enough inner turmoil yet? Josh almost said, but thought better of it.

"The answer is always the same, Stern. You don't need me to lead you through it. Take time in your cell and get before God. But don't keep putting it off; you'll tend to rationalize away faith." Josh reached in his coat pocket. "I'll tell you what. I have something that may help." He slipped him a single sheet of paper with some scripture references. "Read this when you're alone, then make a decision in private. Let me know what you think."

"I promise I'll read it."

Stern suddenly remembered the paper the seminary student had handed him on the plane—the one he'd glanced at, crumpled, and thrown away. He took a deep breath.

The dots were beginning to connect.

The hour expired quickly and Josh rose to leave. Perhaps there was some hope after all, in spite of Stern's serious misgivings. His need was too great for any heady theological discussion. Josh knew the bottom line would still come down to what Stern chose to believe.

That night in the quietness of his jail cell, Stern read and reread the paper that Josh had given him. He pondered the words of each scripture verse. Without fully understanding what he was doing, he prayed a simple prayer to Amber's God. The One he'd spurned for so long, he now turned to for help. If God were a God of mercy and forgiveness as Josh had described, then he was a desperate candidate. Stern prayed for faith—faith to acknowledge that Christ was the answer. He thought of Amber's childlike faith, and how she had lived her life. If it was good enough for her, it was good enough for him.

He broke and wept like a baby, crying himself to sleep.

CHAPTER 39

Julie sat stunned, still not believing what she was seeing. There was a chance she was wrong. The names didn't match and that troubled her. But faces don't lie—there were too many striking similarities. She had to find out more about this Hiram Morton Fenley III. Stern would know, but she needed to talk to someone by phone right away, and there was no chance of speaking with him. Her mind flooded with a thousand possibilities.

Who could she talk to? Jud Tillston? But would he talk to her? She had his phone number on the letter he'd sent. She could call and at least leave a message. She'd been at the library for close to two hours and it was a Sunday evening.

Little chance of reaching Tillston, she reasoned. But it was her only viable option. Her cell phone was in her car.

Earl had a hard time believing that his former boss had held a deadly secret for years. But it made sense after hearing Nattie's disclosure. He wasn't about to judge Gus, but he figured if it had been *him*, he would have spilled the beans to the police.

Curse the D.A.! Earl's jaw tightened in justifiable anger.

"Hiram owned the police. He owned the *town* back then. He had influence, wealth, and connections. People were afraid of him, especially Gus," Nattie finished her story. "Gus was terrified of losing his business he'd worked so hard for. And then he wasn't sure what else might happen. He just kept his mouth shut as he was told—and started drinking. To make matters worse, Hiram offered him five thousand in cash as an added bonus, and Gus took that too. We had bills, you know, and that was a lot of money back then."

"So he was threatened *and* bribed." Earl cracked the knuckles on both hands.

"Yes—and drank himself to death."

"What happened to the kid?"

"Morton? He disappeared shortly after that. Sent away to who knows where? He was never seen or heard of after that."

"People must have had suspicions."

"Maybe, but the story was that he was going away to study law, to take over the law firm when Hiram retired. Everything was soon forgotten."

"So the old man covered his butt and saved his reputation."

"And his power," Nattie added.

"Yeah, he couldn't very well have his son being on trial, now could he?" Earl scowled; his dislike for Hiram grew by the second.

"Everything was quickly covered over. Gus even thought Hiram bought off the sheriff. There was no investigation, you know."

"So I heard." Earl nodded. "You going public with this stuff, Nattie?"

"It's too late now. The damage has been done. Who would believe me anyway?"

"I do."

"You're the exception."

"It's gotta be told. You believe in justice, Nattie?"

"But, I'm guilty too. I could have said something a long time ago."

"You were between a rock and a hard place. I don't imagine no judge or jury would be hard on you."

"But he's the D.A. and he knows all the judges."

"They ain't all crooked. Maybe one of them would like to see him hang. A lot of people would too, for that matter."

"I need help, Earl," Nattie said, clearly distraught.

"I'll see you get it. There's a lot going on here and we need to find that killer."

"You're pretty sure Morton killed Amber, too, aren't you Earl?"

Earl's eyes widened at Nattie's observations. "My sixth sense don't lie, Nattie. It's been right all along."

"What are you going to do?"

"Get in touch with Howie."

"Who?"

"Stern Blankley. I call him Howie."

"You want to call him?" Nattie asked.

"I can't. He's in jail. I'm headed back to New York to see him in person."

"Don't forget me, Earl," Nattie pleaded.

"You're in good hands, Nattie. The Lord's—and mine."

Julie had written Jud's phone number in her weekly planner, which she kept with her at all times. She quickly punched the numbers on her cell phone and waited. The phone rang five times with no answer. She prayed that he would pick up. Jud's answering machine kicked in, to her disappointment, but she still held out hope that he would answer. There seemed like an endless succession of beeps before she was able to give her message:

"Mr. Tillston, it's Julie Fisher—the one you sent the yearbook to. I have some important information that you need to know. I've recognized a face in the book. Someone I believe is the owner of the photograph I found. The odd thing, Mr. Tillston, is that he's in my reading group. His name is Hiram Morton Fenley III. Does that mean anything—"

Before Julie could finish her sentence, Jud picked up on the other end.

"This is Jud Tillston," the voice was distinct and seemed startled.

"Mr. Tillston, this is Julie Fisher. I'm calling on a cell phone from

White Marsh, Maryland. I'm in the parking lot of the library where I work. Did you get my message?"

"I heard it, that's why I picked up," Jud said. "What are you saying about this Fenley guy?"

"I saw his picture in the yearbook—I think he's the same guy that's in a discussion group that meets at my house."

"What do you mean you *think* it's the same guy?"

"He goes by a different name."

"What's the name?"

"Fenton Newman."

"Doesn't ring a bell."

"The faces are the same, though," Julie insisted.

"You're sure? It's been a long time, people change."

"Some things don't change. The eyes, mouth, nose, and ears are the same. Very distinct. A round face."

Jud had never seen Hiram Morton Fenley III, but what an odd coincidence that this woman from Maryland would be calling him on a Sunday evening describing the son of the D.A. who was scrambling to lynch his client.

"He's bald now, and he doesn't wear glasses. But I recognize the face, Mr. Tillston."

"So what do you think the connection is, Ms. Fisher—if any?"

Julie hesitated, but wanted to make her point. She might never get to talk to Tillston again and she felt destined to help Stern.

"I think…" she said, pausing to take a deep breath, "I think he has something to do with Amber Greene's murder."

"*Something* to do with it?"

"Yes." Her heart started to race.

"Could you elaborate?"

"I think he may have killed her."

"And, why do you think that, Ms. Fisher?"

"It's just a feeling."

Jud wasn't buying into the *feeling* thing at all. There had to be something more concrete than that, notwithstanding the coincidence.

"What else stands out about this guy? Was he acting suspicious?"

"Once during a group meeting he fled abruptly, as if he was paranoid."

"What were you discussing at the time?"

"I can't remember—we discussed a lot of things."

"Were you aware of the events here in New York?"

"Yes, we were. We discussed them frequently."

"Where did you get your information from?"

"It's a long story, but we knew about Stern and Amber Greene before the murder."

Jud crammed the phone closer to his ear. "You did?"

"Yes, we had a good source of information."

"And this Fenley guy knew all of this?"

"Yes."

"Were you discussing any of this during the meeting when he left so suddenly?"

"It's possible, maybe probable. I can't remember."

"Does he know you have the picture?"

"Yes—I shared it with the group."

"Does he know you have the yearbook?"

"No."

"Good. Have you told anyone else what you're telling me?"

"No, you're the first."

"Don't tell anyone else until I get back to you," Jud demanded.

"I won't," Julie promised.

"Can you describe this guy further?"

"Yes. He's short. Not much over five feet. Kind of pear-shaped with effeminate features and a high pitched voice."

"Anything else?"

"Yes, something very peculiar."

"What's that?"

"His hands."

Jud sat up. "What about them?"

"He has short, stubby fingers—and puffy hands."

Jud froze. *Those are the exact words that Clifford Weeks used earlier to describe the man that came to Stern's house in Annapolis.*

"What? What did you say about the hands?"

"They're odd. Small and puffy with short fingers."

"Julie," he said, his voice edged with excitement, "I think you're on to something. Where are you headed now?"

"Home."

"How long will it take you to get there?"

"About ten minutes."

"Give me your number and I will get back to you within an hour."

Julie gave Jud her home phone and cell number.

"Mr. Tillston?"

"Yes, Julie?"

"Do you think he's the one?"

"Let's put it this way. We've been looking for a man with the same description that you just gave us. A man who could be anywhere in the greater D.C./Baltimore area. What are the odds of you calling me tonight with this information?"

Julie smiled to herself. "Do you believe in providence, Mr. Tillston?"

"I'm beginning to."

She paused and took a deep breath. "One more thing, Mr. Tillston."

"What's that?"

"If he finds out we're on to him, I'm at risk, right?

"He's not afraid to kill women, is he, Julie?"

The ominous tone in his voice struck her with fear. "No. I guess he's not."

"You have an alarm system?" Jud asked.

"No."

"A handgun?"

"No."

"Just get home and lock yourself in. Chances are slim that he knows anything other than what you shared about the picture."

"That would make him real suspicious though, wouldn't it?"

"Probably," Jud admitted.

"Mr. Tillston?" Julie's voice quavered.

"Yes?"

"I'm scared."

CHAPTER 40

Earl was over three hours from Hollister. It was three-thirty Sunday afternoon and with luck, he'd be home by seven. Too late for a visit at the jail. Visiting hours ended at five on Sunday. He had to get word to Stern somehow. He'd call Jud Tillston when he got to New York. He still had the lawyer's business card in his wallet.

Josh Woodhouse had the church spend an hour of the Sunday night service in prayer—for Stern Blankley, for the trial, and for the town of Hollister.

Julie also prayed on the way home and called Melissa. No answer, so she left a message for a return call, ASAP. It was nine o'clock when she arrived at her townhouse, thankful that there were streetlights. Since her conversation with Jud, she'd felt paranoid. She slipped through her front door as if someone were watching her. Jud had been so forthright, and his words had a sobering effect on her.

It was better to be scared than not, she thought, but *not to the point of paranoia.* She wished Melissa was there with her. The deadbolt sliding into place gave her a sense of security, and she leaned momentarily with her back against the door. She sighed and comforted herself with the thought that Jud would call soon and alleviate some of her fear.

They had known about the man with the puffy hands. That fit the description of Fenton Newman. It was all coming together rapidly. Maybe too rapidly. She thought about what she'd shared earlier in the day at the meeting. What was Fenton's response? She couldn't remember anything out of the ordinary. The more she thought about him, though, the more her skin crawled.

Where is he tonight?

The call from Earl to Jud came at nine thirty-five. Earl had trouble with his truck on the way home and was delayed for over two hours. Thankfully, he was able to do his own troubleshooting and discovered the ignition was malfunctioning. He stopped briefly and shut the engine off, but couldn't get it to start again. Jud's line had been busy for several minutes, and Earl tried repeatedly to reach him. The answering machine finally kicked in. Earl felt stupid talking to a machine, but, it was urgent and he didn't care how he sounded.

"Mr. Tillston, it's Earl, Earl Teeter. I've got some important information for you." He paused. "I just left Nattie Burlew a few hours back and she told me something you ought to know. It's about Morton Fenley."

What on earth is going on? Jud thought to himself as he heard Earl's call come in. He'd just gotten off the phone with investigators in Annapolis after his conversation with Julie Fisher. And now this call from Earl Teeter.

"This is Jud Tillston. What's up, Earl?"

"You ain't gonna believe this, Mr. Tillston, but Nattie Burlew—that's Gus Burlew's wife; he OD'd a while back—well she told me today that Morton Fenley was the guy who forced that Proctor kid off the road years ago."

I'd believe anything at this point, Jud thought. He fit this latest disclosure into the freakish puzzle that, until tonight, had no pieces in place.

"And furthermore," Earl continued, "I'd bet my truck that he's the guy that murdered Amber. Just like I said before."

"Mrs. Burlew shared *that* with you today?"

"Yeah. She's known for a while. Gus hid it for years but spilled his guts to her one night when he was plastered. There's something else you ought to know."

"What's that?"

"She said that Morton's father, the D.A., threatened her husband and bought him off to cover for the kid and save his own skin."

"You sure of that?" Jud was incredulous at the turn of events.

"Heard it with my own two ears."

"Will she swear to it?"

"No reason not to now."

"Now?"

"She wouldn't have done it while Gus was alive. He threatened to kill himself if she said anything."

Poor woman, Jud thought. *She must feel like she's been let out of prison.* "Where are you now, Earl?"

"In Hollister—at my trailer."

"Can you be on standby?"

"Sure."

"I'll call you back tonight. I've got other calls to make right now."

"I'll be home all night."

"Good—and Earl?"

"Yeah?"

"You're a godsend. You suppose it was Him that gave you that sixth sense?"

"I imagine He did."

Jud's belief in providence had just increased tenfold.

Hiram Morton Fenley II went to bed early that night, subdued by scotch. He fell asleep at nine-thirty with a smile of contentment on his face, fully expecting the next day to be a rewarding one as he pressed forward for the trial of Stern Blankley.

Julie didn't dare to shower. She'd seen and read too many murder mysteries to risk it. She had checked all doors and windows and everything was secure. She sometimes left the sliding glass door that exited from her kitchen unlocked, especially if she had been in a hurry, as the case was today, but was relieved to find it locked.

She made herself a cup of herbal tea and retired to her living room to wait for Jud's call. She made sure all the blinds were shut and the curtains were drawn. The tea felt soothing, and as she sipped, it brought a sense of comfort to her frayed nerves. It had been forty minutes since she had talked to Jud.

She decided to go upstairs and prepare for bed, keeping her cordless phone with her in the bathroom. For an instant, she thought she heard a noise in the hallway, but chalked it up to her hypervigilant imagination.

Earl waited patiently by his phone. Both Stern and Hiram slept like babies—but for different reasons. Josh Woodhouse felt an overwhelming urgency to pray.

CHAPTER 41

Julie emerged from the bathroom, wiping her face with a towel, and shrieked hysterically as she ran headlong into Fenton Newman. A wicked smile glazed his face. The gun in his hands aimed directly at her head. She shook with fear, unable to speak.

Her first impulse was to pray and hide her face in the towel.

"Julie, it's so nice to see you," Morton said, softly. The sinister grin remained. "I'm sure you didn't expect me."

She felt dizzy and fought to keep her balance. She reached for the door casing. The face she had been studying so intently just a short while ago was now a living, breathing reality a few feet away. But there was something so monstrous and evil about it now.

"I think you and I need to talk, Julie."

The smile disappeared. He took a step toward her. Julie flinched and stepped backward. She had an urge to make a break and try to slam the bathroom door in Fenton's face, but he read her thoughts and positioned himself against the door. His eyes flashed with dark malevolence.

"Perhaps we should go somewhere a little more comfortable, Julie. Maybe your bedroom. What do you think?" Fenton waved the gun and motioned her toward the door. The cold steel in his hands was a raw contrast to the nasally, effeminate whine of his voice.

Julie froze. Her legs wouldn't move. Any thought of running vanished. She was strangely fixated with this ugly, little man.

"What do you want, Fenton?" she asked.

"What is it that you know about me, Julie?" he shot back.

Should she lie? Feign ignorance? Buy some time?

"I don't know what you mean."

"Don't lie to me! I know you know who I am. I overheard you and Melissa talking about the yearbook today."

The heinous little demon had been eavesdropping. He probably heard everything. "I, uh, I know you're not Fenton Newman," Julie said, her voice quavering.

The statement seemed to shock him. "Who am I, then?"

The question begged an answer Julie couldn't give. She decided to stay with the minimum of facts.

"Hiram Morton Fenley III."

He smiled at the sound of his full name, as if hearing it for the first time. "You can call me Morton."

I could call you accursed. The words rang in Julie's head.

"I have no regard for the name Hiram. In fact, it repulses me," Morton continued.

And you repulse me. Her silent monologue gave her courage.

"It's too bad you've caught me in this little web of intrigue, Julie. You should have left well enough alone. What else do you know?"

His paranoia is getting the best of him. "What are you hiding, Morton?"

"What makes you think I'm hiding anything?"

"You keep asking me what I know."

"You know more than you are telling me. But you will tell me all you know soon enough."

You smug little moron! If it wasn't for that gun, I'd be more than your equal.

Morton continued, "Like I said, why don't we find a more comfortable place." He advanced toward her, waving the gun spastically. "Turn around!"

Julie did.

"Let's go to your room."

The fear increased as Julie headed down the hallway toward her bedroom.

"I can kill you, you know, and no one would know who did it." He placed the barrel of the gun at the base of her skull as they entered the bedroom.

Now the fear was suffocating. For the first time in her life, she thought she might die. This man was a killer already and apparently had no conscience. The thought of Amber Greene flashed through Julie's mind. The news hadn't indicated any sexual assault, just a cold-blooded murder.

A relief followed by a shudder.

God, there's a reason for this. You'd better be in control here. She prayed that Morton's evil wouldn't succeed again.

Morton forced Julie onto her bed and stood within a few feet of her. The phone in the bathroom rang. Julie knew it was either Melissa or Jud. It rang five times and the answering machine in her bedroom kicked in: *please leave your name and number and I'll get back to you as soon as I can...*

"Julie, if you're there, pick up. It's Melissa. I got your message. I was at the mall and just got in. I'll be up for a while. Call back if you want, otherwise I'll catch up with you tomorrow sometime. Bye."

"How much does she know?" Morton seethed at the interruption. "She was with you in the kitchen, wasn't she?"

Oh God, don't let him involve her, she's innocent. "She only knows I have the picture of Amber, and the yearbook. Nothing else."

"You're lying to me, aren't you?" Morton raised the gun and aimed it directly at her face.

"I swear I'm not!"

"If I have to, I'll kill her too."

"She's not involved. I swear she knows nothing. Please leave her out of this."

"I know where she lives, Julie. I've been by there several times before. It's not far from here, is it? Five, maybe ten minutes. Not far at all, is it Julie? She's such a pretty girl too."

The more Morton spoke, the more crazed he seemed—as if something was controlling him. Julie shut her eyes, her heart pounding. She couldn't bear to see his contorted face.

"Look at me when I speak to you!" he screamed. "Don't shut your eyes! I want you to see my face, Julie. I want you to see my face the way that Amber saw it before I shot her. She knew me." Morton laughed. "She *knew* me."

The phone rang again. Julie knew this time it had to be Jud. It had been over an hour and he hadn't called. She prayed that he wouldn't leave a message. The answering machine clicked on but there was no voice, just the sound of a phone hanging up.

"Where you expecting another call, Julie?"

"No," she lied.

"Who would be calling you at this hour on a Sunday?"

"I have no idea. It happens all the time."

"Are you expecting company tonight? A male friend?"

"No."

"I hope for your sake you're telling the truth. But then, it's not really going to matter if you do or not."

His words bore an ominous finality. Julie feared the worst. The only chance she had was to buy as much time as possible. Maybe Jud sensed something was up. It was pointless trying to reason with this man who was growing more unhinged by the moment. Morton was working himself into frenzy, and frighteningly toward another brutal climax.

The phone rang again, and this time there was a message: "Julie, honey, it's Jim. Sorry I missed you. I'll call again tomorrow."

"Who is Jim?" Morton demanded.

"He's a friend." Julie frantically read between the lines, recognizing Jud's voice. It was a decoy. He knew she was in trouble. She would play along with Morton's game, stalling for as long as she could.

"Was he planning on coming over tonight?"

"No—he was just calling to chat."

"I swear if you're lying to me—" Morton's eyes bulged. The veins in his forehead looked like they were going to pop.

"I'm not lying, he's just a friend. I met him at college and we've been dating."

"He'll be looking for someone new, very shortly." Morton appeared satisfied with her answer, and the veins in his forehead relaxed. "I have something I want to tell you, Julie. It's something I've never told anyone before, and you're going to listen to every word. After I've told you, I'm going to kill you just like I killed Amber Greene. I promise you Julie, that I *will* kill you. It will all be over so suddenly. You won't suffer."

Strange, but her fear was completely gone.

If I die, I die.

She was assured of heaven. Her life was in God's hands, the same way that Amber's was.

Julie wondered if Amber sensed the same peace before she died that she was feeling now.

The smallish man with the rounding shoulders and effeminate voice began his narrative. Julie purposed to be a good listener, hoping that his story was a long one.

CHAPTER 42

"I was named after my father, Hiram Morton Fenley II, whom I despise to this day. I refused to use the name Hiram and adopted the name Morton instead. My father was aloof and arrogant—probably the richest man in Hollister, and certainly the most powerful. My mother was passive and weak. I didn't hate her, but I resented her weakness and inability to protect me from his abuse." Hiram clenched his teeth before continuing, "He would often belittle her in front of me, entering into fits of rage and verbal tirades against her. She was not his intellectual equal and was a poor fit for his lifestyle—an embarrassment to him. It bothered him that he had married so poorly, but he was too proud to divorce her. He was more concerned about his *reputation*." Morton accented the word with disgust.

"My father drank heavily and launched his abuse against me, calling me an impotent dwarf, an equal embarrassment to him as my mother. He wanted a third generation lawyer," Morton said, scoffing. "And I had *no* interest in law. The older I got, the more I resented him. Bitterness grew within me, Julie—a desire to get even with him somehow. I hated him. I hated myself, my appearance. I had no power.

"That's when I began reading books on the occult—everything I could get my hands on. I had a secret life that no one knew about. A fantasy world I escaped to. Whenever my father abused me, I would go to my room, imagining ways of getting even. At times, I sensed a force with me—something dark and sinister. I knew it was real, Julie. It was so real to me. But I kept my distance—at first."

Morton continued, "My father is a big man, Julie—well over six feet tall and heavy, with a loud voice. Intimidating. Look at me—Julie, look at me." His voice softened to a whimper.

Julie hated to look, but she didn't dare refuse.

"I *am* a dwarf. Look at my hands, so small and helpless. I think that's why my father hated me. I took after my mother. But I was nobody's fool. Do you understand me?" Morton's appearance began to change, and the tone of his voice was now more menacing.

"Night after night in my room, I indulged myself in an evil fantasy. The more it grew in my mind, the more real it became. The force was always there, but I never fully let it inside. I knew I could though. I knew if I did, I would have power. I had a disease in my mind, Julie. A morbid, hateful disease that grew more and more intense. Something devilish was trying to take over.

"And then Amber Greene entered the picture. She was an escape for me, too—an escape of a different sort. She was part of my fantasy. I pretended that she was in love with me and we would be together someday. I even wrote her a poem once and sent it to her. When she discovered who wrote it, she was furious. Amber was not a kind person, Julie. She stunk with conceit—partly due to her looks, and partly due to her parents' indulgence as an only child. I knew no such indulgence. She tore the poem to shreds and humiliated me in front of her friends. I was a joke to everyone—a little puppet whose strings had been jerked. *She* was the puppeteer. That fantasy crumbled, Julie, leaving me dead, empty, and still impotent.

"When Heath Proctor heard about the, poem he went berserk, threatening to tear my arms and legs off. He slammed me into my locker and tried to shut the door. It took three guys from the football team to pull him off.

"And so it was, Julie. I vowed revenge. Somehow, somewhere. Revenge! It gave me a cause and a purpose, a driving force. There was so much violence within me, but I had no way to release it. No way to perform it. But a plan was forming in my head. A plan to get even.

"Every time I withdrew into my world, the plan grew clearer, and the presence of evil was so real. It was becoming my master. But who or what was the force, and where did it come from? There was a barrier beyond which I had never gone. I was too afraid. Too much unknown. Like approaching a cliff. The closer I got the more I was seized with fear.

"But...I gave in to it." Morton paused, as if considering the weight and consequence of his decision. Julie couldn't tell if there was a hint of remorse or merely self-pity.

"The question became who? Heath or my father? Heath was a more obvious choice, Julie. I made him the object of my plan."

Julie sat motionless, letting Morton drone on, mesmerized by his own words.

"I ran him off the road!" Morton's eyes went dull. "Yes, it was me! I waited one night for him as he left Amber's house. It was close to midnight, and I was parked along Sullivan Creek. I knew when he was coming. I knew his car. I waited. Waited until he passed me, and then I pulled my red Thunderbird behind him and closed in on him. I kept pushing at him, blinding him with my high beams...sixty, seventy miles an hour.

"I was in control, Julie. Can you see it with me? Close your eyes and see him trying to get away from me. But he couldn't—my car was newer, faster, and I was the master for the first time. We approached a curve and I pulled alongside him. I could see his face in the moonlight.

"Such fear! He knew who I was, too, Julie. It gave me such a sense of satisfaction." Morton was gasping as he continued his story.

"Then I backed off and hit him in the rear bumper. The car flipped over and over. Down the bank, into the water. He was gone—or so I thought. I slammed on my brakes and backed up to where he went over, got out, and peered down the bank into the water. I felt an unbelievable urge to go down the bank to the water's edge—something was leading me. No. Driving me. The bushes were sheered off where he went over, and I slid down where his car had torn away part of the bank.

"And then, I saw him. Somehow, he'd survived and gotten out of his car. Knee deep in water, he staggered forward to the shore. I could see him clearly in the moonlight. The star athlete, the one with such a future, broken and bleeding. He saw me too, and fell to his knees. He kept reaching out to me with his *big* hands. He wanted me to help him to shore.

"You see, Julie, Heath's life was in the balance, and I had control. He kept reaching out—reaching out to me, pathetically, with fear in his eyes. He knew I could save him. I, Morton Fenley, had the power of life and death for him. I could have helped him to the shore. Maybe he would have lived, but my mind flashed back to the locker scene. My body, crushed into the metal by his massive weight. His hot, stale breath spraying me with spit. I felt again the force of *his hands* against my face as he shoved my head against the cold metal.

"I had always felt so inadequate Julie, so unmanly, deficient—but something was there with me. Something horribly evil and sinister. The same force that was in my room. I let it take over. I relinquished my will to it. As Heath reached for me again, he stumbled face first in the water. I approached him then, with no fear, forced his head underwater, and held it there—mercilessly, with *these* hands, Julie."

Morton held up his hands in front of her, clutching the gun in both. Julie recoiled at the thought of Morton holding Heath's head underwater. She again wanted to vomit, to escape from this hideous creature. But he went on, totally absorbed in his monstrous monologue.

"The struggle was pitiful. May I use that word? His muscled body, now helpless. The life ebbing from him.

"Oh, the irony of it all. Who was strong now? Who was the impotent one? The victim? I felt a surge through my hands—a strength I'd never known. Then it was over. No more struggle. Just a limp and lifeless form that floated like a leaf away from the shore. I had no remorse, Julie. Not a twinge of conscience. Just a massive sense of release, like something had been discharged from my body. I felt the same way after I killed Amber. She was such a pretty girl..."

Morton had a maddening, desperate look in his eyes.

Julie knew it would take a miracle for her to escape from this cold-blooded killer. She prayed.

"I was the Master, Julie," Morton continued. "Can you see it with me? I, Hiram Morton Fenley III, was the Master!" He stopped and looked at her as if waiting for a response.

Julie spoke, "*You* were being mastered by evil, Morton."

The words disturbed him, and he waved the gun in her face. "But can't you see the irony of it all? The poetic justice?"

There's no point in speaking—it might drive him over the edge again.

"I drove home, Julie. My father was waiting up. It was about twelve-thirty and I knew he would be there. It didn't matter to me because I now had sway over him too. I could destroy his reputation and bring him down. I told him what happened, but not all. I told him I'd run Proctor off the road, hit him with my own car, but I didn't tell him I drowned him. To this day, he doesn't know. I could tell he wanted to kill *me* but thought better of it. He bought my silence. Financed me for life. Sent me away, out-of-state, where I would never be found. Helped me change my name. A new identity, everything. I never went home, except for when I killed Amber. Never saw my father after graduation...or my mother."

Morton cast his eyes to the floor for a brief moment.

"My father threatened a man named Gus Burlew who had gotten Heath's car from the creek. Poor Gus put two and two together, and my father bought him off too. Dark little secrets, Julie. Sad, isn't it?" He looked at her again with vacant, lifeless eyes.

"And what about Amber?" Julie asked.

"She knew too much. Digging stuff up with that idiot Blankley. Sure, I read all his novels, not because I liked them though. I was searching, expecting that someday he'd revisit the scene and write about it. I was right. Too bad he dragged Amber into it. I think she knew I did it, you know, killed Proctor. She was ready to disclose it to Blankley. I had to act fast and cover myself.

"I killed her with his gun. It was foolproof, Julie. I went to his house in Annapolis posing as a computer technician. I couldn't believe my luck. Some painter let me in, and I had access to Blankley's office and his bedroom. No trouble picking the lock to his bedroom. I figured he had a gun, but where? I found it in a nightstand beside his bed. Never touched it with my hands. Gloves and a briefcase, Julie. I was gone within ten minutes. Slipped out with no one seeing me—except for one man and he never looked at me very closely. Then on to New York.

"My plan was to kill Blankley first and then kill her. I was going to plant the gun on him like it was a murder-suicide, but I changed my mind. I waited until he left and slipped into the house through the backdoor. She hardly knew what hit her, Julie, although she saw my face. An awful look on her face, but she didn't resist or run. What could she do? Pray, like you must be doing right now? The story was about to be completed years later. I remembered her shredding the poem in front of her friends and laughing. I guess I had the last laugh, right Julie? Two shots and it was over. I hid the gun so it could be found. Luckily, Blankley's fingerprints were all over it."

Morton's mouth turned up at the sides in a macabre grin that sent chills through Julie's body. The fear was back. He again had a crazed, empty look in his eyes as he fastened them on her. She could feel a strange presence in the room drifting in like a dense fog. Morton was breathing it in.

"It's so sad, Julie. So sad. You now know everything, and you're the only one. I had to tell you." He clutched the gun tightly with both hands. "I had to release it."

Julie faked empathy, trying to buy some time and look for a way to escape. Maybe try to distract him and make a bolt for the door he had closed behind them. Startle him. Push him away from her and make him off-balance for a moment, then make a run for it. Her heart was beating so loud she thought he could hear it.

He elevated the gun slowly. She waited for the precise moment. His eyes flickered, as if reflecting on his life's story, satisfied that he'd finally shared it. Then his hands dropped slightly from the weight of the gun. Julie's mind was keen in spite of her fear. This was her chance—maybe her only chance for escape. Another second might be too late.

She lunged at him with all the force she could muster. The weight of her slender body pushed him off-balance. If he recovered, maybe he would lose aim—or maybe she'd be wounded. She could run wounded. She was sure of that.

Every muscle and nerve fiber in her body was primed for the next explosive moment. But it was a nightmare frozen in time. No movement. Trying desperately to flee from a dreadful enemy. Paralyzed with fear.

This was no dream.

Hell was in her room, a living, hideous, palpable hell surrounded her. Then, like a taught spring, Julie's body mobilized in a flash of adrenalin. She broke for the bedroom door.

So distant!

Ten feet of infinity before her. Hell in pursuit.

A shot fired out and whizzed past her head. She heard the dreadful sound of hot lead as it crushed into the door in front of her. Another shot, but no pain. She wasn't hit. She fumbled for the door handle, clutching it in her hands, twisting and turning the lifeless knob.

Stuck.

Just as it had been for the last two years. A split second too late.

Morton regained his focus. Possessed with rage, he lunged at her. Clutching the gun in one hand, he struck her head with the butt end and tried to drag her down to the floor. Her head went black and her legs buckled under her. A horrible ringing in her ears. Conscious but dazed, she heard Morton's baleful cursing and felt his groping hands.

The gun pressed against her temple—his free hand reached for her throat. Julie pictured Heath at the creek side with Morton's hands forcing his head underwater.

Would he shoot her, or strangle her? Overcome with fear, but still with enough reserve to fight, Julie bit Morton's arm and kicked as hard as she could. She pushed herself free, again trying the door.

It opened!

She bolted for the stairway.

Another shot rang out, splintering the spindles of the staircase railing. She descended the stairs with a burst of fear-driven energy— her feet barely touching the steps. Morton, in ungainly pursuit, shot a fourth time, missed her head by inches, and began his descent. Catching his feet on the carpeting, he lost his balance and pitched head-over-heels down the steps, vaulting violently and crashing into the wall at the bottom of the stairs.

Julie stood, her chest heaving wildly.

Morton lay twisted from the fall, the gun somehow still in his hand. Stunned, but conscious, he regained his senses and fixed his eyes once more on Julie.

There was a loud banging on the front door as the police tried to force their way in. Another shot rang out. It was from an officer's gun, blasting away at the lock on the door. Another shot and the door broke free. Three uniformed police rushed into Julie's living room. Julie stood motionless in horror—eyes shut, hands over her mouth.

Morton raised himself to his knees, still aiming the gun at her. A final shot. The gun and part of Morton's right hand disappeared. He screamed in agony, slumping to the floor, his body covering his mutilated hand. Two of the officers rushed toward him. The third officer, a woman, comforted Julie.

The nightmare was over.

CHAPTER 43

"I knew when you didn't answer something was up. I tried a little decoy to let you know I was onto it," Jud told Julie from the phone at the police station.

"I did everything to stall, hoping you'd have enough time," Julie said. "I have his whole story. He confessed everything to me—you won't believe it."

"I'd believe anything right now. Nothing would surprise me."

"Does Stern know yet?"

"Not yet. I'll let him sleep and tell him in the morning."

"He won't believe it either."

"He'll probably think he's dreaming," Jud agreed. "What a difference a day makes."

"Or, an evening."

"Yeah, an evening."

"You saved my life, Jud."

"And you saved Stern's."

"It was meant to be."

"How so?"

"Providence," Julie said. "Remember?"

"Yeah, Providence. We've got disclosures on this end too. Same night, same time. Obtained by a man named Earl."

"Earl?"

"Yeah, says he has a sixth sense." Jud laughed.

"Providence again, Jud."

"No doubt."

"Can you do me a favor?" Julie asked.

"What's that?"

"Arrange a meeting with Stern for me."

"I think I can do that."

"It's very important."

"I'm sure he'll agree."

"I want to tell him the whole story."

"I'll get back to you, Julie. And by the way—"

"Yes?"

"You're a remarkable woman."

"I have a great God."

"Providence again?"

"Yes."

Jud hung up the phone and sunk slowly onto the bed, shaking his head. Then he blew a huge sigh of relief.

"Providence," he said aloud.

Morton made a full confession to the police. Nothing was denied. To his distorted thinking, fate had dealt him a *bad hand* and he was the consummate victim.

The meeting between Stern and Julie took place shortly after his release from jail. He was astonished when he heard her story and over-whelmed with a deep sense of gratitude. What could he say? What were the odds of events playing out as they had? It wasn't a matter of chance, he was convinced.

And Julie never entertained notions of chance, notwithstanding her occasional doubts about providence.

It was unremarkable that there was an immediate rapport between Stern and Julie. It seemed the logical consequence of something or-dained. Their greatest bond was their mutual faith. They spent the next few days talking endlessly, like old time friends meeting again after years of separation.

Several Months Later

Stern, Julie, and Earl met together at the Lakeview Cemetery. A slight mist was falling in the spring afternoon. Patches of new grass were beginning to grow on the earth that covered Amber's grave. They placed flowers next to the headstone. On the back of the headstone was engraved the words from Genesis 18:25, "Shall not the judge of all the earth do right?" The words had a special meaning to Stern—something profound that reached back into the past and pressed his conscience with a sublime and transcendent truth for the present. It was at that moment he knew within himself all injustices for all time would one day be redressed.

Earl sat in the park gazing at the Civil War statue, wondering again if any of the passersby would stop and reflect upon its meaning. He thought about the events of the last year. It was like he'd been picked for a leading role in a preordained drama. Now he had left the stage and was returning to his normal life. Some things, however, had changed forever—his faith, his values, and his friendships. He thought about the initial meeting with Stern in the park, and how their friendship had started and grown.

He and Stern had made a pact to keep in touch, and he was already planning a trip to Annapolis with Candy to visit.

Julie kept her job at the library in White Marsh, but had an open invitation to visit Stern, which she did more and more frequently, upon his insistence.

Nattie remained in Pennsylvania with her mother. She had started attending a new church. In time, she healed. Although she testified in Hiram's and Morton's trials, no charges were ever filed against her.

Josh Woodhouse continued visiting the county jail once a week.

His church was lively and growing. He also kept in close contact with Stern, answering questions regarding his newfound faith.

Morton's insanity plea was rejected. He was convicted on two counts of first-degree murder and given two life sentences. Josh visited him at the county jail while he awaited trial.

Hiram was convicted on counts of obstruction of justice, tampering with physical evidence, bribery, and other charges. His disbarment from law practice was swift and final. Ironically, before his trial, he was placed for a short time in the same cell that Stern had occupied. He refused visits from Josh, sneering at any notion of God.

Mrs. Fenley died of a heart attack shortly after her son and husband were convicted. By the time of her death, the whole town was aware of the dreadful abuse at the hands of Hiram. Small consolation for a life lived in misery.

Frieda Baker was given an honorable discharge from Stern's service, and resumed her life of discourse with Erline Slicer and her circle of socialite friends in Annapolis.

Jud Tillston became a firm believer in providence and started attending a church regularly.

Stern never wrote the book. The publisher understandably voided the contract. After all, the story had been told and retold in the media scores of times. It was a chapter written and closed in Stern's mind. There were new horizons and a brand new life, one with a different set of values; one that included Julie Fisher. In a way, she was an extension of Amber. Not a replacement, but an extension of her life and faith.

He visited Hollister with Julie one final time. She walked at his side along the sandy beach at Friendship Point where he and Amber had walked. Stern raised his eyes to the sky above, and then closed them. He squeezed Julie's hand firmly in his own, silently praying and thanking God for His mercy.

TATE PUBLISHING & *Enterprises*

Tate Publishing is commited to excellence in the publishing industry. Our staff of highly trained professionals, including editors, graphic designers, and marketing personnel, work together to produce the very finest books available. The company reflects the philosophy established by the founders, based on Psalms 68:11,

"THE LORD GAVE THE WORD AND GREAT WAS THE COMPANY OF THOSE WHO PUBLISHED IT."

If you would like further information, please call
1.888.361.9473
or visit our website
www.tatepublishing.com

TATE PUBLISHING & *Enterprises*, LLC
127 E. Trade Center Terrace
Mustang, Oklahoma 73064 USA